THE
BOYFRIEND
SUBSCRIPTION

THE
BOYFRIEND
SUBSCRIPTION

STEVEN SALVATORE

Recycling programs for this product may not exist in your area.

ISBN-13: 978-1-335-04159-3

The Boyfriend Subscription

Harlequin Enterprises ULC
22 Adelaide St. West, 41st Floor
Toronto, Ontario M5H 4E3, Canada
www.Harlequin.com

Printed in U.S.A.

for every gay man

who has felt like a seed in need of nurturing,

waiting to bloom

Welcome to

VERSTL

Switch Positions

Click Here for Intimacy

Customize Your Sexperience

⇕

Support Creators

⇕

Become a Member

SUBSCRIBE!

One
Estimated Time: A New York Minute

Teddy Hughes

Nothing is better than sinking my fingers into fresh soil.

Okay, maybe sex.

No, scratch that. Not even sex compares to moist dirt, rich with nutrients, sliding between fingers, wedging into the spaces between nail and skin, knowing that once I prep and till and plant the seeds, something beautiful will sprout.

Life, firmly rooted, in the exact place *I* plotted.

Sun, water, shade, patience, love—knowing that if I tend to them, they will grow—has been the only thing I've been able to depend on, aside from Kit Davis, my roommate and childhood best friend. But I'm about to lose her, too.

Looking around the space that was once Plant Daddy Nursery and Garden, now nothing more than empty shelves and plant beds, stacked planters on top of palettes, and painted concrete floors with small piles of soil I didn't bother sweeping, my entire body feels broken. Every bone shattered, every tendon shredded, every muscle weakened.

All that's left is a single African violet, a parting gift for Kit.

Plant Daddy used to be so vibrant: A queer-owned jungle oasis with budding vines growing up walls and spiraling from the rafters, stocked with rare flowers of every shape and size and color from all over the world. Walking in was entering Oz, another dimension entirely, an escape from the gray concrete of Manhattan and into a Technicolor playground of life, blooming and thriving and breathing. I lived for the moments when newcomers would stumble upon my hidden plant oasis inside this old art deco building. With wide eyes, they would explore, inevitability leaving with something verdant and thriving—a seed of possibility.

I thought that was enough.

For years, it was. I sustained a damn nursery in New York City. And it was successful, despite the massive business loans and handouts from Kit to stay afloat, including her covering my half of our monthly rent, which is a whole other bag of manure. Not to mention, all the legal fees from the fucking lawsuit—

The chime above the door dings. I could've sworn I locked the door and papered up the windows with a giant "PERMANENTLY CLOSED" sign, complete with a weeping flower I painted because Kit said it would be good for me to channel my "inner artist" with some art therapy. Turns out, I cried harder staring at the flower's giant tear-soaked eyes.

Because apparently it's possible to let down a cartoon drawing, too. Who knew?

"We're closed," I choke out.

"Apologies, Mr. Hughes. I assumed you'd be gone by now." Her voice is ice in my veins. Keys dangle from her perfectly manicured fingers as she checks the thin gold watch around her wrist.

"I have until 5:00 p.m." My fingers dispel the soil and I wipe them on my jeans.

Her foot taps impatiently. "My client is eager to get into *his* space." A black town car idles on the street. "You agreed to vacate the premises by Friday, May 24, at 5:00 p.m. It's—" She checks her watch. "4:43."

"He's here?" A breathless anxiety rattles against my ribs. My ex-father-in-law, the man who took my life from me. Is Murray, my ex-husband, here, too?

"Mr. Hughes," she begins, a mix of pity and condescension in her voice. "My client—"

I muster a modicum of strength. I won't allow her to see me sweat. For what, so she can report back to her client, who will no doubt tell Murray? This family can't continue to have a chokehold on me. "For the next fifteen minutes, it's still mine."

"Very well." She nibbles on her bottom lip. "For what it's worth, Plant Daddy was quite the business. I have both of your books, too. My husband's a big plant guy, and—"

"No offense, and thank you, but I'd like to be alone."

She hums as she ambles toward the door, running the soles of her heels through a pile of dry dirt. "I assume someone is coming to remove the remaining contents?"

"As per the settlement," I chime robotically.

Daylight streams through the dark, dusty space, a glimmer of what it used to be flashes in my mind like an afterimage, an old Polaroid that got overexposed and never fully developed. Still, I see hints of what was.

Pressing against the door, she stops halfway out. "Mr. Hughes, you seem like a nice man. A pillar of the community, if the testimonies of your customers are to be believed." Her smile scrubs away the stony, ruthless, high-powered attorney hired by my ex-husband's father to persecute me out of spite. Gone is the woman I saw nearly every day for months of litigation, replaced by someone vaguely sweet. Sympathetic, even. It's fucking unnerving. "I don't love this part of my job, but I have to warn you. If you aren't out by 5:00 p.m., you'll be forcibly removed. I don't want to see that happen."

"I'll be gone," I say. "And thank you."

She bows, and disappears through the front doors, brown paper covering the glass windows peeling back in her wake.

I'm compelled to fix it, but what's the point?

I walk the perimeter of the old shop, tracing the walls with my fingertips in remembrance of how it used to feel to walk in here every day and lock up every night after helping clients discover the perfect plant companion, *the one.*

Plant gays were always my favorite customers. Connecting with another gay dude over something beautiful and delicate, a shared love of a green aesthetic that became a lifestyle, always made me feel alive. Maybe it's the instinct to tend to something small but very much alive—a desire to have children, a family, that more often than not feels like a fervent daydream, the stuff of high fantasy for gay men.

How did I end up here?

Alone, broken, with nothing but a failed dream. Where I once had purpose, now is a hole I've dug myself. And I can't see bottom. My lawyer said I was lucky the Whalton Estate agreed to drop the lawsuit if I surrendered the storefront. But I don't feel lucky. I feel cheated out of my life, everything I worked hard for and built. Lost my marriage, in-laws I foolishly considered "family," and my livelihood. I had no strength left to think it through, past all the debt I amounted to hire a lawyer to keep a business afloat that a lawsuit succeeded in destroying. I thought once I finally left greater New Orleans, Louisiana, behind, the nothing I had growing up poor as hell would fade into memory, not come roaring back with a vengeance.

I officially filed for bankruptcy this morning, the proverbial cherry on top of today's cake. All the years spent building credit, gone. Zeroed out. My name no better than oversaturated mud, no potential for growth in muck and mire. The skyscraper of debt might be bulldozed, but so is the last seven years of my life, including my ability to rent another apartment—which is why I'm moving in with my momma, back home to Louisiana, at the end of the month.

For a fleeting moment, I almost call Murray. Pointer finger hovering over his name in my contacts, trembling, wanting to push down and hear his voice. I haven't seen or heard from him in over a year, since he shattered me.

Right now, I miss him.

I need someone to hold me and tell me everything will be okay, that I'll survive, like an aloe plant. Murray never was a balm for me, as much as I wish he could have been. He was a violent storm and the drought that followed, and I was doing all I could to store water for when I needed to survive him.

As quickly as thoughts of him entered my mind, I push them away.

Notifications light up my vibrating phone screen. I forgot about the timed Instagram post set to go live on @TheOriginalPlantDaddy. It's a curated ten-slide scrapbook of the last seven years of Plant Daddy Nursery and Garden, with a farewell caption to my 100K followers.

Seems fitting, being alone in this hollowed-out space while thousands of people tell me how much they'll miss me. Crying-face emojis and heartfelt DMs pour in, and everything hits me so fiercely that my body goes numb.

Again, the chime above the door dings, and my blood boils. "I have a couple more minutes—"

"Sorry, I know you're closed, but I had to see it one last time."

I look up and immediately wipe the rogue tear from my cheek.

Ben, a short, clean-shaven muscle gay with a propensity for tight color-blocked shirts tucked into even tighter dress pants, has been a loyal customer since I opened. He's holding his phone up. He's a producer on Bravo's *Watch What Happens Live*, and last year he booked me as a bartender after finding me on Instagram. In his words, "Who doesn't love a hot ginger plant daddy?"

"I saw your last post on Insta and I was on my way into the studio and—" He sucks in a breath. "Wow. It's really gone, huh?"

No words come.

"It's so weird." His lips are stretched tight, looking at me expectantly. "I was kind of hoping you might have a last-minute gift for a friend's birthday." Ben looks up at the rafters, searching. He smiles sympathetically. God, I feel like a widow at a funeral for her late husband.

"I might have something left in the back," I say.

"Really?" He perks up.

"Don't get your hopes up." I offer a small laugh as I make my way toward the storeroom. It's empty, save for a shelf that houses one monstrously large glass orb-shaped terrarium I couldn't sell or donate. I was planning to leave it here and let the bastards who stole my nursery from me deal with it, but Ben needs a last-minute gift, and this is the sort of thing I do best.

In the corner are some leftover succulents and mosses. They're not in the best shape, nor are they the brightest or biggest, but I can make magic with them. In the midst of sorting through what I have—different species of Echeveria, a stone plant, even a baby rubber plant—I spot a short bamboo stalk, which is great for someone with a new job.

I work fast, my hands knowing what to do without having to think. I create a drainage layer using some remaining crushed stone I also couldn't get rid of at the bottom of the terrarium. There's enough activated charcoal around to go on top of that. Grabbing the moss, I drape it over the previous layer, and step back to get a better look. It's looking like an earthy layer cake, and a jolt of life runs through my body. I'm smiling, humming absentmindedly as I start to add in soil and fertilizer.

Then, my favorite part: Teasing the roots of the succulents, pruning some of the longer roots, then shaking off excess soil, and using my fingers to dig out small holes for each plant until the terrarium is nearly full, the bamboo stalk near the front.

But it's missing something.

I'm out of the usual accoutrements I would add to make it feel more whimsical and extra and gay, so Ben will have to make do with what he gets. But that's not it. It needs height. Color. Something visual to pull the eye.

Then I remember the African violet, the lone plant left at the front of the store, and I run out, my eyes scanning the empty storefront for Ben, who is on his phone near what used to be the checkout counter. Next to him is the beautiful purple flower with fuzzy leaves. It's perfect.

"Any luck?" he asks.

"I might have some magic left in these hands." Even though I don't know if I believe it.

"You're good people, Teddy."

Back in the storeroom, I toil with the last plant, fluffing the roots, patting the soil around it, making sure it's as flawless as it could possibly be, given the circumstances.

When I carry it out, Ben's eyes widen. "Careful with her. She's heavy, the last vestiges of Plant Daddy."

"How much do I owe you?"

I shake my head. "Nothing."

"Stop that." Ben's brows crinkle. "It wouldn't feel right."

"I don't want anything."

His brows crinkle, and he offers another sympathetic smile. "How about I take you out for drinks once the dust settles?"

I'll be gone long before the dust settles. Plus, a pity date? No thanks. "Sure."

"I'll DM you, handsome," he says as he carries the terrarium out the front door, the chimes dinging one last time. I watch him walk out, knowing I'll never see him again. But at least I got to have one last customer in the city.

The silence left in his wake hits me hard, sucking all the air from my lungs.

I don't want to be alone.

My phone buzzes with a text from Kit: I love you. We're getting smashed tonight. I'm not taking no for an answer. Prepare your liver.

My heart races when I realize it's now 5:01, and I'm officially a trespasser.

How do I say goodbye to the fantasy-turned-reality of my art deco New York space that was never meant for me, despite the tangled history that brought me here?

I close my eyes and suck in a deep breath, inhaling. Without my babies, the air isn't as clear or fresh, but it still has that earthy floral musk that makes me feel like I'm home. As I walk out, it hits me: I've lost my home.

I'm a dug-up plant, unrooted, born to bloom and wilt.

Cole Vivien

Firefly lights zigzag across the penthouse balcony dotted with high-top cocktail tables. Caterers build mouthwatering hors d'oeuvre towers on sparkling sterling silver trays. New York never fails to disappoint when it comes to staffing the most beautiful servers, who trickle in to get outfitted in crisp white shirts with leather harnesses embossed with the VERSTL logo.

This is it.

VERSTL's Content Creator Appreciation Gala, the symbolic culmination of everything I've worked my ass off for over the last few years. Until this week spent meeting with investors to take VERSTL public, my company still felt like a niche space that existed inside my laptop. If we hit our current projections, we stand to become the first publicly traded sex work company and I'll have done the impossible: Made my own empire, away from Father's name, money, and expectations.

Empires aren't built in a day. They're carefully curated online over time.

With a few minutes before my scheduled *New York Times* interview, I whip out my phone and stream a tour of my penthouse at The Mark Hotel. First to TikTok, then Instagram, and most importantly, to my VERSTL subscribers. It's second nature to transition between platforms, altering what I'm capturing to best fit each app—showing far less clothing and more dick by the time I reach VERSTL.

Engagement is immediate, likes and comments beget virtual tips and paid subscriptions. Thousands of followers validate me. It's a rush whose heady effects only last so long before reality sets in and nerves get the better of me.

This is *it*.

Out of the corner of my eye, a tablecloth is clearly uneven, and I move to fix it. I dance around it's edges, making sure the lengths match on all sides.

"Everything looks great, boss." Jason's voice is steady, hypnotizing. He's narrowing his eyes at me, studying me like a rat in a lab. "Nothing will go wrong."

"Stop calling me boss, Jace." Technically, I *am* his boss, but he's been my best friend since I moved to Los Angeles nearly eight years ago with nothing but hope in my wallet.

"You know my power dynamic kink." He winks.

"Also, saying nothing will go wrong is the kiss of death. So thanks for that."

"Loosen up, you're giving ice sculpture realness."

"Excuse me?"

"Ice sculpture. Gorgeous, unique, chiseled to perfection, but conditions have to be perfect and sustained or you'll melt, or smash to the ground in a zillion imperfect pieces."

He knows me too well.

Jason Meyer is a tall, wickedly handsome frat paddle of a homo. When we first met, he was a finance guy for a major film studio looking for a roommate in West Hollywood and he immediately took me under his wing. We've been inseparable ever since. Jason transitioned to management when I started VERSTL and he pitched me on hiring him as a brand manager, and he'll soon be onboarded as our CFO, if all goes as planned. I expressed hesitations with working together, but he assures me time and again nothing will come between our friendship. Though he does joke about the amount of time we spend together, saying, "Just don't fall in love with me." I laugh it off, but I've sworn off love. There's no room for those emotions in my day-to-day.

"I hate you," I tease.

He winks. "When you're ready, April Fitzgerald, the *Times* reporter, is waiting for you in the upstairs gallery." He straightens up, avoids eye contact. "Nickolas Lund is here, too." The mere mention of Nicko's name sets my teeth on edge. He's the top-grossing male performer on VERSTL. Jason thought it'd behoove VERSTL to have him here to speak to the app's power in connecting to audiences, and the outrageous success it's generated for both of us. A part of me wanted him here for support, but now that he is—

"You good?" Jason asks.

Inhale air through my nose, exhale out through my mouth. "Always."

April Fitzgerald's eyes focus on mine, then down to my crossed arms like a scanner studying my body language. "Over a million unique followers, the second-highest grossing male sex worker, and you—"

"*Entrepreneur,*" I correct her.

Her gaze travels to Nickolas Lund seated next to me, like she's waiting for him to react. He's here because it's "good PR." Nothing more. I've never been able to escape him, no matter how hard I try.

I clear my throat to redirect her attention toward me.

She leans forward, locking eyes with me. "*Entrepreneur,* apologies." She's unflinchingly good at pretending she's enlightened enough to believe "sex worker" and "entrepreneur" can be one and the same. I respect her effortless Boss Bitch energy and the well-worn Louboutins she probably wears to live up to a *Sex and the City* fantasy of being a writer in New York. I did my research on her: Law degree from a state school, loves adopting elderly dogs and posting about them on Instagram. Her bylines include pieces on queer politics, book banning in schools, investigative work on senatorial corruption, and coverage of protests calling for the legalization of sex work. Her fierce tenacity is admirable. She continues, "You founded VERSTL at the age of twenty-seven."

"My Saturn return," I add, with a flourish.

"It's since become the largest, most reputable sex worker–centered interactive content-sharing platform that empowers *entrepreneurs* and leads with body autonomy, all during a time when protests are breaking out in major cities across the country to decriminalize and legalize consensual sex work—some of which you helped organize with VERSTL. You've garnered the attention and support of activists, legislators, celebrities. Not to mention sex workers of all genders. You've made it onto the *Forbes* 30 Under 30 list. It's all quite impressive." She narrows her eyes. "What's next for VERSTL?"

"We're just getting started. Legitimate brand recognition across all markets. My goal has been to change the view of sex work, to humanize it. And our policies, future trajectories, and plans for expansion reflect that undertaking."

The corners of her mouth twitch ever so slightly. "Are the rumors true, about VERSTL potentially stepping into the *traditional* online dating market?"

"Rumors?"

"Is it true VERSTL would appeal to more investors if you cornered that market?"

"I'm not sure where you're getting your information, but no. And I don't like the insinuation of a word like *traditional*, especially in queer spaces."

She nods in acknowledgement. "Switching gears. At twenty-nine, how do you balance that distinct type of fame and success with a private life?"

Before I can say anything, she turns to Nickolas and asks,

"Is what we see, what we get? Is the Cole Vivien on camera the same man behind the scenes, who is often described as a 'prince' by collaborators and clients?"

Everything I do is directed, scripted, produced to within an inch of its life, choreographed to death. Including this interview. But not *these* questions, and I don't have answers prepared. I've worked tirelessly to build my company and image, and there's too much at risk if my personal life becomes public knowledge.

"More or less," I say before Nicko can respond.

"Quite an unusual way to describe por—"

"Porn?" I finish for her. She's most likely viewed at least some of my most popular videos and read the thorough client reviews after I gave her unfettered, Diamond-Tier Member access. Which means she's seen every square inch of me. Her eyes widen at the script flip. "There's nothing shameful about porn. Porn, as a *word*, is taboo, but as a concept, it's the purest, most beautiful and connective form of entertainment."

"So is *that* your ethos?" she asks.

"Well, VERSTL—" I begin, but she cuts me off.

"Not the company's ethos. *Yours*."

This question also catches me off guard. The company *is* my ethos, I thought that was self-explanatory. I hear Father in my head: *Vous êtes propriétaire de votre maison.* You own your house. Only you can build and defend it. Control the narrative.

"Intimacy," I redirect. "Do you know how many people lack intimacy? Especially queer folks. Take gay men who spend an exorbitant amount of time on hookup apps where you're the next best thing until the next best thing, trying to make a connection, but it's never satiable. For some, a quick anonymous encounter works. Others want something more meaningful. VERSTL is about meaningful connections, using real intimacy, without...*complications* to fulfill sexual desire."

"Complications?" The word tumbles inside her mouth. "It sounds like you created the algorithm for human emotion."

Nickolas grabs at my hand. "You're damn right he did. He's a genius. Cole understands that most people want love, or something like it. And he gave it to us." His fingers intertwine with mine, and I resist the urge to wriggle out.

"Commodifying love," April says, scribbling notes.

Wrong. Safe, healthy intimacy *without* love complicating things. "I—"

"And Mr. Lund." She shifts focus. "You're the highest grossing *entrepreneur*. Many have expressed interest in a collaboration between you both." Her line of sight falls to our hands, where Nickolas rubs his thumb against the outer side of my own. "Have you held off because there's something happening behind the scenes, a romance perhaps?"

"Are you trying to find a scoop?" My insides squirm, but on the outside, to them, I'm impenetrable. I reach into my pocket and grab a small, clear quartz crystal and squeeze it so tight I wouldn't be surprised if I bleed; I collect crystals to maintain spiritual stasis and channel calming energy.

"It would be quite a splash if, behind the scenes of a forward-thinking sex worker–fronted company, an actual romance had blossomed between its two brightest stars. A penthouse fairy tale." She gestures around her, and her eyes sparkle in wonder at the space: Five bedrooms, six bathrooms, a library, a private rooftop terrace with panoramic views of Central Park, pure, unadulterated luxury. "The Mark Hotel penthouse *is* called the 'Castle in the Sky.' Built for a modern-day love story."

Nickolas scootches closer, our thighs touching. He's all lean muscle and tattoos, blond scruff and blue eyes, a veritable god among gay internet circles. The optics alone of a romance between us would break the app, overload servers, and entice investors. The revenue would open doors. But not like this. Not with a lie.

The crystal turns in my hand as my heartbeat quickens, thumping against my ribs.

What is Nicko's game here? Faking love for publicity?

Nickolas Lund was one of the biggest gay content creators and sex workers across OnlyFans, JustForFans, and Twitter. When he moved exclusively to VERSTL, we saw a massive spike in revenue. Last year, he flew to LA from New York to make content with me, and our chemistry was off the charts. We spent a week together in Palm Springs, cameras set up all over the house—in ceiling corners, camouflaged into the furniture *Big Brother*–style, to capture the week naturally. No cheap sets with staged stop-and-go shots. I wanted to shoot naturally animalistic sex in a gay vacation paradise. But he broke all my rules, and all that raw footage remains unpublished on my private VERSTL server. After that, we spoke only through Jason.

Until yesterday, when we met for a drink.

One thing led to another, and we fucked all night.

Hot sex. That's all. I was clear this time.

April wants a story that doesn't exist. And it's getting too personal for my liking.

I flash an undeniable smile and take back the reins, ending the interview: "What do you say we head to the party?"

★ ★ ★

Moody electro pop hums infectiously in the air as a warm breeze blankets Madison Avenue. VERSTL's East Coast sex workers, cis and trans men and non-binary folks, fill the expansive balcony. There's a camaraderie among these brilliant content creators because they can all exist together here without judgment. Their stories of struggle and hardship, of body shame and body love, of sex liberation inspire me. I want to do right by them.

A deep sense of pride fills my chest as I finish making my rounds, connecting with each person, when April, martini and vape pen in hand, approaches.

I wave to a group of creators who call me over, but it's too late.

April tips her glass at me. "You're good at pretending."

"Excuse me?" A waiter walks by with a tray of champagne, and I grab a flute.

"You *are* Vivièn DuBois-Deplantier of The Deplantier Corporation, right?" she asks, and my knees buckle. "Does your family know about your legal name change? Your father has some pretty wealthy, influential, religious clients, and a reputation for being a family-oriented construction company."

I can't breathe. *Vivièn DuBois-Deplantier,* the son who walked away from an inheritance because I didn't want to step into Father's shoes and helm the family ship. My family name comes with a great deal of expectation, and I carefully made sure VERSTL would be free of the weight of the Deplantier name.

My sister, Mallory, is the only person in my family who knows about VERSTL. I've hated making Mallory run interference on my behalf to keep VERSTL a secret from Father and his clients and investors. Changing my legal name wasn't stressful, it was freeing. Mallory assures me that if anyone in Father's network stumbled upon me in secret, they'd be too afraid of Father to say anything to him. I request my face obscured in periodicals my family might read. They would never search out gay porn, so my face—and cock—are safe, but a *Times* feature with my *real* name in print? Undeniable.

I started this company from nothing, ostracized from the Deplantier namesake, and I *want* to tell my family, but on *my* terms. When I am certain the house I've built is sturdy enough to stand. Someone like April doesn't get to hold that over me.

"*Family-oriented?* Sounds like a microaggression." I'm trying to center myself, but my ice sculpture is melting. As a child I developed a series of coping mechanisms for my anxiety. To make my heart rate slow, I touch my thumb to each one of my fingers while repeatedly counting to twelve: *Onetwothreefour, fivesixseveneight nineteneleventwelve.* "You've been busy connecting family dots. Why?"

She has the poker face of a high roller. "So that's a confirmation?"

I wince. Did I confirm? *Fuck.* Name change records are public, but I paid good money to close them. Still, she can't see me sweat. "What's your angle?"

"The commodification of love," she says, coolly. "Powerful stuff."

"That's not—you're missing the point. I built VERSTL on one foundational belief: everyone deserves intimacy. Not all connections are about sex, but *all* sex is connective."

"Hmmm." Then she disregards everything I said: "Your sister is getting married in a few days. That's a big deal, especially as she's poised to take over as successor to the Deplantier fortune. How does that make you feel?"

"Let me not mince words. My sister has earned every ounce of success she's garnered. And I would appreciate it if my family were not contacted for the article. Assuming it's still a piece about the merits of VERSTL and not some cheap family scandal." I take a deep breath. "I would *hate* for anything to ruin my sister's day. Now, Ms. Fitzgerald, if you'll excuse me."

The bustle of the party drowns out the noise in my head, the sounds of chatter and laughter and clinking cocktail glasses. For a few minutes, an hour or two, maybe, I'm riding the high and able to push April's interview from my mind.

There's one moment, when all eyes are on me and I'm searching the crowd, and one thought smacks me in the face: I have nobody.

Then Nickolas Lund sidles up beside me, smiling. "Don't worry, babe." He pulls me to the center of the patio. Everyone goes silent, followed by gasps as he kneels down.

"Cole Vivien." He pulls out a velvet ring-shaped box. His words come out at half speed, and partygoers react in slow motion: phones whip out, flashes blind me, murmurs drown out my heartbeat. April Fitzgerald records everything.

This is *my* party, *my* story. I must take it back.

I swiftly pull Nickolas into a hug, carefully nuzzling my chin into his shoulder so I can whisper in his ear. "We need to talk."

I lead him inside and into the bustling kitchen, a mess with chefs and servers.

"You okay?" Nickolas asks. "I thought—"

"Don't." If Father were here, he would tell me I can't lose my biggest star. Plus, there's April's story to contend with.

I need to handle this delicately. *Plus*, he's clearly unpredictable. I take a deep breath in and exhale. "Sorry, Nicko, I'm stressed. Why don't you go back to your apartment. I'll meet you there later. We'll talk. About everything."

He leans in for a kiss, despite knowing my rules:

1. No kissing.
2. No falling in love.

My teeth grind as I walk him to the elevator.

Once he's gone, the realization sets in: *Nicko almost proposed, surrounded by press.*

I have to get out of here.

I hold my breath until I'm outside The Mark Hotel. I exhale from somewhere deep in my diaphragm once outside, hoping the memories of Nickolas escape into the air.

Frank, the impeccably dressed Italian doorman asks, "You okay, sir?" A modicum of concern dots his eyes. His head tilts before his back straightens. He smooths out his suit jacket, and I mimic his movements, slipping back into character. He immediately recognizes the intended stoicism. "Very good. Shall I order you a car, Mr. Vivien?"

"Please." I send Mallory a text: Emergency drinks. Carlyle.

Teddy Hughes

"Dearly beloved, we're gathered here today to mourn Plant Daddy, remember the beautiful years spent, and pay our respects to—"

Wrong. "No, fuck that," I interrupt Kit and she looks at me like I've killed a puppy. I slam my beer on the bar top. "*Respects?* Plant Daddy doesn't need a funeral." I resist the urge to say, "*I* do." And instead say, "Fuck respect! Let's roast the assholes who took Plant Daddy from me."

Kit sucks at her teeth. "You're grieving, so I'll accept that, but interrupt me again, and I will plant you." Her tongue has always been sharper than a blade.

"Punny."

"Too soon?" she asks.

"Plant Daddy's body is still warm," I say.

"Right. Well, a roast. Dearly beloved, we're gathered here today to spit on the graves of the lawyer and the assholes who took Plant Daddy from my brother-from-another-mother, Teddy."

"They're not dead," I say, imagining their tombstones, which is super macabre, but it brings me a modicum of comfort.

"They could be. I know a guy," Kit says, and I raise an eyebrow. "Joke!" She sloshes her beer mug. "Also, spit on our landlord who is raising rent as if living in New York isn't fucking extortion already, and, uh, am I forgetting anything?"

While we're at it? "And Murray. Fuck that guy."

Kit raises her perfectly manicured brows and glares at me. She licks her plump lips before saying, "Fuck that guy."

There aren't many patrons in American Trash, a very hetero dive bar within walking distance of our six-floor walk-up shoebox studio with the makeshift wall/divider that cuts across it, separating her space from mine. Kit likes it here because, according to her, "Being in a straight bar is like going to the zoo without the animal cruelty. We get to observe heteros in a controlled environment."

Whoever is in earshot shouts, "Fuck that guy" along with us. I love this level of blind support from a couple of supremely straight dudes at the other end of the bar by the pool table, who are clearly shit-faced. They shout, "Fuck that guy" back and forth to each other. They get me on a spiritual level.

Raising her glass, Kit clinks it against mine and takes a swig of the hoppy, foamy beer, but like everything with Kit, one swig turns into the entire glass and before I can blink it's empty. She eye-fucks the hopelessly straight bartender, moving her glass toward him, and he pours her another.

"Why do you lead him on?" I whisper.

"Because it's fun," she says. "He doesn't need to know I'm not into cis dudes as long as I can get free drinks. The straights take so much from us, this one can give a little back."

I laugh and try my best to catch up to her, but she can drink me under the table.

"The real question is," she begins. "Why did you bring up Murray?"

I choke on the room-temperature beer.

"Did you text him?" she asks.

"Did you see his latest Insta post?" I swerve away from her question. "On Fire Island with his new boyfriend?"

"You texted him, didn't you?"

"Fuck you. I'm lonely." I shift awkwardly on the wobbly, ripped barstool.

"Aaaaand there it is," Kit says. "Look, I know you think Doctor Murray McFuckwad was the love of your life, yada,

yada, blah, blah, but he destroyed you. Do you remember what he told you, because I do. Vividly."

There's a baseball game playing on the TV screen over the bar in front of us. "So, how about them Yankees?"

"You forfeited your entire business," Kit starts.

"*Technically*, it was just the building." I cut her off because I don't want to talk about the sordid history and the desolate present right now. "I still own the Plant Daddy name. Not that it does me any good, because bankrupt! Silver linings? Glass half whatever?" I burp and she glares at me. "Let me hold on to what I can."

"You suck at dealing with loss, Teddy," she says. "On a thousand different levels."

"That's why we're here." I hold up my beer mug. I stand up to get the bartender's attention because I'm going to need more liquid courage if this is where the night is headed: Therapy with Kit. The wooden floor of American Trash is sticky, and the soles of my well-worn Converse peel off the planks like plastic-wrapped Kraft singles.

She grabs my face and gives me the most pitiful look I've ever seen and, fuck, that makes me feel worse. "I want to protect you," Kit admits. "I don't know how."

"Danger!" I shout robotically. "Abort mission, abort feelings, abort, abort, abort!" I laugh, but she doesn't. "I'll be okay. This was a long time coming." Last year, the universe decided my life was the punch line of a cheap joke when Murray filed for divorce, kicked me out, and moved in with a past-his-prime twink. Then Murray's father, Murray Whalton II conveniently discovered…*bookkeeping* discrepancies linked to my retail space and decided, hey, let's go after my son's ex-husband's entire fucking life for sport. He never liked me, thought I was below his son's station. It's like, I moved out of Murray's large Tribeca loft and into Kit's five-hundred-square foot Upper East Side studio and never truly got to process the loss of Murray. Now it's all hitting me at once. In nine days, I'll be back in Louisiana living with Momma without a dime to my name and a heart space full of tainted memories. Momma has always lived within her means because we never had a choice; pennies were pinched, counted, and accounted for.

"I wish you could stay," Kit says. "What about your books?"

"What about them?" I ask.

"You're a published author, you got like a hundred thousand followers on Plant Daddy's IG. You're famous. Can't you, like, get an advance on a new book or something?" Her question is hesitant and frantic. Bless her art dealer heart, she knows nothing about publishing.

I shake my head. "Publishers only care about Instagram followers if and when it makes them money. I never earned out either of my advances, and it's been years since my second book pubbed. Nobody is breaking down my door for a third book. Believe me, I've tried to submit proposals. At this point, I think my agent presumes I've died."

"You're a writer?" the bartender asks, suddenly interested in me.

Kit swipes across her phone screen, then swivels it to show the bartender. Glancing over her, I see a selfie with both of my books. "Teddy is brilliant. You should absolutely buy his books. Twenty copies, I think."

"*Plant Daddy: How to Embrace Your Inner Horticulturist* and

Plant Daddy in the City?" The bartender squints while reading the titles of each book aloud. "I know that shop! That's you?"

"Was."

"I heard it shut down. Tough break. My ex-girl used to go in there a lot." Normally, I would probe because I love hearing about customers, but he made it awkward by bringing up an ex, so. "Your books are, what? Nonfiction? You know, I've always wanted to write a book." Next he'll say something about how a friend of his cousin's cousin published a book once, and then he'll ask me if I can help him write his book. Right on cue, he tells me about *Dasher Dancer Prancer VixXxen: Santa's Little Helpers*, an erotic tale of reindeer-clad strippers hired by Mrs. Claus to fuck the joy of Christmas back into a downtrodden Santa.

"That sounds, um, wow." Are the straights okay?

"Thanks! So tell me more about your books."

I clear my throat. "I'm a horticulturalist by trade, and I always wrote—Insta-blogging, #plantstagram, that sort of stuff. The Plant Daddy Instagram and TikTok accounts blew up and my home nursery took off and got picked up by a media outlet due to it being LGBTQ-owned, and I was approached by an agent who thought I would be able to put together a book she could sell to publishers. Then I moved to New York and opened the brick-and-mortar. The first book was sort of a how-to for novices who wanted to learn about horticulture and get into gardening themselves. Big focus on sustainability. Stories about my life are woven in. Incredible portraits of hundreds of beautiful, unique, exotic plants from all over the world that I took. The second book is about being a 'plant daddy' in a concrete jungle, which didn't do as well as the first. But it was gay, and the nursery was thriving."

"Cool. Sounds intense." The bartender's eyes are glazed over. "You still write?"

Kit and I exchange a knowing look. Not going down this rabbit hole. I shrug. This is the longest conversation I've ever had with the dude, and I'm ready for it to end.

His methodical, exhausted nods make it clear he does not want to hear my life's story, anyway. "How does she fit into the picture?" His gaze lands on Kit.

"She held me up when things got tough," I say, holding back tears that pull at the corners of my eyes.

"We know each other from back home in Nawlins. He's my bestie," Kit adds. "Don't worry, Sugar, you know you're still my number one guy."

He blushes and someone at the end of the bar calls his attention.

"I've built my life here," I say, turning away from him and demanding Kit's full attention. I don't want to talk about my books or the nursery. I want to drown my sorrows for a little bit. It's our last week together, my last few nights in the city, and I don't want to waste them crying. "It's all gone."

She pulls me into a hug. "You're my person." Her nails dig into my upper arm, and I pull her closer. "No matter what happens or where you live. I just wish you didn't have to leave."

"Maybe it's a sign," I say. "No nursery, no books, no money for rent, no—" I resist the urge to say *Murray*. "Prospects. Maybe I need a good reset."

"Or could you stick it out? I'll spot you next month's rent. Again. I sold a stupid expensive painting at the gallery and my commission is more than enough to cover both rents for a couple months."

"You can't keep doing this." My voice is resolute, unwavering.

"I mean, I *was* gonna spend it on sex toys, but this seems like a more worthy cause."

I chuckle. "I appreciate it, Kit. I do. And I love you for even suggesting it, but—"

"But your damn cis male ego," she says.

I concede. "I'd rather hook on the corner than move home, but I have no more cards to play."

I feel a set of hands on my shoulder. It's the supremely straight dudes from the pool table earlier. One of them says, "Fuck that guy, am I right?"

The other says, "Solidarity, brother!" and fist-bumps me.

"Thanks, bros." I deepen my voice and puff out my chest.

"Fuck yeah!" they both say in unison, then bust out in laughter. And with that, they stumble out into the street, but before they disappear completely, I hear, "Fuck that guy!" one more time.

"I don't get men," she says.

"Same." I sigh. "If you want to help me, get me laid before I leave this city. You know the trade back home is—"

"Pitiful!" She releases the grip on her beer mug. I search her eyes for understanding, but they're cloudy, wet. She bites her lip. I've known her most of my life and I know what's going through her head right now. She's trying to find a way out of this, a compromise to keep me here, a get-rich-quick scheme of some kind. "You know, you can totally make a VERSTL account. Two birds, one stone! Your gingery lumberjack aesthetic is in high demand with guys who have daddy issues." She fondles the collar of my red flannel shirt. "And beard fetishists."

"Thanks?" I involuntarily pet my beard, which is well-kept and short, but full.

"I can sleep at Tara and Naomi's tonight, assuming you can make a dick appointment. Or, oh! I can be your winglesbian." She winks. Tara and Naomi are Kit's triad partners; Kit met the couple two years ago on a polyamorous hookup app. They've invited her to move in to their brick factory-turned-Brooklyn loft, but she didn't want to leave me. I think that excuse is a front for her fear of commitment. Maybe once I'm out of her studio and she's alone again, it will be the push she needs to move forward. Sometimes, I think I've held her back because she's always taking care of me. "How do we find you a dick?" She looks around American Trash. Not a gay in sight. "Not in this straight monstrosity." She holds out a hand, expectantly. "Grindr."

"You love any excuse to fuck with gross men."

"It's the best," she admits. When I hand over my phone, she loses focus on the conversation. I snap my fingers in front of her face to break her trance, but she swats me away. "Do that again and I'll break your hand. The men on here are nasty with their ill-lit dicks and incessant one-word messages: 'Pics?' 'Into?' 'Looking?' Ooh, but what about him?" Hands on my shoulders, she swivels my body on the barstool until I'm facing the most beautiful man I've ever seen.

Two
Click Here to Subscribe!

Cole Vivien

Mallory's infectious donkey laughter fills the bar at The Carlyle. Seeing me, she hops off the stool, sashays toward me in her white Dior floral midi dress, and flings her arms around me, so tight I can't breathe. She pulls back and squeezes my brawny shoulders. "You've filled out, *petit frère!* Puberty finally hit you. Only took twenty-nine years."

With a laugh, I flex. "I've been bulking."

She gasps, playing it up to make me feel good about my physique. I'm fifteen again, blushing from my older, much cooler sister's compliments.

"Mother will be happy. She worries you're not eating." Mal gestures toward the bartender. "I ordered the Vivièn special: extra dirty martini."

I plop onto a leather barstool. "This is why I love you."

Nearly a year since we've seen each other, but we slide right back into a rhythm.

My index finger anxiously tap-tap-taps the stem of the crystal martini glass as my eyes dart around The Carlyle's Bemelmans Bar, studying the breathtaking murals on the wall. The whimsical storybook paintings are in jarring juxtaposition to glittering glass bottles full of amber liquid, leather banquets, mahogany furniture, and golden accented lamps. It reminds me of Mallory.

"Talk to me, tell me what vexes you," she says. "I need a distraction after spending all day in Midtown meeting with a new contractor."

Slowly unspooling everything from the *Times* reporter to Nickolas—Mal's the only one who knows my history with Nickolas—I brace myself for a lecture along the lines of "Why would you put yourself through *that*?"

Mal plays with the mint sprig jutting out of her sterling silver julep cup. "Nothing can take away what you've built." Her voice is warm butter and honey on crusty, freshly baked bread. "Not even Nickolas. Though *he* is a whole other story." Her nostrils flare. "I'll make some calls, squash the story—"

"No! A favorable front-page business section headline will entice investors who might not be willing to take a chance on a queer-led company built around sex work. But the personal information, my *name*, the Nickolas of it all—"

She grabs my hand. "Breathe, *petit frère*." She looks so much like me: amber eyes, high cheek bones, angular jaw, but softer around the cheeks and with slightly more wrinkles around the eyes—I told her baby Botox would take care of that. Her chocolate brown hair falls in waves around her face and spills over her shoulders.

We were inseparable until I moved to LA. Though we FaceTime often, it's not the same as our once-a-week Sunday dinners and all the time we would spend gossiping over coffee about our tragic men *de la semaine*. I miss her, and worry that once she officially takes over for Father and starts her own family, there won't be much left for me, especially living on opposite coasts. But I push those intrusive thoughts from my mind.

"Consider it handled," she says. "You're so tense. Your aura is muddy."

"I don't know how to relax."

"I know." She sighs. "You get that from Father."

"How's he been?" I ask hesitantly.

"Ask him yourself when you see him Sunday." She takes the smallest sip of her mule. Father hangs in the air between us, and neither of us pull at that thread. I respect her decision to run his empire, though she knows I would have loved to poach her for VERSTL's CFO. But her allegiance is to Father, and she keeps my secrets. *C'est la vie.*

"Right." After fishing the last olive from my extra dirty martini, I pop it in my mouth. "As your man of honor, I know all we talk about is wedding stuff, but how are you and Mikey right now? Mentally, spiritually handling everything?"

"I love my fiancé, but he's useless. Between Father and the increased workload, and Mother's wedding hyperfixations, I don't get much *me* time." She shrugs.

"You were *supposed* to take this week off."

A laugh spurts from her lips. "Yeah. I 'took off.' You know

Father." She sucks her teeth. "But I refuse to work on our honeymoon."

"When I'm home—" I start.

"I'll book us crystal alignment massages!" she interrupts. "It'll bring your energy field into balance."

"I'm balanced!" I lie.

She rolls her eyes. "You're dodging. You're keeping mammoth secrets from Father. *And* Mother. You can't sustain that."

"I know. I *will* tell him. *Them*." She stares me down. "Soon!"

"I mean, don't ruin my wedding, but *after*. I want my brother back."

There it is. The warning.

"You underestimate him." She pushes her hair back behind her ear.

"*You* underestimate how much *he* resents me." I down the rest of my martini in one gulp and hold out a hand for the bow-tied bartender who is already sliding another drink my way.

She sucks in a breath and winces; it stings her too because she was Father's consolation prize. It was me who was supposed to take over for him. I'm the disappointment, which is also why I stay away. Without bothering to refute, she says, "I hate the thought of you being in LA alone."

"Alone?"

"You don't have family out there. Or a man. *Love*."

Tension pools in my temples.

She plays with her obscenely large diamond engagement ring, the one she bought herself because her fiancé doesn't exactly come from money. "I worry about you. You need people. You keep yourself so walled up and I've seen what happens when men like you isolate their hearts." She looks down. I don't know what she's referring to, and I realize that maybe I *have* missed a lot of her life all these years away on the West Coast.

But I don't want her worrying about me. Not with everything she has on her plate already. "Who says I don't have someone?"

Immediately, her eyes perk up. The way the worry melts off her face almost instantly releases some of the tension in my chest.

Before I can stop myself, more lies slip out. "I was going to surprise you, but I've been seeing someone."

She nearly shrieks as she jumps to her feet. "What's his name? Why didn't you tell me you were dating again! Tell me everything."

I move my fingers across my lips like a zipper. "You'll meet him at the wedding."

A flat-out lie—there is no boyfriend—but she doesn't need to know that. If it makes her happy for her wedding day and eases her worries, I'll figure out how I'm going to pull a nonexistent boyfriend out of thin air later.

She squeals. "Ahhh! Fuck, I have to go, my car is waiting. But—" Flinging her arms around me, she exclaims, "I'm so, so happy you're not alone!"

I want to tell her I prefer being alone. At least if I'm alone, nobody can break me.

Afterward, ambling across 77th Street, I consider getting lost. Stop into a Rite Aid, grab a trashy "I heart NY" hoodie, ditch these clothes, and wander. Maybe walk along the East River down to South Street Seaport. I spent a lot of time there during college, wandering the cobblestone streets late at night.

The summer between freshman and sophomore year, I met a guy there on Grindr. **100 feet away.** We started chatting, sent pics, and discovered we both went to NYU, but he was one year ahead. He was tall and gangly, blond, nerdy, wholesome. Before sunset, he saw me overlooking the East River, watching the brown waves rush by, and asked if I wanted ice cream. We spent the entire night wandering around the financial district, holding hands. We found a secluded spot by the ships and blew each other. In the morning, we split a Lyft back to the dorms and shared a long kiss goodbye. He ran his fingers through my hair and bit my bottom lip gently. He told me it was a "perfect date," asked if he could see me again, *officially*. While I enjoyed our night, anything more would be too hard for me to sustain. He stepped back, sensing my inertia. "Kissing you is like falling in love." He sighed, looked up to the sky, and walked away.

Lost in memory, I continue until I reach 1st Avenue and hear a raucous "Fuck that guy!" followed by hysterical laughter and "We gotta find pussy, bro!"

A laugh escapes my gut as I see a relic dive bar from Route 66, complete with a marquee welded from old road signs and bits of scrap metal, riddled with 1990s neon signage. Orange construction cones line the front—maybe it's closed to the public?

Nope, on a closer look they're decorations arranged as an ironic post-modern sculpture, though I doubt the MoMa would agree. There are two motorcycles parked out front directly on the curb, illegally, one of which is an NYPD bike, which is so thoroughly New York City. Through the dark windows, outlines of a few bodies dot the bar.

The perfect place to escape. There won't be a single gay guy here, so virtually zero chance of being recognized.

I must've activated a silent alarm because the second I push open the door, the bartender narrows his eyes at me. I shove my hands in my pockets, which are tight against my thighs, duck like the ceiling is low, and walk to the counter.

Is there a menu? This isn't the type of place with leather-backed, engraved drink cards. The back of the bar is lined haphazardly with old bottles, and the TV screens above them are playing sportsball and an outdated reality show about a tattoo shop. Between the screens are old signs with plastic letters wedged into their faces. They're hard to read from here, so I walk closer.

But someone is staring at me.

He's a shorter, stockier, slightly younger Richard Madden with a full, perfectly kept ginger beard in the cutest teal beanie and red-and-black flannel shirt. Long, thick fingers decorated in tarnished rings of gold, silver, and tungsten grip his frosty beer mug; workers hands, strong, sturdy, steady. Freckles dance across his cheeks and he's doing his best not to stare.

"Talk to him," she hisses. Her hair is a gorgeous Afro. Her skin is rich and dark, popping against her acid-washed jean jacket littered with patches: Black Lives Matter, the Black power fist, a green planet symbol with text too small to read, and the lesbian flag.

He takes the biggest swig out of his beer mug, glugging every last drop until a foamy mustache coats his own which is so adorable what's left of my insides knot.

"He's hot. Shoot your shot, bitch." She's not exactly trying to be quiet, and I have to respect her I-don't-give-a-fuck attitude.

Another quick scan confirms he's clearly checking out my body, undressing me with nervous glances he doesn't realize I clock. Guys who recognize me from VERSTL act differently, more dominant, like I'm an easy target because I fuck for money.

He lightly pounds his empty beer mug on the bar, and the bartender looks up, a terse nod of acknowledgement.

I change my mind and turn back toward them. "*Excusez-moi*—" Continuing in English, I ask, "Do either of you know how to get the bartender's attention?"

The guy looks up.

Our eyes meet.

I stop breathing because he has two different color eyes, one green, one blue.

Beer foam rests on his upper lip before he promptly wipes it away. His irises sparkle, and his mouth drops open slightly; his breath catches. He takes a sip from his mug, but it's empty.

His friend nudges him. "Say something."

Coughing, his cheeks turn an adorable shade of pink. "To grab the bartender's attention—" I'm immediately captivated by his boyish Southern drawl, slightly tainted by New York. "I usually bend over the bar and shout, 'Hey, Sugar, looking for a date?'"

Teddy Hughes

I have a huge thing for:
Men who speak French fluently.
Jawlines that can cut glass.
Cheekbones built for the runway.

And this man in front of me checks every box. His beauty defies logic: Curly and coiffed, yet somehow messy dark brown hair with the faintest strands of gray that obviously indicate a stressful job for someone who can't possibly be older than twenty-five. It looks effortless but probably took hours to craft.

Honey-brown eyes, thick syrupy pools I could drown in. The perfect amount of groomed scruff on his face. The area around his eyes is darker, like he hasn't slept much in the last ten years, and fuck, even that's hot.

And a *real* body. Not a smooth twink or an ultrafit muscle god or an airbrushed Insta-gay. His broad-shouldered frame is solid, built, but naturally so. All confidence and swagger, and mixed with his model height and cut jawline, I'm a goner. He's a *tacca integrifolia*, exotic and breathtaking and completely unique.

So obviously I choke on imaginary beer and make an absolute fucking fool of myself in front of this guy who stumbled out of *Vogue* in skintight Armani wielding the ability to absolutely destroy me. But then! I have the balls to say some shit like, "I usually bend over the bar and shout, 'Hey, Sugar, looking for a date?'"

He starts laughing. Like, from the belly, and the skin around his eyes crinkles and his lips make the most beautiful shape, and I'm drawn to them like a hummingbird to the nectar of a flower, or an insect lured to a carnivorous plant. Either way, wreck me.

I breathe out, ragged and uneven, in relief, and when I look over at Kit—who I forgot existed for a hot second—she's Cheshire cat cheesing.

"Does that work around here?" Frenchy asks, motioning to the dire dive-y scene around us, and oh my god, what is someone like him even doing here? My cheeks heat in secondhand embarrassment because what must he think of me, so clearly a regular in a place with *Trash* built into the name? But the beer is dirt cheap, and I'm broke and unemployed and about to move home at thirty-four years old. My stomach winces because wow, that's somehow even worse than the bar itself.

When I don't say anything, Kit shrugs her shoulders and says, "Try your luck."

Without missing a beat, Frenchy says, "Sure. For five bucks."

Kit reaches into her bag and slaps a crumbled five-dollar bill on the counter. "Let's see who can get the bartender's attention first."

I bury my face in my hands.

"Something tells me you have me beat here," Frenchy says. There's a calm confidence in his voice that makes my jeans tight.

The bartender immediately makes his way to Kit, and she orders Frenchy the cheapest tap beer in the place to match ours. After he pours it for her, he lingers in front of her a bit too long. "On the house," he says.

She smooths out the crinkled bill and pushes it toward him. "You're the best, Sugar." She yawns and stretches exaggeratedly, turning her back on Frenchy, and says, "I'm exhausted! You'll be good here, right, Teddy?" Her eyes widen before darting to the side in his direction. Leaning down to hug me, she whispers in my ear, "Go for it. You look hot. He's hot. See you at home, roomie!"

I try to grab for her, to keep her here as a buffer, my wing-lesbian, but she's swift and slips away quickly, waving good-bye to Frenchy and Sugar and the rest of the bar patrons like she's some sort of local celebrity.

Then we're alone.

Neither of us says anything.

Awkward.

"Beer's not bad," I say, realizing I never got a refill and am currently sipping an empty glass yet again. I'm truly not built for this world.

He smirks, and the honey of his eyes glitters in the dim light of the overhead bar lights. "I haven't had a tap beer in forever. Or a beer in general, really. It's nice. Frosty."

"We love frosty." *We love frosty?*

Biting his lower lip, he hums, "Frosty the Snowman." He's unhinged. Cool.

Sweat beads my brow and I almost remove my beanie, but my hair is probably a disaster and that's fifth date level of intimacy.

"It's hot in here," he says, unbuttoning the few top buttons of his shirt. Black curly chest hair pokes out; the suggestion of hair on his body makes me feel dizzy.

It's like I've been in the Sahara for a month without water and he's the outline of an oasis, drawing me closer and closer.

Get a grip, Teddy.

He probably wants out of here. I don't blame him. I want out here.

"I, um, was about to head out."

"Oh?" Frenchy's face falls.

"You wanna come?"

"We need drinks first." He winks, teetering on the heels of his ridiculously expensive designer shoes, which peel off the floor with a *squelch*. He tries to call over the bartender. "Hey, Sugar!" The way he says it, too! Seductive.

Without Kit, my lesbi-shield, I have no idea how Sugar is about to react to what sounds an awful lot like a catcall. "Oh god, no, uh—" I place my hand on his to stop him, but his fingers are so warm it sends a bolt of electricity through me, and words elude me.

"What'd you call me?" the bartender asks, venom lacing his voice.

And we're about to be hate-crimed. So much for drinks.

"Love you, Sugar!" I say to the bartender, whose cheeks redden before I turn to Frenchy and shout. "Run!"

Cole Vivien

"What are you laughing at?" cute ginger-bearded Richard Madden asks.

Doubled over laughing on the edge of the curb around the corner from the bar, I try to swallow my breaths so I can answer. "That was the most unplanned excitement I've had in a long time."

"You don't get out often, huh?" he asks.

"You scare easy, huh?" I mimic.

He blushes and gnaws a bit on his bottom lip. "I'm cool." He looks down at his Converse and kicks the concrete impatiently. "Where to now? Rob a bank?"

"Did that already," I say. "I've never been to The Big Apple before." I feel slightly bad lying to him about never being in the city before, but this is a move that'll put him in the driver's seat. He'll lead the way, and I'll go along for the ride.

He winces. "Oh, wow. Rule number one, nobody calls it The Big Apple. That's the verbal equivalent of an 'I heart NY' hoodie."

"You have one, don't you?" I ask.

"That's…neither here nor there."

I stifle a laugh. "I think it's relevant."

"Okay, fine, it was an ironic Christmas gift from my roommate, Kit."

"New Yorkers sure do love their irony."

He squints. "Lucky for you, I'm from the suburbs outside Nola. We're not about irony. Just jazz and blow-your-socks-off cuisine."

"Is that where you're taking me? For jazz and étouffée?" I ask.

His laughter is magic. "I'll take you to my favorite tourist trap, which'll be quiet and perhaps a bit sketchy this late. That cool?"

"Lead the way."

He turns and walks west on 77th and we're heading back in the direction of the hotel. I have to jog a bit to keep up. I can't help but notice his ass as it bounces.

"I'm Teddy, by the way." He slows down for me.

I catch him looking directly at me. Our eyes lock.

There's something magnetic about his energy; his face is a source of comfort, which is so foreign I'm not sure what to do next.

This is the moment where I have to negotiate how much

of myself I give away to this stranger. If I tell him who I am, he could either get disgusted or turned on. If I keep that information from him, am I lying, or lying by omission? I could fake-name him, make up a story about how I work in fashion or something. It wouldn't be entirely false information, merely contextually inaccurate. But he seems like a sweet guy, and the fake-name game works when I want a one-night stand without the burden of performing as @TheColeVivien. He doesn't seem to recognize me, so at worst, we'll go our separate ways here and he'll exist as a tiny memory, and at best, I can continue to escape, pretend with a cute guy for a little while longer.

Pivoting on my heels, I swerve directly in front of him and start walking backward.

His breath catches as we maintain eye contact. Without saying a word, his eyes and the subtle movements of his head guide me so I don't trip over obstacles.

And I no longer have to negotiate the options.

Teddy Hughes

He holds out his hand for me to shake like this is some sort of business interaction.

Are we sure he's not straight?

I can't remember the last guy I picked up who shook my hand in a proper greeting. Then again, the last time I picked up a guy was in the bathroom of The Eagle right after Murray left. I didn't even get the dude's first name. I had moved in to Kit's and she wasn't home, so I brought him back. He left immediately after he came on my face, without finishing me off, and I spent the rest of the night crying over a framed picture of Murray in the shower while listening to "All Too Well (Taylor's Version)" by Taylor Swift on repeat, all ten minutes and thirteen fucking seconds of it, until the steam and water worked its way into the cheap frame and the picture became waterlogged, his face warped beyond recognition. I still have that picture tucked in a drawer.

Anyway.

"I'm Cole," he says.

Cole. Dashing, angular Frenchy with a gait like a fucking god or something, has a name to match his swagger. The way he's walking backward, trusting me to guide him, is super fucking hot so obviously I'm fully imagining that he's some type of Ryan Gosling or Henry Golding who will take me on a journey of obstacles and wit to find love, culminating in a grand romantic gesture and a mansion-on-the-beach-set wedding complete with fireworks where Celine Dion makes an appearance to sing "It's All Coming Back to Me Now."

Maybe I'm getting ahead of myself.

I hear Kit's voice: *This is only for the night.*

Cole's still holding out his hand and it's getting a bit awkward because I haven't taken it yet. And now we've passed the threshold of acceptable amount of time to take his hand and he probably thinks I'm rejecting him, except I want to take it! His ears get red and he stumbles a bit, and I'm probably to blame because I'm not entirely paying attention to what lurks behind him as I wander into the autumn forest of his eyes and completely ignore the small older woman pushing an even smaller white fluffy cat in a baby carriage who screams something unintelligible at us, making Cole jerk and his whole body flails.

Lurching forward, I quickly grab both of Cole's hands and somehow manage to catch him before he tumbles to the ground as we both yell "SORRY!" to the poor woman, who hisses. Or maybe it was her cat? Either way, in the end, I *do* take both of his hands. And also his body, because we're somehow chest to chest.

"I like your name," I say, and my dry mouth tastes like beer. Does my breath stink? Am I giving him beer breath? There's something hard and familiar underneath his shirt, strapped across his pecs. Is he wearing a harness?

"I like your flannel," he says, not missing a beat.

I let out a howl of a laugh and my stomach jiggles against his. I let him go and do a short runway walk to the end of the block.

This prompts him to clap and yell "incredible" in the most adorable French accent: *"UN-CROY-AHBL."* Good god, I'm toast. "Your laugh. It's infectious," he says.

The Mark Hotel is to our left. Men in perfectly pressed suits dip into bougie cars with drivers named Jeeves or something that will surely take them to their private helicopters to the Hamptons. Meanwhile, here I am, tugging at the bottom of my Target shirt, which is threadbare and coming apart at the seams, hoping Cole doesn't want to go anywhere outside of a hot dog cart.

I snort. "It bodes well for me that you like my laugh."

He turns his head away from the hotel and stares up at the brownstones curiously and intensely examining the architecture as if he can see right through the bricks and mortar. A sexy, pensive Clark Kent; I do the same thing, pretend I have X-ray vision to see inside the homes of the people who aren't me, to see if they found a way to love what they had. I wonder if that's what Cole is doing, too. When we reach the end of the block, he snaps back to the moment and registers the weird stare I'm giving him, so he hooks his arm around mine hesitantly. "This okay?"

All my questions melt away due to him being closer than he was two seconds ago.

We continue walking toward Central Park. I direct us uptown, and we walk along the cobblestones that border the stone wall around the park until we reach The Metropolitan Museum of Art.

"The Met?"

"Have you been?" I ask, not knowing how long he's been in the city. It's perfectly reasonable that he's found the time to go to some of the museums. "There's this exhibit here now through the end of the summer I've been dying to see. It's this interactive gardening experience. Like, nature as living art. It's experimental and hands-on. I'd die to go." I point to the colossal banner above the main entrance: photoSYNTHESIS. Plant Daddy was originally contracted to secure some of the most exotic plants, but they severed the deal once they found out about the lawsuit against me. I would go if it didn't devastate me to have to think about the what-ifs of it all. He doesn't need to know any of this. Not for one night. "Maybe one day."

"Fascinating." With squinting eye, he's clearly deep in thought as he studies the building's architecture.

We settle onto the steps, and he leans back, looking up at the sky. It's smoggy, but a few select stars peek through. Maybe it's the beer going to my head, but I can't stop thinking about the potential harness beneath Cole's shirt. Then Cole's entire naked body. Now I'm sweating and wishing he would say something because for me, all silences are uncomfortable.

"So where are you visiting from?" I ask.

"LA." A man of many words.

"*Oui, oui*, big West Hollywood gay energy," I say, and his eyes widen at my *modest* French. "But more polished. WeHo gay energy is not far off from Hell's Kitchen gay energy. Both are like succulents, you know, beautiful and hard, can thrive in harsh conditions, and have a reputation for taking care of themselves but actually do need to be tended to. Also, they prick, so…" Why am I still talking? He probably thinks I'm unhinged. And yet I can't stop. "I like plants." Wow. That's what I go with? I shut my eyes tight and expel my awkwardness like a dog shaking off water after a swim. "I'm such a nerd. Sorry. I shouldn't be allowed to talk to cute guys."

He examines me like I'm a prickly pear.

"I don't mean to say that like, you're a bitchy cactus or something."

The corners of his lips twitch, like he's stopping himself from laughing. "A bitchy cactus? Is that the genus or species name?"

"Oh, she's got jokes!"

"An arsenal."

I grab his bicep and squeeze. "I'd love to hear them."

He smiles so big I want to dance on the balls of his cheeks. "Play your cards right." Then he puts on his best poker face, all stern and smolder. "So, you think I'm cute?"

"Who said that?" I scoff.

He chuckles. "Playing hard to get, I see."

"Who me? Never," I say. "But I'll answer if you answer something for me."

"Go ahead." He checks his phone.

Deep breath: "Are you wearing a harness?"

Cole Vivien

Past midnight, Teddy asks something I don't hear because my phone buzzes with rapid-fire texts from Jason asking where I am, telling me about all the filming requests from the creators in attendance, the buzz online about the app, hundreds of new subscribers. When I don't respond, he adds: BTW I wrapped up everything with the Times reporter. All good. Hotel's clean. Heading to a club downtown with some of the V guys. I borrowed one of your jocks. Don't wait up ;)

I silence my phone and shove it in my pocket. "Sorry, my friend is going out with some guys to a club."

"What about you?" His voice is tinged with disappointment.

"Not my scene." I'm more interested in how this will turn out.

"Same. I'm a house plant. Would much rather be home with my plant babies." His nostrils flare. "I mean, like, not now, obviously. This is so much better than being home alone." He's sputtering.

"*You're* cute." I sidle up beside him and he blushes again. At this rate, I'm going to give this guy rosacea.

"I am?" His voice is small. "I mean, thank you. You are. Too. Also. As well."

"I gathered that already."

He buries his face in his hands.

"So what were you asking me before my phone blew up?"

"Oh, um—" He laughs again, a bit nervously, but it's still music. "Are you wearing a harness under your suit?"

"Could you feel it?"

He shrugs. "I like harnesses. Plants and harnesses and guys named Cole."

"Bold."

"It's true." He clears his throat, then looks around. The steps, and the surrounding area, are empty, except for us. "Can I see?"

"Very bold." But I stand up anyway and start unbuttoning my dress shirt. Then I stop. "I'll trade you. A good look at the harness for the flannel."

He flicks the collar of his shirt. "*This?*"

I shrug. "Looks comfortable."

He scratches his beard, then reaches up and tugs the brim of his beanie down over his eyes and nose. All that's visible is his mouth, which smirks. "This is nuts."

Then he stands up and unbuttons his shirt, which comes unhooked quickly due to its wear. He pushes his beanie back above his eyes, then gets back to his shirt. He's wearing a white ribbed tank top underneath that hugs his sturdy, thick upper body and accentuates his hairy pecs.

"You really want this old thing?"

"Why not?"

He shrugs.

"I'm so uncomfortable in these clothes." I shake my arms and the lack of slack and movement is apparent. "I thought about buying an 'I heart NY' hoodie earlier." I wink.

After dethreading his arms through his shirt, he takes it

gently into his hands and folds it perfectly. His broad shoulders escape the flannel and all I can do is stare at the definition of his collarbone. A cool breeze ignites a wave of goose bumps down his strong forearms. It was warmer earlier, but May nights in this city change in a New York minute.

"I can't believe I'm doing this, though it's not the strangest shit I've seen in this city." He shivers. "Where did you come from, anyway?"

"Like, in life?"

"Existentially, yes. But also physically, tonight." He gestures toward my monkey suit. "I'm assuming some sort of highfa-lutin business-y thing."

"Highfalutin? That's a choice word."

He tips his beanie toward me. "I know things."

"Existentially, I—" I glance up at the night sky, at constellations that resemble castles like penthouses and Greek gods like Nickolas Lund. "That's a thought for another night. Maybe one with more wine. Wouldn't want to scare you off with deep thoughts."

"I enjoy deep thought," he says in an almost whisper.

My shoulders relax. My interactions with men are always so methodical, with my go-to moves, an intimacy checklist I tick off with my fingers, lips, tongue. No-brainers. But nobody has made me as breathless yet comfortable as Teddy. And I'm not anxious around Teddy. Which is strange.

"Anyway—" Back to negotiating how much I reveal: "I'm here on business. Tonight was an appreciation gala for my employees."

"*Your* company?" His eyes widen. "And you really want my whole Target shirt?"

I chuckle and, with a wink, say, "Nah, a sleeve'll do."

His brows raise. "I should—"

He stops talking when I take off my shirt, revealing the leather harness.

Teddy Hughes

I don't subscribe to organized religion, but my single momma raised me Catholic. When Cole's shirt comes off and I see his body, I say a whole-ass Hail Mary followed by an Our Father and do the sign of the cross because I've seen the lord.

I'd subscribe to him.

"What?" he asks, as if he doesn't know he's beautiful.

Every muscle, tendon, fiber of my being yearns to reach out and touch him, but I don't have his consent.

"I'm average, at best." He flexes, fishing for compliments, confidence oozing off him in buckets. He knows what he's doing, and I'm hooked.

"There's nothing average about you," I say. Once upon a time, as a thick guy, a comment like that would have sent me into a spiral of body shame, but I've learned to love my soft big boy dad bod and that body dysmorphia in the gay community is the common denominator that connects us all.

A gay couple walking by hand in hand catcalls us, jolting me back to the reality that we're undressing outside in public. To the naked eye, we definitely look like two dudes about to fuck on The Met steps. I press my folded flannel against my stomach instinctually.

Cole doesn't flinch. He puffs out his chest a bit more.

"Show off," I tease. "You *know* you're hot."

That makes him deflate a bit. "It's all a show." He rolls his eyes, not in a sarcastic way, but in the way Kit rolls her eyes when she's being vulnerable. I can spot avoidant behavior miles away. *Thanks, babe.*

Normally I would comment on that, but we just met and I could use one night of hot, sweaty sex. Deep vulnerability is off-limits. If I'm lucky, I'll get a glass of water after fucking before he says, "I have an early morning, but this was great," and promptly deletes me from his mind the second I'm gone.

Look at me, assuming he'll invite me back to his hotel room. Judging from Cole's attire, his perfect Armani suit and designer shoes and that harness!—which is not your run-of-the-mill sex shop harness, it's definitely more intricate, leather woven together in a statement piece, one hidden beneath all those beautiful clothes—he'd look down on my tiny-ass "two-bedroom" studio with Kit.

With my eyes still fixated on the harness, he asks, "You really like it, huh?"

"Can I?" My fingers twitch.

He steps closer, lessening the gap between us, and raises an eyebrow. "You don't have to ask, Teddy." His voice is deeper, huskier, and breathier all at once and all the blood in my body rushes to my dick.

I take another look around because I'm not one for an audience and I feel like this is my shot to kiss him and level up the flirtatious energy between us. Coast is clear.

My fingers reach beneath the harness, brushing against his warm skin and soft chest hair, and wrap around the strap.

Gripping it tight, I lock eyes with him, and with force, pull him impossibly close to me, his lips hovering above mine.

His hot, heavy breath tickles my chin. I move to kiss him, but he tilts his head slightly, missing my lips. But he doesn't move away. Instead, he wraps his arm around me, resting at the small of my back. Licking his lips, he says, "Sorry, I don't kiss."

Cole Vivien

Teddy squints, scanning my face for any sign of playful pillow talk.

Instead of explaining, I move to his neck and breathe against his skin.

My fingers dance across the back of his neck and his flesh ignites, sending a shiver down his spine that makes his entire body quake.

"Fuck," he groans, breathing heavily like he ran a marathon. He tugs harder at the leather strap across my chest.

"Wanna try it on?"

"Fuck yeah."

His dick is rock solid against my thigh, straining his jeans. I don't want to pull away, so when he lets go of the strap, I do my best to unhook it and take it off without losing body contact.

Once it's in his hands, he takes a step back, and a rush of cold air assaults me.

Offering me his flannel, he says, "Here, babe." Every guy I've hooked up with outside of contracted filming for VERSTL has called me babe in the "flirting stage," between sending nudes and introducing their names. It's lost all meaning. Yet Teddy's tender expression of the word makes my ears prickle. Curious.

I tuck my black Armani shirt inside the back of my pants so I don't have to put it on the nasty Met steps, and slip into his warm flannel. It smells like sandalwood and vanilla and manly musk; I could get lost in it if I allowed myself.

"It looks better on you." He wriggles into the harness after adjusting it for size.

"I disagree." Now it's my turn to grab onto him, loop my fingers into the metal hook at the center of the harness, leveraging my strength to pull myself into him.

"You're killing me."

"Can't do that," I say. "But I do have an urge to cuddle you."

"I bet you're a good cuddler." He clears his throat. "We could, er, go back to my place but it's a dee-saster. Plants everywhere." Nervous laughter takes over. How often does he do this sort of thing? Probably never, which is even more adorable. "And bras. Did you know living with a woman would mean bras everywhere?" His voice trails off and he looks himself up and down, avoiding me entirely. He scratches his head and a rush of adrenaline I haven't felt in a lifetime hits me. I don't need sex, or even want it. I'm not lacking in that department. But a night where I'm not alone, falling asleep next to a warm body, would be new. Invigorating.

"We could go back to my hotel." Though, if I take him back to my hotel, I *have* to be honest with him. I have an obligation to let him know what I do. He should have the opportunity to decide if he wants to be with me knowing I engage in raw, bareback sex. I get tested regularly, so does everyone I fuck, but I don't want him finding out after the fact and thinking I was deceitful by omission. Every man has an agenda, and I want him to know I would *never* take advantage of him. "We don't have to," I add quickly.

"You're fucking hot. I would love to."

I let out a deep breath, knowing this sweet, beautiful man might say goodbye to me here and now.

"But?" he asks.

"There's something you have to know about me first."

Teddy Hughes

He's a murderer. That's what he's about to say, isn't it?

If he were, he wouldn't tell me. Unless he's genuinely psychotic?

Suddenly, his body is so damn tense. "My name is Cole Vivien. *The* Cole Vivien," he says, as if he's Meryl Fucking Streep. I go through the Rolodex of gay celebrities in my head. It's a short list, so it takes like ten seconds. Nothing.

I hedge my bets: "Oh, you were in that movie? Show?"

His face softens as he sighs in relief. "You don't recognize me." It's not a question, but a statement.

"Am I supposed to? Are you some sort of social media influencer?"

Lips pursed, his head tilts back and forth diplomatically. "You could say that."

I swallow a laugh; it's preposterous when social media influencers think they're *that* important. But mocking him is probably not a cute look for me right now because I'd like to fuck him.

"I'm a sex worker, an *entrepreneur*," he stresses, handing me his phone, app open:

VERSTL
Switch Positions

Cole Vivien ⊘

@TheColeVivien

CEO and founder of VERSTL. "In case I forget to tell you later, I had a really good time tonight." Here to make dreams come true. My only rule: I don't kiss...on the mouth.

SUBSCRIBE!

"Whoa," is all I can say, and when I look up at him, he's looking at the ground. Is he nervous that I'm going to judge him? "I know this app!"

He looks up, all puppy dog eyes. "You do." Not a question, not a statement.

"Grindr meets OnlyFans meets Match.com meets Sugar Daddies for queer entrepreneurs who want to interact with real consumers and develop intimate connections? Every gay in my world knows VERSTL." I scan his screen again: *CEO and founder of VERSTL.* Oh. Oh, shit. "You're *The* Cole Vivien." A little laugh escapes my lips because I chose not to subscribe to his account. It's like following Mark Zuckerberg on Facebook. Big egos and all. "I get it now."

"You're not turned off?"

"Why would I be?" I hand his phone back.

He shrugs. "I—"

I cut him off. "I have a few friends who have VERS accounts and make decent side money. It's legitimate, hard work, and I'm a huge advocate for sex work and its decriminalization. And the work VERSTL does has been extraordinary." I'm babbling, and I'm sure he hears this all the time. "I would never be turned off by this. Or you. Unless your goal is to entice me into making content?" I laugh at my own punch line because of what Kit and I discussed earlier, but Cole isn't laughing. I realize what I said—*how* I said it—and all the air leaves my lungs. "Obviously that's not what you're doing," I say, quickly, but *fuck*, I think the damage is done.

Crossing his arms over his chest, he offers a tight-lipped smile. "I would never do that. I tell everyone I might be intimate with what I do before it gets to that point." His voice is not exactly monotonous, but it's sure as hell not anywhere near as warm as it was five minutes earlier. "There's a lot of guys who, once I tell them what I do, shame me. Those people are easy to deal with. Then there are the ones who ask to be scene partners. For my ego, and from a financial standpoint, that's—" His words sound breathless. "It becomes a business transaction and I'm not looking for that tonight." He goes silent for a few seconds. "I understand if you're not interested—"

"I am!" I cut him off again. "Sorry, I totally get all of that." I'm not about to make this more awkward. Time to start over. Backtrack. "Well, I'm *The* Teddy Hughes. And I'd love to spend the night with you."

Three
A Value Proposition

Cole Vivien

Frank's gargantuan stature is easily visible halfway down the block.

"The Mark?" Teddy asks. "*That's* where you're staying?" He stops walking. "I'm dressed like I'm going to Folsom Street Fair! I can't go in like this."

"That harness is more expensive than this." I pull at the opening of his flannel, still draped across my body.

"I'm *naked*!"

He has a point. Though I'm sure Frank and the front desk clerks have seen playboys of all kinds, the drug-induced party boys from new and old money stumbling in and out of their lavish lobby at all hours of the night.

It's late now. We can easily get up to the penthouse without drawing attention.

"I have an idea." I yank his shirt off my body and tie the arms around his waist.

"Very '90s leather bar," Teddy says. "Which is very my aesthetic. If I had any money, I'd hire you as my stylist."

Stepping back, I say, "It's a look. You fill out that tank top and harness *so* well."

Teddy bites his bottom lip. "Oh, yeah?" Placing his warm hand on my bare chest, I realize I'm still very much shirtless. I yank the Armani out of the back of my pants and quickly button and tuck it in, and I do a full-body check in a nearby window.

"You look sexy as fuck," he says. "Am I good?"

That's a loaded question. "More than good." I hook my index finger inside the lip of his jeans and tug him close to me. The back of my finger grazes a tuft of warm hair, and a shiver electrifies my body. I want to see, feel, kiss every part of him, nuzzle my nose between his legs and dive deep, coming up for air only when I need him to breathe for me. "Damn near perfect."

He blushes. "For The Mark, I mean." He scratches the top of his head.

I fixate a little too long on his beanie, and while I love how adorable it makes him look, it's tattered and looks worn in a very unchic way. "You mind if I—"

He shrugs. "Do your worst, handsome."

Beneath his beanie is a mess of sun-kissed red-by-way-of-strawberry blonde curls, tampered down by the hat, but still breathtakingly beautiful. I run my fingers through the tangles, and he closes his eyes, leaning into my touch. He moans softly. His lips look like pillows I want to lay my head and curl up on. They part ever so subtly, and it takes all of me not to nuzzle my nose against his cheeks.

Slowly, he opens his eyes. "How do I look?"

I hold my breath, not wanting to break the moment.

Michelangelo's David *couldn't compete with you.*

Like every single star in the night sky in human form.

Like the most beautiful thing I've ever seen.

What I say is, "Good to go."

Teddy Hughes

How did I manage to convince a sex god to invite me to stay the night at The Mark Hotel?

My body is riddled with nerves, all synapses firing at once.

Play it cool.

What Would Kit Do? Probably an ironic finger gun and a wink to break the tension.

"Mr. Vivien." The doorman bows his head to Cole.

Cole straightens his posture. "Evening, Frank."

"There's a note for you at the front desk," Frank responds, an air of class in his voice.

Cole's eyebrows crinkle. "About what?" he wonders out loud.

Frank doesn't react. Or move. Like one of those guards at Buckingham Palace.

"Thanks, Frank. Hey, is the kitchen still open?"

"For you, sir." Frank's eyes wander to the harness strapped across my chest. "What would you be needing tonight? I can radio the kitchen for you, save you the trouble." He doesn't take his eyes off me, tracing the outline of the ratty flannel tied around my waist down to my dirty Converse, examining my hairy chest and bare shoulders because skin is far too garish for the lobby of The Mark. Frank clearly smells the middle-of-the-night-hookup on me.

Cole looks to me. "A bottle of—"

"Rosé!" I immediately regret the choice. Feels so pedestrian. Rosé?!

He smirks. "And some chocolate-covered strawberries."

"Right away. I'll send up your note with that, if you'd like to head *straight* to the elevators," Frank says, eyeing me.

I feel cheap. I'm used to feeling poor—or at the very least, squarely middle-class—because I am, but cheap is a new one. I don't belong here, and I want to crawl right out of my skin and disappear through the walls and back out onto the streets so I can quietly make my way back to my shitty apartment, alone.

"You okay?" Cole asks as we wait for the elevator.

There's a young straight couple who look like they've returned from a night at the opera. The woman, blond hair styled and pinned to perfection in a curated bun and a blush ball gown that sparkles under the soft overhead lights, has her arm hooked to a man in a navy blue tuxedo with slick hair parted off to the side. The diamond engagement ring on her ring finger is Mount Fucking Everest, and her fingers delicately stroke his wrist, which dons a gold Apple Watch with a braided brown leather Hermès band. Both stare at me like I've killed their Maltese, Muffy, because in my mind they totally have a floofy dog the size of a decently flashy BULGARI clutch.

You know what? Fuck this. "Oh, babe," I say to Cole, "my chastity cage is tight." I shift my weight leg to leg as if I'm picking a wedgie, and Mr. and Mrs. Muffy are clearly sipping on this like poison-laced tea. "Can we use the pup masks tonight? I've been a good boy." I tug on the harness as the elevator doors open.

Cole rushes in and hastily whips out a key card on the panel, looking at the corner of the elevator where the wall meets the floor.

The man starts to walk in, but his wife holds him back and turns her nose up at us.

"I don't have a chastity cage." I wink at them as the doors close.

He lets go of a held breath. "Did you have to?"

Flashing my best puppy dog eyes, I hope he isn't a surly, uptight wench because god forbid I embarrass him in front of his rich peers. But he's clearly trying to bite back a smile; his nostrils are flaring and he's purposely avoiding me.

So I dip and swerve around him until we're face-to-face.

We stay like that, suspended in the center of the elevator, neither of us breathing, until it stops at the top floor and the doors open directly into the fucking penthouse.

The grandeur of it takes my breath, holds it captive. I can't help but feel like I'm suddenly in the middle of my own BDSM-flavored fairy tale.

Cole Vivien

"Holy shitballs!" Teddy's face is all wide-eyed wonder and awe as he twirls, arms spread open. His steps become hesitant as he peeks into the lounge with the grand piano and fireplace. His eyes trace the outline of the space, taking it all in like he's won a brand-new house on an HGTV show hosted by a tragically heterosexual designer wife and her contractor husband. As he wanders into the white living room with the cathedral ceiling and skylights, he lets out a breath. The dining room, which looks like a Michelin star farm-to-table restaurant, is set for twelve right off a state-of-the-art kitchen.

"What do you think?"

Running his fingers along the marble countertops, he says, "This old thing?" He turns toward me. "Modest. I've been here at least a few dozen times."

"You have, huh?"

"You think you're the first hot Frenchy to pick me up at a straight dive bar and trick me into taking my shirt off at The Met, all in an effort to seduce me into going back to this very penthouse?" Teddy starts opening the kitchen cabinets. "Last time I was here, it was for a wild bareback sex party. I think I left my chastity cage here." He reaches into one of the drawers and pulls out a wildly elaborate cooking utensil with a metal spiral on the end. "Right where I kept it." Another drawer, another gadget, this time an electric wine bottle opener. He presses the button and it buzzes. "Good to know my electric penis pump still works."

He's overcompensating. On the rare occasion that I do hook up with a guy for fun, who genuinely wants *me*, not @The-ColeVivien, they tend to talk big games thinking that I want wild, kinky, no-holds-barred sex. To fuck like a porn star: lights, camera, fetish.

"Hey." I place my hand on his. "You don't have to do this. We don't have to do anything you're not comfortable with."

He moves in closer to me, and he hovers near my lips for a few seconds, silence suspended between us. I swallow, hard.

Closer.

Impossibly close.

Sandalwood and beer and vanilla and sweat.

He opens his mouth, tilts his head, and I almost stop him because of my no-kissing rule, but his head swivels. "I bet this place has a great view," he whispers, and promptly turns to march right out of the kitchen.

He's a giddy child playing hide-and-seek, and I chase after him, laughing and doing my best to indulge him, and maybe myself a bit.

Dashing between the different rooms and up the stairs to the second floor, he ends up on the patio overlooking Central Park, in the same spot where April found me out, then Nickolas almost proposed marriage. I shove those anxieties down and focus on Teddy.

"I can see the park from here," he says, his eyes glassy. "It's beautiful."

"You okay?" A sadness radiates off him in low frequency waves, and I want to turn it off, find the button that makes him laugh that hearty, witchy cackle again. Or at the very least, make him feel safe. I carefully place my hand on the upper part of his back.

"Feeling...*strange*."

"Being here with me?"

Teddy shakes his head. "My nights in this city are numbered."

"Oh?"

"Couldn't keep my business afloat, rent hikes and—" He leans over the railing and gazes longingly at Central Park. "It's like nothing here ever belonged to me. But I loved it. *Love*. It's surreal."

"You wouldn't be the first person to fall in love with some…thing that couldn't love them back." I want to tell him to protect himself better, but it's not my place.

He looks away. "Falling in love is a lot like cracking your own chest open and hoping you don't die from blood loss or infection. Especially when it ends and you go your separate ways and hope you find some*thing*, *one* who works." He shrugs.

That's a brutal visual which accompanies my own reasons for never allowing myself to fall in love.

"But I can't *not* love," he says. "Maybe that's why I'm a constant wreck."

I don't understand why some people open themselves up that way. The reality is, everything ends. Why not mitigate the damage by steering clear altogether?

"Are we still talking about the city? Or was there a man?" I ask.

"Isn't there always?" Teddy asks. He lets everything unsaid hang in the air.

"Sorry, I don't mean to pry."

"It's a tale as old as time, really. Plant Daddy," he points to himself. "That's me," he whispers. "Meets a man who promises him the world but can't deliver. Ends up meeting another who is ready to commit, but then changes the parameters. Wants an open relationship, and suddenly hole and pole becomes his priority over Plant Daddy. I mean, how can one person compete with a city full of dick?" He sucks in a big breath, and leans into me, so I meet him there and rub the spot on his back where my hand rested. The facade of Teddy's self-characterization falls away. "*I* wasn't enough." He picks at dirt beneath his fingernails.

I try to speak, but all that comes out is air, like a slow leak in a tire. "Teddy—"

He cuts me off with a big, heaving sigh, followed by a long, drawn-out groan and a little screech that sounds like a spider monkey. He shakes out his limbs. "Ugh, gross, emotions," he says. "Nothing says, 'Fuck me, stranger I met in a bar' like weeping on your dick appointment."

"This isn't— You don't have to censor yourself with me."

He sighs and I urge him to continue. "In that case, I'm a real catch! No money, moving back home to my mom's at thirty-fucking-four! Turns out all New York did was bleed me dry, heart, body, mind." He wipes his eyes with the back of his hand.

"I know how you feel," I say.

"I doubt that," he says.

I could say a million things right now to prove how wrong he is, that he knows nothing about me. But I let his comment sit.

"Agh," Teddy grunts. "Sorry. That was unfair."

Like I thought, his comment isn't about me. It's easy for anyone to look at my life and see a chasm between reality and fiction created by our permanently online brains.

"Don't worry." I move closer to him to let him know I'm here. He's a sweet soul looking for someone to see him.

The room service attendant announces his presence. We see each other through the glass windows separating the living space from the patio, and I wave in acknowledgement. He bows, leaves a sterling silver tray covered in decadent milk, white, and dark chocolate-covered strawberries on the coffee table, and a bottle of rosé chilled in a matching ice bucket next to the couch.

"I didn't set out to meet anyone tonight," I confess. "I needed to escape this party I was throwing here. I—" I contemplate telling him about Nickolas and my complicated family ties, but decide against that. "Life is never what it seems on the surface."

Teddy wraps me in a bear hug so warm and tight I have to actively hold back tears.

It's overwhelming. Too much for my body to manage.

So I pull away. "I'm going to take a shower."

"You want company?" he asks.

"I need to decompress for a few minutes, if that's okay. Make yourself at home. Whatever you need, it's yours."

Teddy Hughes

YOU'RE *WHERE*? Right on cue, Kit is both flipping out *and* mildly jealous over text messages. OF COURSE you meet a walking sex toy and end up in a scene from Pretty Woman!

Except I'm no Richard Gere, I text back as I shovel leftover caviar and buttered toast points I found in the fridge into my mouth.

Within seconds, she fires back: No, he's obviously both Richard Gere AND Julia Roberts. OMG are you texting while he's inside you?

I gasp at her borderline bottom-shaming, reminding her I'm *very* versatile.

Cole walks into the living room with a white towel loosely wrapped around his waist and I chuck my phone across the floor. Beads of water dot his chest and stomach. He leans against the wall like James Dean, all shoulder muscles and smoldering stares. I hadn't noticed until we were on the patio and he was talking about wanting to make a connection—his eyes aren't just dark from sleep circles, but from something he carries around with him. Fear, maybe. Loneliness.

"What're you watching?" he asks.

It takes me a second to respond because I have zero words. "How do you not know about *Schitt's Creek*? Have you been living under a rock!"

He tosses his head back, and there's something about a man's neck—especially Cole's with his model aesthetic face and everyman body—the way it elongates and his Adam's apple bounces, that makes me want to lick every inch of him.

"I don't keep up with pop culture."

"I don't understand," I say flatly. "What do you do with your time?"

"Work a lot, build the company." He bites the inside of his mouth.

There's so much more to his story, and I know I shouldn't pry for a billion different reasons—after tonight, I'll never see or hear from him again. And that even if, on the off chance I do, he's a sex worker, so there will be a limited capacity to our exchanges.

I pat the couch next to me. "Join me. I have a caviar and strawberry picnic going."

"I'm salivating." Slowly, he makes his way toward me. He grins sweetly, and his eyes travel down my body.

He spreads his legs, towel creeping open enough that his bare knee is visible, which presses into mine. I want to be respectful and not look between his legs, but it's taking every single muscle in my body to keep from getting on my knees.

"So what is *Schitt's Creek* about?" he asks.

"Rich family with two adult children loses all their money, so they move to this rural town that they forgot they owned where they live in an old motel. Hilarity and hijinks ensue."

Cole's doing his best to listen, absorb, and watch what's going on in the current episode on the screen. His eyes are bright and he even lets a little laugh escape.

I place my hand on his bare knee. Cole doesn't flinch. Instead, he spreads his legs further, and stares at my hand.

Gradually, my fingers tickle his skin until I'm rubbing the underside of his thigh, moving into the towel and up his leg.

"Is this okay?" I ask.

"More than okay," he says.

I move to the floor, wedging my knees between his legs on the carpet.

His raises his eyebrows.

"Someone's eager," he says as both of my hands run the length of either thigh, stopping near his waist where the tension from the towel prevents me from easily traveling up his torso. I like to tease, go slow, take my time devouring.

Massaging his thighs slowly, I say, "Mmm, you're so solid."

"You like that?" he asks.

"Fuck yes."

I lean forward and kiss his abdomen, traveling lower and lower until I reach the white towel. I playfully bite the fabric, tugging at it gently to see if it comes loose. I look up at him, and he's watching me with great intensity. My eyes widen, asking him without words if this is okay.

He places his hands on my shoulders, but it's not in an aggressive, dominant way like how some inexperienced guys do, which is always so selfishly unaware. No, Cole's touch is caring, attentive, the way he strokes my shoulder blade then squeezes lightly in tandem with deep moans that radiate from his core.

As I tease the outline of him beneath the fabric, kissing the terry cloth, nibbling the cotton around its perimeter, his breathing steadily increases; I could spend all day here, teasing him, responding as he bucks his hips by either pulling back or pressing my nose into the tent of his legs and groaning.

I love it when he bucks, bucks, bucks, his back arching, begging me to stop, to keep going, to go further.

With my teeth, I grab the lip of the towel and yank at it until it untucks from around his waist, revealing all of him.

But I don't go directly for him.

Instead, I hoist myself up, swing my legs over him, and settle on his lap so that his dick presses into the seat of my jeans.

Both hands reach around the back of his neck; my fingers run through his thick dark hair, massaging his scalp.

His eyes are closed, but he grabs onto the center strap of the harness I forgot was still on, and pulls me down until our noses graze.

A wild fervor takes over, my body a current of untamed electricity.

Up and down, my hips find their rhythm against him until he's pulling at me.

"I want to kiss you," I say, breathily.

"I know, but—"

"There's plenty more we can do with our mouths."

Cole Vivien

A tangle of limbs and bodies.

His heart beat beat beats so fast fast fast.

Beads of sweat dot his brow.

My fingers move up both of his arms until I reach around his back and pull at him until his chest is against mine and we're hugging.

He's waiting for me to say something. Or to make a move. And I want to; I do. I want to unbuckle his jeans and take him in my mouth until he finishes.

But I also want to stay here, to feel his body pressed against mine, to hold him and hope that maybe he holds me back. So I squeeze him.

And he wriggles his arms underneath me and matches my hug with one of his own. He exhales and nuzzles his face into the crook of my neck. His breathing steadies, his chest settles.

We stay like this for a full minute, but it feels like a split second, over too soon.

"Vif-feers-ice," Teddy mumbles into my neck.

"Excuse me?" I say with a chuckle.

Picking up his head, he clarifies, "This feels nice."

"Can I be honest?"

"Please do," he says.

"I want to do ungodly things to you, don't get me wrong," I start. "But I also want *this* tonight." I hold him again as he lays his head back down on my chest. "Is that okay?"

"I like that." He nestles into my chest hair.

"Maybe we can lose the clothes," I suggest.

He butterfly-kisses my chest before he stands up.

Towering over me, he never breaks eye contact.

Not as he slips off the harness.

Not as he sheds his white ribbed tank top, revealing his solid, hairy upper body.

Not as he slowly unbuttons his jeans and bites his bottom lip, not as part of a show, but in a show of vulnerability, like he's about to reveal something sacred.

Not as he lowers the zipper, revealing the hidden beauty underneath that springs up, because I guess he likes to go commando; he's natural, but trimmed and shaped enough to accentuate all of his six girthy inches.

Not as he shucks his jeans, even after they get stuck on his tree trunk thighs and grapefruit calves.

Not as I study him like he's the ceiling of the Sistine Chapel, the *Mona Lisa*, every great work of art by every great artist who ever lived and ever will; he's the Roman Colosseum, the Great Wall of China, every natural wonder of the world.

He gazes into my eyes as I reach under me, toss the towel onto the floor, and reposition myself diagonally on the long, plush sofa, inviting him to join me.

He presses his warm, naked body against mine, and burrows his head into the crook of my armpit. Inhaling deeply, he buries his nose further in. "Yeah, I like this."

"I'm glad." I pull him closer. "Ask me something. Anything."

Teddy Hughes

"If you could have one superpower, what would it be and why?" I ask Cole as we cuddle together in the massive king-size bed in the master bedroom. We've spent hours talking about our favorite TV shows (his are *Succession*, *Shark Tank*, and *Project Runway*, the classic Heidi Klum/Tim Gunn seasons), movies (the J-Lo stripper movie *Hustlers*, and a whole bunch of French films I've never heard of), musicians (classical musicians whose names sound like fancy menu items at a Paris bistro), and favorite places traveled (Tuscany and Portugal). But then he said he's never truly felt comfortable anywhere. That made me pull him closer, stroke his hair, hold him tight, and switch to something lighter.

"That's a hard one." He intertwines his fingers with mine, playing with each one. "What would yours be?"

I yawn. It's nearly 4:00 a.m. and I could stay up with him forever, but I'm also exhausted. I haven't pulled an all-nighter since edits on my first book, and I haven't spent all night talking to a guy without fucking since, well, ever.

"I'm obsessed with Poison Ivy, the Batman villain." I laugh, showing Cole YouTube clips of the '90s animated *Batman* TV show. "Immune to poisons and toxins—I'm assuming that includes toxic men—and can make plants bend to my will? In my mind, I am her. Only with hairier tiddies."

Cole rubs my pecs and says, "*She's* hot," his voice low and gravelly.

I close my eyes. "A true gay icon." I stick my tongue out, playfully.

He laughs. "That makes sense, Plant Daddy." The way he calls me that makes me think he knows a bit more about me than I told him. I lift my head and glare at him, triggering him to admit, "I might've googled you. When I was in the shower. *Teddy* plus *Plant Daddy* yields a couple immediate results. I had to make sure the man I invited into my penthouse wouldn't murder me." He grabs for his phone on the nightstand and swipes through some apps, pulling up his email. "I ordered copies of both of your books." He flashes me the receipts.

"So your superpower is stalking?" I say, coolly.

"I'm sorry, I didn't mean—"

"Oh, honey, please, I checked out your VERSTL page when you were in the shower. It's totally fine. I didn't subscribe because I'm broke, though. You're expensive. But—" My free hand grabs his ever-hard dick and strokes it, long and deep, feeling its impossible hardness and knowing I can easily control him. This is something we've been doing on and off all night: talk, laugh, stroke, talk, laugh, get deep, deep throat—a beautiful balance. "I make up for my lack of finances with other skills."

"You should put them on your résumé," he says.

"Now, that's an endorsement!"

We both go quiet, and I don't rush to fill the silence.

I move to lick the underside of his chin, then down his neck, tracing his collarbone with my tongue.

Laying my head on his chest, I close my eyes, lulled by the way his chest rises and falls, rises and falls.

His breathing slows.

I'm almost asleep when I hear him say, "Teddy? You awake."

I haven't drifted off yet.

He pulls me in and grips me.

"If I had one superpower," he whispers. "I would fly away. Find someplace I belong, where I don't have to perform." He pauses, and so faintly says, "For anyone."

Cole Vivien

Light streams in through the expansive windows, bathing the room in soft golden tones.

It's so quiet I forget I'm in the city. The past few days, I've done a lot of wandering as the sun came up, weaving through each of the rooms, and then when that didn't satisfy me, I'd end up lost in the maze of Central Park. But not this morning. Instead, I spent it in Teddy's arms. For the first time in a very long while, I felt peace.

Teddy is passed out on his stomach, his freckled back bathed in the sun's rays. His hair looks even more red, but also blond, in the morning light. There's something peaceful about the way he sleeps, grinning as he dreams. He strikes me as the type to wake up and immediately process the wild adventures his dream self went on.

Draped in the softest cotton robe, I find myself on the patio after ordering room service. The city is serene at this time of the morning, that golden hour when only the most ardent joggers are out before tourists fill the sidewalks. It's only a matter of time, especially the Saturday of Memorial Day weekend.

I lie down on the couch and soak up the sun, and find it easy to doze off.

"There you are!" Jason's voice breaks through the silence.

I eye him. He looks like the morning after, disheveled. "Good night, eh?"

He grins. "Hot as fuck. I crab-walked back."

"Pig," I say, standing up.

"Oink." He leans against the railing. "Could say the same for you."

"Low-key, quiet," I say, and he narrows his eyes at me. "Me, myself, and I."

He yanks the drawstring of my robe swiftly open to reveal my naked body.

"I sleep naked."

"So does the hunky ginger in your bed, apparently," he says, and I hiss at him. The penthouse is big enough that Jason is staying with me, in his own wing, so I rarely see him. "*Relax*, Casanova. I popped into your room to wake you up and saw a very bubbly ass that was not yours and left. He's sleeping. What do we know about him? Room service put your breakfast in the sunroom. Worked up an appetite, huh?"

I would normally tell Jason everything I learned, but that feels like betraying Teddy's trust. One recent item about Teddy that came up when I googled *Plant Daddy* again while he slept is that he declared bankruptcy after "discrepancies" were discovered, connected to his recent divorce. Bankruptcy filings are public, but the wording of what I saw is so nebulous I found it interesting. Jason would twist this information and make Teddy out to be some sort of money-hungry leech.

"Speaking of an appetite! Are you dying at that invitation?"

"What invitation?"

"This one." He holds it up. "I left it for you at the front desk. You didn't open it?"

I replay last night in my head, but once Teddy got naked all bets were off. I snatch the note from Jason and immediately all I see is an iconic golden monochromatic rainbow. "This is from Alessandro Arcobaleno!"

Mr. Vivien,

My team read your proposal and were quite impressed. I think a partnership with VERSTL could be quite advantageous for us both. As a queer designer with a strong ethos and a businessman with a strong brand, it's important my values align with anyone I do business with. I'd like to meet and see if our visions align. Me and my partner (in business and life) have a table reserved at Per Se at 8pm tomorrow evening.

All my best,
Alessandro

I plop hard on the couch and study it. "I thought we wouldn't hear from him."

"I've been in contact with his assistant for weeks—do you not listen when I talk?" he responds. "Here's the catch. He's wary of being attached to a company like VERSTL. From a brand perspective, he's focusing on propelling his name forward. If he's going to help you design clothing to expand the VERSTL brand, he wants to be sure you're interested in broadening your brand beyond sex. It's—"

"Hard enough being queer and making clothes for queer folks," I finish for him. "I know. That's why I want to work with him. He designs such fantastic gender-neutral items, but he also plays with fetish in a high fashion way. I love his blend of—"

"Save it for the meeting tonight." Jason throws a hand up,

urging me to stop. "I RSVPed for you. Oh, but you *do* need a date. I'm talking boyfriend material. To make a good impression. Reflect his values."

"Fit heteronormative values," I add, half joking. Market research Jason's firm conducted showed us that queer consumers are much more critical of queer artists and brands than nonqueer brands, making it hard to garner their support financially. "How are you not running some sort of multibillion company?"

"One day." He pauses. "Actually, I was thinking—" His tone curious. "*I* should go with you."

"I don't know if we'd be convincing as a couple," I say.

Jason shrugs. "I *would* suggest Nickolas instead, but."

"No." Unequivocally no. "I could—"

"Don't even suggest it," he says. "Horrible idea, taking your one-night stand to a business meeting at one of the most exclusive restaurants in New York? Uncontrolled variable." Jason presses the back of his hand to his forehead and feigns fainting like a Southern belle. "It smells like sex in here. Or is that syrup?"

"Both," I say with a grin. The sugary cinnamon-laced smells of the breakfast food are making my stomach growl. "I'll figure out tonight."

"Great, boss. I'm out. Got a date to fuck a couple after brunch in Chelsea. Hoping to get my eggs poached." Jason's sexual escapades are borderline fiction. He talks a big game, but it's all for show.

"Happy for you."

He opens one of the sterling silver trays and picks a slice of French toast up. "I'm taking this for the road." Hurricane Jason leaves as quickly as he came.

Teddy yawns as he ambles into the great room. "Did I hear another voice?" He's still naked, and I drink in his form.

"I got us breakfast," I say coolly.

He stretches before making his way to my front, hopping into my lap and straddling me. Our noses graze again. "Morning, handsome. What'd you get us?"

"Everything," I say. "God, how are you more beautiful in the daylight?"

"I'm immortal." He wags his tongue at me.

As I look into his eyes, gemstones in the daylight, one fleeting thought crosses my mind, and it's so fucking mad that I almost don't want to bring it up. Then again, he hasn't left yet, and he easily could have. Maybe Jason is wrong about it being a terrible idea to invite a "one-night stand" to a business dinner, not when that person is Teddy.

Teddy Hughes is a calming presence, and I need that. Plus, he said himself last night that he needs money, so there's definitely a way we can help each other. I want to help him, and keep him around a bit longer, if I can, and there's nothing safer for me than a good business deal.

"Actually," I say as he reaches for the serving cart, Jason's non-suggestion ringing in my ears. "There's something I want to run by you, a business proposition."

Teddy Hughes

"A business proposition?" I repeat, demounting him. "Romantic."

He winces. "That sounded cold."

I look under the closest tray to find a waffle. "Don't be sorry. I'm listening." I settle in beside him, drooling over his form. And the food—warm pancakes, crisp, buttery Belgian waffles, cinnamon-swirl French toast, a crystal fucking bowl of plump red berries and green melon balls. But mostly Cole.

"I have an important business dinner tonight, and my sister's wedding upstate Monday. Before you ask, yes, it's a Memorial Day wedding."

"The straights love co-opting national holidays for their weddings," I add, wondering about the nature of this business meeting.

He snickers. "Always. Anyway, I'm checking out tomorrow morning and renting a car for next week. Would you be interested in spending that time with me?"

Is this guy serious? "Like, the whole week? It's my last in the city, and—"

"I would hire you," he adds, a touch of hesitation on his lips.

"Again, romantic." I wink.

"That's my brand." He playfully elbows me.

I stop, reflect on his offer. "Color me intrigued. So how would that work, exactly?"

"I'll pay you to pretend to be my boyfriend. I need to impress a potential business partner tonight who wants to see me and my brand go beyond sex. It would go a long way to look coupled up." He rolls his eyes with a smirk. "And my family is, well, *interesting*, and there'll be no place for me to hide at my sister's wedding. *Unless* I have someone I can get lost in." He licks his lips and looks away, as if he's let slip something too vulnerable. "I haven't been home in a long while and it'd be nice to have a shield from all the questions. They'll be so consumed with *you*—"

"Even though your sister is the star of the show?" I ask.

He laughs again, but this time it's pitched and melodic and beautiful, different from how he laughed last night. Almost like whenever he laughed last night he was putting on a show, using a fake, deeper laugh as armor. Now he's letting his guard down.

"One would think," he says. "My *father* is the real star. We—" He stops himself from saying something else.

"The patriarchy is strong," I say.

"You have no idea." He pauses.

"Wait, your sister is getting married in New York?" My wheels are turning.

"My family lives outside of the city," he confesses.

"I thought you'd never been to New York before."

He swallows hard. "I'm sorry about that. I didn't mean to lie to you."

Technically, Cole doesn't owe me anything. It's not an egregious lie. It didn't harm me. I understand not wanting to tell a random guy you met in a trashy bar intimate details about your life. So I move past it. "I get it. I mean, I don't, but I do."

"Sorry—I understand if you don't want—"

"Did I say that?" I smirk. "But there's nobody else? I'm your last resort?"

"First and only."

"Nice line. So you're contracting *me* to play the role of your boyfriend?" This is certainly a twist I didn't expect. *From One Night Stand to Hired Boyfriend: A Memoir* by Teddy Hughes. I laugh out loud, despite myself.

"What?" His eyes pierce right through me.

Fuck, I'm a goner. "Your entire business model is built around subscriptions, yet *I'm* the one *you're* subscribing to. I'm your boyfriend subscription."

"Has a nice ring to it." He licks his lips.

I want to kiss him so badly, our bodies are magnetized. Suddenly, I'm inches from his lips. "If you coin that, I get royalties."

He turns away, whispers, "Deal," his breath hot against my cheek as he moves closer to my earlobe. His pillowy lips nibble at them delicately. "I trust you." His words are hesitant, like he's waiting to believe them. "And I like your company."

"So you'd be paying me to be at your beck and call," I say, though it's more like a question.

"Essentially." His fingertips running up and down my arms tenderly renders my entire body his.

"I *could* use the money," I say out loud. For years with Murray, I felt like I was at his beck and call, but that he never saw me as someone worthy of the task. I was there for him, but never enough. The way Cole touches me tells me I'd never be invisible to him, that he'd never discard me the way Murray did, even if this is *just* a business transaction.

"I'll pay you fairly. Seven days, seven nights? The hardest parts will be tonight, tomorrow, and Monday for the wedding. After that, it's hanging with the family but we'll have plenty of alone time." He ruminates. "Five thousand?"

I do some fast math. Seven days times 24 hours is 168 hours is $29 an hour. Not bad. Look at me, figuring out the cost of spending a week with an insanely hot guy when I have no job and nothing to do but move out of my apartment by the end of next weekend. Hell, I'd do it for free, but I'm not about to tell him that.

I'm about to accept his offer when he says, "Seven thousand? A thousand a day."

Reflexively, I shout, "Deal!"

Then I step back.

What did I agree to?

I take a cursory bite of waffle. "What are the ground rules? Now that we're business boyfriends, I'd like to know what's included in the, um, price." I wash it down with a glass of orange juice. "Is this an all-you-can-eat buffet? A la carte? Do you expect a side of cock with an Oscar-worthy performance?"

"I didn't think that far in advance. I would never want you to feel pressured. This is not about sex. Though I definitely would like to have sex with you. If you want to."

"So nookie is not expected," I say, touching his arm. "I appreciate that. Only if I want to?"

"Only if you want to."

"Abso-fucking-lutely."

Expertly eye-fucking me, he takes a step forward and my breathing snags.

As a reminder, he says, "No kissing."

Four
Terms and Conditions May Apply

Teddy Hughes

What the hell is this no-kissing thing? I want to be all, "Who hurt you?" a totally reasonable response to a "boyfriend." How exactly are we supposed to sell this without kissing? Murray hated PDA, refusing to kiss me in public or even hold my hand. I got used to it after a while, but his internalized homophobia, which he constantly projected to strangers, wore on me. Even in places like Provincetown and Fire Island, where gays blow each other on Boy Beach, he refused to kiss me. I never wanted to be fucked on the street, but is holding my man's hand while strolling through the park too much to ask?

"Out of curiosity, why don't you kiss?"

"Kissing complicates everything. Business, pleasure—blurs every line. So even when I'm not performing, I don't kiss to keep my—" His hand moves to his chest, right above his heart. "Head clear."

That's a load of manure, but I'll challenge him on that later. "What else?"

"Spend nights with me like we did last night."

I'd do that for free. But again, I don't tell him that.

"Be convincing." It's more of a question than a request.

"Easy." I grab hold of his arm. "How's this?"

Softly, I brush my nose against the side of his face, his stubble soft and itchy at once. I give his cheek three soft kisses, the first two quick, but the third lingers a bit longer.

Breath catching, he moves to lock eyes with me.

My fingers slide down his arm and between his legs, resting high on his inner thigh. Maintaining eye contact, his body moves parallel to mine.

He reaches to the back of my neck and pulls me into him.

I open my mouth. Exhale.

He opens his mouth. Inhale.

His free hand reaches around my back and down to my ass, squeezing it hard.

Before he starts to beg, I remind him it's a game and pull away.

Panting, lapping for air, I ask, "Like *that*?"

He bites his lip, head bobbling in ecstasy as he coos, "Convince me."

"Always leave them wanting more."

Sighing, he says, "*More, please,*" and I oblige.

This is a job, I repeat over and over to myself.

This is a job. I get to my knees, take his hard dick, run my tongue on the underside of his shaft, memorizing his veins and the weight of him over me, while staring straight into his eyes. He moans as the length of him hits the back of my throat.

This is a job.

Cole Vivien

Teddy's hairy stomach expands and contracts in short bursts as his ragged breathing slowly steadies. The rest of his body is coated with a thin layer of sweat, highlighting the musculature of his upper arms, thick thighs, and pecs with big perky nipples that he loves to have pinched.

He's utterly spent, his wet body limp atop damp bedsheets.

"You okay?" I ask, laying my head on his lower abdomen, inches away from his plump dick. My nose lightly grazes the tuft of curly hair, and I breathe in his musk.

"Heaven," is all that manages to escape his lips as he tries to catch his breath.

My fingers dance across his soft yet somehow firm belly until his skin feels slicker, and I stumble upon a rogue puddle of cum I must've missed. I position myself over him, and when he looks directly into my eyes, I flash him a sly smirk. "What kind of boyfriend would I be if I didn't clean you up?"

"Oh, f-fuck, Cole," he stammers as my tongue licks up every drop of the bittersweet and salty pool. His cock twitches beneath me, chubbing back to life against my chest. He makes a hissing sound from the sensitivity of the head rubbing my skin, so I don't take it further. His lips are too lickable. My whole damn body resists the urge to make him taste himself on mine.

I need to distract myself, not continue to stare directly at his beautiful face. You know what they say about Icarus flying too close to the sun.

Crawling up the bed, I intertwine my legs with his, wrap my arms over him, and lay my head on his soft chest hair. "Tell me something about you nobody knows." I don't realize what I'm asking until the words spill out. Too bold. Too...intimate.

But he takes it in stride. "I've lived so much of my life for the last year in fear."

His stomach stops contracting. He's holding his breath.

I grip him tight to let him know I'm listening, that I'm not judging him. *I have, too.*

"I was twenty-one when I met my now–ex-husband. He was in Nawlins visiting family, and I was young, dumb, full of cum, and damn naive," he says, and I press my ear to his chest to hear his heart beat faster faster faster. "And broke. I kind of grew up without much. *Nothing.*" He waves the thought away, and I wonder what he thinks about the way I live. "He was a doctor. Fancy, right? Eight years older, which seemed like a lifetime. I thought he was wise beyond his years." He laughs, but it's full of venom. "At first, he nurtured my dreams of opening my own plant nursery—"

"Is that what you went to school for?"

"Horticulture. Bred flora. I have a thing for tending to seeds, nurturing them until they flourish into something beautiful." The way he says that, the break in his voice, makes my heart ache. "His family comes from money. Like, old money." His voice takes on a British accent as he recites what he tells me is a scene from *Titanic* with Kathy Bates's character, which makes him laugh. I echo it, but only because I want him to feel at ease.

He tells me about his ex's family's estate, the gardens that enraptured him—sprawling acres of tall cypress trees imported from Tuscany that lined the property like flames. The outside gardens were global paradises. There was a sweeping grove of weeping willows that created a ghostly New Orleans allure around an Olympic-sized swimming pool treated to look like a natural bayou. The Japanese-inspired garden was Teddy's favorite spot, with different-sized trees sculpted with cloud-shaped boughs, cherry blossoms, pruned pines, Japanese maples, and bamboo. A peaceful stream that trickled into a waterfall ran around its perimeter and round, natural stone walkways led to a tea house.

The way he talks about plants is the closest I've ever come to touching raw passion.

"What happened to your ex?" I ask.

"We were long-distance for a few years, him here in the city, me back home in Nola, still trying to figure out how to make my dreams a reality. I had started the @TheOriginal-PlantDaddy Instagram account, curated shots of gorgeous gardens, most of them his family's estate, but a lot were from my own makeshift greenhouse in my apartment, where I started to breed, grow, and sell plants. My followers exploded overnight, and I was getting contacted by some major people and companies. I kinda rode that social media rocket for a bit, and after getting featured on HGTV and going viral across different platforms, the book deals came. For the first time, I was making real money. I needed a central hub, you know? So when he proposed and told me he'd help me open my nursery in the city, how could I say no? I was his Teddy Bear, ya know?"

His body shivers, and he stops talking.

I want to say he doesn't have to tell me anything, but he beats me to the punch.

"*Lesson du jour.*" His French is adorably acute. "Never give yourself up to get involved with an entitled man who comes from old money. Momma warned me. 'They stick to their kind—they'll never let someone like you in.'" He shrugs it off. "I never really had two pennies to rub together, but I have my plants. *Had.* Okay, now you go. Tell me something nobody knows about *you*."

"That's a long list," I say nervously, Teddy's warning tumbling around my head.

We stay quiet for a long while as one particular memory floods me:

A white Cadillac pulled up in front of Washington Square Park. Tinted windows slid down to reveal Father peering out at me over the brim of gold aviators. His secretary had emailed me a month prior requesting a three-hour time block in my schedule labeled "Pre-Graduation Dinner" with the name of the restaurant linked. He was trying, I thought. He'd been in meetings all day. Closing on a development deal with the Walton Group to "take The Deplantier Corp to new heights."

Checking his gold Rolex, he said, "Be on your best behavior, investors will be joining us."

Of course he couldn't show up for me, be present, spend time one-on-one the way other fathers did with their sons. There was always a motive, an objective, a lesson to learn. I was born to take over his company, a dream I never asked for or wanted. It was a yearlong battle between him and Mother to even allow me to pursue a degree in fashion. He wanted me to go to Harvard Business School, and I wanted to go to Parson's School of Design or FIT. Mother didn't often get involved, but when she did, Father listened. She collected favors by playing the dutiful wife and sacrificing personal opportunities that came her way early in their marriage—Mother was an aspiring actress when they met, but once they were married, he wanted her at home, tending to the household, so she gave up her acting career and never let him forget it. She cashed in one for me, convincing him that a dual fashion and business degree at NYU was a compromise.

"Is Mallory coming?"

"Your sister has other things to do." He waved thoughts of her away.

"Mal would be a better fit for your dinner, Father."

"Vivièn, I won't hear another word." He muttered something in broken French under his breath, an old world curse he broke out when he didn't want to hear something we had to say. "Your mother tells me tall tales about plans to move out to Los Angeles."

She was supposed to keep that to herself, *I thought. "Have to put my fashion degree to good use." I knew that would cause a reaction, given the nature of his visit.*

He snickered. "Foolish. When will you grow up, Vivièn?"

"I think I've done a good job at that on my own."

"You've never been on your own, son." He shifted his weight to face me. "You have the illusion of independence." As we drove past some of the NYU dorms, he motioned toward them. "You're only where you are because I allow it. I'm funding your playtime but after graduation, The Deplantier Corp is your future."

"No." The word propelled out. I couldn't stop it if I wanted to.

"No?" He looked gobsmacked, waved me away.

"Stop doing that. Shutting me up. You always do that."

"Don't speak to me that way, Vivièn." His voice was a stern warning. I was suddenly five years old and sneaking into his office on a dare from Mallory while he was in a meeting. I thought he would

find it funny, but he never found anything funny. I would always be an insubordinate child who needed to learn.

"I apologize." I couldn't breathe. The air in the car was thick, and my head was dizzy. "All I'm trying to say is that I want to make my own way—"

He laughed. "You're not making your own way in this world, son. Not as long as I'm paying for your way. I won't hear another word about what you want. You have two choices: step up, be a man, and accompany me to this dinner with the investors, or I will have no choice but to cut you off."

"No choice?" I repeated.

He cleared his throat. "Remember this, son, in this family, every move you make reflects on us and our business. With our name comes a great deal of expectation. Every interaction you have is a deal, and it'd be foolish to think otherwise. I wouldn't want to do it, but you'd leave me no choice." He paused so I could catch up to his train of thought. But the train was barreling down the tracks at max speed. "No inheritance. No more me paying your rent. Or your bills. No allowance. Nothing." He sat up straighter, if that were possible, and stared at me, waiting.

He knew he had me on a string. No, a leash. And I didn't want to be chained anymore, money or not. In that moment, I knew I would never be enough for him.

"Driver," I shouted. "Stop the car, please."

Father's face twisted. "Viv—"

"I appreciate the offer, Father." I pulled on the door handle. "But I choose me."

That was the last time I saw him.

I wandered the streets until I stumbled upon a dive bar in Union Square.

Yanking on the brass handles, I threw myself inside the empty bar. One server. One bartender. And a single patron, at the far end of the bar. Skinny, lanky blond, round tortoise-framed glasses, a total nerd nursing an ice-cold beer in a frosty stein. It was him. The guy I met at South Street Seaport three summers ago, after freshman year. The one who said, "Kissing you is like falling in love."

I plopped onto the leather barstool to his side and let out a sigh.

"You don't remember me," I said. "But—"

"Oh, I certainly do," he responded. "The most beautiful boy I've ever met that I let get away without learning his name." He held out his hand, and my heart leaped into it. "Nickolas Lund. Friends call me Nicko."

But I don't tell Teddy any of this. Our silence swells until my own heart is beating faster than his and I want more than anything to get up, run out of bed, lock myself in the bathroom, and wait out the weight of this memory.

Sensing my discomfort, Teddy squeezes me, applying the perfect amount of pressure around my upper body until my heart rate slows.

We stay like that for a while until my work alarm goes off. Realizing Teddy has nothing to wear—for dinner tonight or Mal's wedding—I sit up, grab my phone, and fire off a few key texts I know will get immediate attention.

"Everything okay? Did I do or say something—"

A confirmation text chimes through, and I snap into business mode.

"I have some work to catch up on before we head upstate tomorrow, since I know my family and the wedding is going to occupy my time. I don't want you to be bored, or worry about dinner tonight or the wedding, so I booked you a fabulous personal shopper at Saks Fifth Avenue."

He sits up slowly, covering the lower half of his body with the comforter, bunching it in his fists. Scratching his head, he asks, "When?"

I hand over my titanium black card. "One hour."

Teddy Hughes

The elevator doors open to the lobby of The Mark.

"I don't understand." Kit's eyebrows crinkle; her scowl, even over FaceTime, is epic. "He's hiring you? Paying you to fuck him? You're a hooker?" she says, motioning for me to move out of the frame of the camera so she can see the lobby. "My goddess, that lobby! I'm wet!"

Immediately, I feel the stares. Even on a Saturday, there are men in suit pants and button-downs—those top few buttons undone in a show of "relaxation"—women in Versace pantsuits, and young twentysomethings in Givenchy shoes and ripped jeans that cost more than a down payment on a car.

It's like they can smell Target on me, even though I used the same fancy-ass Mark-branded soap to wash my pits and ass that they did. You would think I'm wearing assless leather chaps, a dog collar, and Cole's harness with nothing else the way these hoity-toity folks are staring. It's unnerving, but I learned a long time ago that people who live in this world will never see a person like me worthy of existing on *their* level. And I refuse to focus on what other people think. Mostly.

Lowering my voice to a whisper, "I like to think I'm more

of an escort, but in the classy sense." I flip the camera to give
her the full tour. "Remind me to show you Cole's bathroom
later. Everything is Tiffany Blue."

"That place drips money, dahhling!" Kit stands up to grab
something out of frame and I notice the walls behind her—she's
at her art gallery. She puts the phone down and all I see is the
underside of her chin. "No, I told you already your client can
not touch that far wall outside noninvasive hooks. I don't care
if he wants that wall for an installation, the New York Histori-
cal Society won't permit it." Her smile stretches and she nods
before picking the phone back up. "I swear, artists think they
own the galleries they show in."

"Breathe. Keep your eye on the prize," I say.

"I know." Kit has made a name for herself in the art world
over the last few years, built up her gallery to be one of the
most sought-after spaces in the entire city focusing on breaking up-and-coming artists to the point where some of the
world's most renowned are seeking her out. Her goal is to
buy out her partners and expand to newer, bigger spaces and
eventually become affiliated with art schools in the city and
offer scholarships to artists of color. A few months ago, she
was spotlighted in the *Brooklyn Rail* for her mentorship pro-
gram focusing on helping women of color start their careers as
art dealers. "I love artists, but I hate dealing with their teams.
Anyway, back to *your* new business venture. You're actually
going to do this, Teddy?" There's a bit of judgment in her
voice. I'm surprised; I thought she'd find this amusing and
jump at the chance to celebrate my newfound seven grand.
I thought she'd joke with shit like, "You finally fucked your
way to the top!"

"Why not?" I ask. "I have no money, and this will really jump-start my savings, moving back home." Her face drops, eyes pierce through the screen. "Fuck, I forgot we were supposed to spend my last week together. I'll tell Cole I can't."

"No, don't," Kit says. "You need the money."

I feel like the biggest ass in the entire universe for bailing. "It *could* give me a bit of cushion *and* help me rebuild a new nursery. I don't wanna be at Momma's forever."

"I don't want to see you get hurt." She's giving me The Eyes. Kit's specialty, her superpower, the ability to question your life choices so deeply that you actually feel it in all 206 bones in your body.

"How would I get hurt?"

"Do I have to show you receipts of your emotional fragility? I saw the way he looked at you at the bar. And I know you. You're a hopeless romantic and probably into him big-time already. Add to the mix meeting his family and going to fancy dinners and spending every night together. You really don't think that, at the end of this, when he goes back to LA and says goodbye to you, that you're going to be better off than you would be if you left now on *your* terms?" Her jaw is clenched and she's staring directly into the camera lens, doing everything she can to penetrate my better senses.

"You're overreacting. I'm doing this on *my* terms."

Then, like a sniper, she goes in for the kill. "For your sake, I hope I'm wrong and Cole isn't another Murray."

The call ends.

Silence pounds in my ears. People are staring, their noses turned up, their eyes looking me up and down. I try to pull my beanie down over my face, but it doesn't go past my eyes, so that's awkward. They probably think I'm some bearded home-less dude, and they're the type who believe being homeless is a direct result of "not working hard" instead of systemic issues and environmental factors out of their control. I may techni-cally be homeless, but they don't need to know that. I could be one of those B-list actors who spend exorbitant amounts of money to look shabby.

"I'm staying in the penthouse." I curtsy, exuding Sassy Fag Energy.

The cute Mafia bouncer Frank is still at the front door. His eyes subtly move up and down, checking me out *and* judg-ing me at once. His lips purse. "Your car is waiting. Will Mr. Vivien be joining you?"

"Just me, Frankie."

"Frank," he corrects. "*You're* going to Saks—" he coughs. "Like *that*?"

Be cool, Teddy. "I'll have you know, this is vintage *Tarjay*."

He straightens his back. "We had some...*complaints* last night after a few guests saw your *attire*."

The straight opera couple in the elevator. It's *always* a straight couple, isn't it? I hold in a laugh.

"We expect any *guests* of our guests to dress and *act* appro-priately." Frank points toward the exit like an air traffic con-troller at the airport. "Your car is waiting, sir."

My clothes suddenly feel ill-fitted for my body.

Acid settles in my stomach as I rip the beanie off my head. Running my hands through my hair—it's been a while since I've gotten it cut—I feel more out of place. Nothing gives a gay a sense of power quite like a fresh fade and rejuvenated curls, and with Cole's money, I can go to one of those fancy salons before Saks. A great way to decompress after Kit and Frank.

I'll show him how well I clean up.

Cole Vivien

HORRIBLE IDEA. ABORT MISSION. Jason blows up my phone after I tell him about my Teddy boyfriend subscription plan. He's untested goods!

Ignore.

The beauty of this plan is that Teddy is real, his lack of professionalism in escorting is endearing, a plus, not a flaw. Anything too polished can come off as inauthentic.

As I hold in a breath, my phone buzzes again, this time with the results from the STD and HIV rapid tests I took yesterday. Negative across the board. *Deep breath out.*

Cracking my knuckles, I step into CEO @TheColeVivien mode. My assistant calls from LA with a brief rundown of the endless emails, televised interview requests, including CNBC about rumors of going public, teed-up media coverage from international magazines and newspapers, local and national gay media outlets, updated ads from advertisers.

There's an email from April Fitzgerald, a follow-up request from the other night.

Ignore.

After a quick Zoom meeting with the chief talent officer, who oversees the quality, standards, and practices of our content creators, it's more Zooms with investors before I do a quick run-through of the pre-recorded and edited content set to go live on my page this week. Like always, I end up in my protected drive, hovering over unedited footage of Nickolas Lund and me in Palm Springs. Jason believes it'd instantly go viral across gay media and generate a lot of revenue for VERSTL, but I can't deal with the Nicko of it all, and everything that was caught on camera. It's Too Much™, so instead, I shift focus to editing my man of honor speech at the exact moment Mallory starts blowing up my phone. When I don't immediately answer her texts, she FaceTimes me.

"Before you say anything," I take hold of the conversation before she unravels. "I need you to take a few deep breaths. For me." I ex out of the VERSTL drive window.

Mallory goes silent and together we close our eyes and inhale smooth, deep breaths. At first, she wheezes, but after a good minute, she mellows out and sighs.

"Hey, sis," I say. "You okay? Talk to me, what's happening with the venue? And why isn't the very expensive wedding planner Mother surely hired handling it?"

"The wedding planner is useless," she says. "Father is donating good money to the governor for use of Castle Rock." Castle Rock is an historic castle-like estate nestled on top of a mountain in the Hudson Valley overlooking the Hudson River. It's on a sprawling, hilly natural reserve owned by the state. Father had to call in favors with the governor and make a hefty donation, but they're letting us have run of the property. Or so I thought. "They're giving me the runaround, hitting me with extra fees and more restrictions. Listen to this shit."

She reads off her screen; her voice mechanical. "'*Guests can't walk into the castle, make sure to stay a safe distance away. Did you hire security? We haven't yet received the contract from the caterer.*

When the tent service comes, make sure they do not ruin the grass. Guests have to be off the property by midnight.' Like, the fuck!"

Teddy's voice pops into my mind, and I can't help myself. "Allow me to play the world's smallest violin for you."

Her eyes widen. "Oh, she's a bitch today." She cracks a smile, and we both laugh.

"Everything's going to be great, sis. And I'll be there early tomorrow with Teddy to help you deal with Castle Rock and the wedding planner. Promise."

She lets out a tortured screech. "His name is Teddy!? Tell me everything! Where does he work? Where's he from?"

"Would you like his social security number, too?"

"Preferably. It'll make the stalking process run smoother." I know she's joking, but with our familial connections, she's also dead serious. Nobody gets within a ten-foot radius of marriage without a full private investigation.

"Be good, Mal."

"I'm not the ones you have to worry about," she says. "You know they're going to be all over him."

Exactly.

"RIP Teddy," she says with a giggle. "Thanks for letting me vent. Who knew weddings were so fucking stressful?"

"Everybody. Ever." I'm interrupted by the penthouse phone ringing. "Let me go, Mal. I have to grab this. Deep breaths. It'll be amazing."

"Love you, *petit frère*!" Her face disappears.

Frank's calm, stern voice booms through the penthouse phone: "Mr. Vivien, a gentleman from the party last night, Nickolas, is here to see you. He's quite adamant I let him up."

I had Nickolas's number silenced on my cell before I left

The Mark last night, and there are over twenty muted texts from him, most asking when I was coming over. *Fuck.*

Not wanting Nickolas to make a scene in the lobby, I count to twelve on tapping fingers, breathe in and out, and when I'm steady say, "It's okay, Frank. Send him up."

Teddy Hughes

Lounging in the back seat of a damn Bentley(!), I shoot Kit a grimacing selfie of my new haircut. We have shared locations on for each other, so I'm certain she's tracking me, even though she hung up on me. Though we argue big, we love big, always, and I know she'll appreciate the selfie-slash-update.

The first time I went to Saks Fifth Avenue was to see the Christmas window displays when I moved to the city for Murray, then a new resident at New York-Presbyterian. He had switched shifts to take me to see the Rockettes and tour the window displays. I always wanted to do Hallmark movie activities with someone special. I had visions of snow falling and handholding and kissing under the glow of twinkling red and green lights. I'd gotten my first big contract, to design a spring floral display for Saks and as I told him my grand vision, he yawned. Work exhaustion. And, apparently, fucking other men behind my back. I spent years pretending we had a fairy tale, planning and executing a wedding, creating alternate versions of us to make the real one tolerable, before I realized that, like the Saks Fifth Avenue window display, we would only ever appear happy from the outside.

Sidewalk bodies inconspicuously peer at me through the

tinted windows of the car. When the driver opens the door for me, they watch, their gazes burning into me, sizing me up, trying to figure out who I am: Slob or celebrity?

Walking through the store entrance, I realize I have no idea where I'm going, or who I'm supposed to meet. I didn't think to ask Cole, and I also realize I don't have his fucking phone number. Am I supposed to saunter in and expect a butler to greet me with a glass of Dom Pérignon in a Swarovski crystal flute, whisk me away to a private fitting room where there will be clothes perfectly tailored to my thick-ass body?

That's not at all what happens. Nobody notices me at all. Actually, the employees look through me. Like invisible trash, out of sight, but the smell lingers.

Everything is so bright and white that my eyes hurt. Beneath chandeliers made of diamonds and magic, I weave between curated displays with barely any clothes on the racks. Nothing has price tags. Which means everything here is worth more than the sum of my being. If I offer up my firstborn, maybe I can purchase a snagged thread off a coat in clearance. Who am I kidding; there definitely isn't a clearance section.

I keep my head down as I make my way toward the men's section. An expired twink with Big Fem Energy bustles by with someone in a fine tailored suit with a golden name tag talking about custom wedding tuxedos for him and his husband-to-be. They both give me a once-over.

I teeter on my heels and rock back and forth, unsure what to do once I reach the men's section, like the pimply new kid in ill-fitting secondhand clothes in the hallway of a brand-new high school.

It should be easy to ask for help. I'm a grown adult. Not a

hormonal teen afraid of being taunted. But this place is like high school on drugs, if high school were full of über-rich snobs in designer clothes. My insides are on fire, and part of me wants to pull a Francis Conroy from *American Horror Story: Coven* and scream out "Balenciaga!" as I burn in shame flames. I'm Andy Sachs at the start of *The Devil Wears Prada*, waiting for a flawlessly primped worker to lecture me about the history of cerulean sweaters. The thought makes me laugh and now I look unhinged.

I could turn and run. Get back outside. The Bentley should still be there. If I go back to the penthouse, would Cole be furious? I could order a Lyft and get the hell home, evade Cole entirely; it's not like he knows where I live or can track me down. Right? Unless there's some sex worker Mafia and he's the don.

What am I doing here? I wish Kit were here.

My body jerks forward, and I'm about to book it out when I hear, "Teddy Bear?"

Cole Vivien

"You never came to my apartment." Nickolas eyes the silver trays of half-eaten breakfast foods. "I waited all night." His dark circles take me back to our summer together after NYU graduation, when we happenstanced at that dive bar, before I moved to LA. How we spent every moment with each other, up all night, sleeping all day, looking disheveled as we stumbled into brunch for our second wind. Then back to his apartment to fuck until we fell asleep, only to wake up and do it all again. Nickolas wanted me to stay in the city, for us to be together. He'd been working at his uncle's accounting firm since he graduated the year before and he said he could take care of me after Father cut me off, but he was already burned-out and jaded from his work. The light in his eyes faded and the weight of carrying his happiness wore at me. I had my own dreams to chase.

"Nicko, we've been through this so many times." I motion for him to join me on the couch.

He shakes his head. "Cole—*Vivièn*." That's how he knows me. But I shed that name years ago. "I know I shouldn't have tried to propose last night, but I lo—"

"Do you understand the weight of that, Nicko?" My heart beats hard and fast against my chest, but I remain calm as I grab onto his hands and hold them in mine.

He exhales and his whole face sinks. The pain around his eyes is too great that I pull him into me. He sobs into my chest.

"You don't know what it's like to love you, do you?" he cries softly into me.

"Nickolas, you don't love me."

Slowly, he peels himself off my body. "Remember what you said to me when you left New York? Because I do. I think about it almost every day." When I shake my head, he says, "You said, 'In another life, maybe we beat the odds.' When we connected last year, I thought it was a sign, like when we met three years after hooking up at South Street Seaport. The universe keeps bringing us together."

My heart aches for him. Because I think I could have loved him, in some way, all those years ago, but now all I see is appreciation for the space he filled for me after I walked away from my family. He'll always be the nerdy, scrawny twenty-year-old I met when I was nineteen, even though his shell is that of a Greek god now.

Nickolas touches my face gently and pulls me toward him. But our lips are repelling magnets, and my head pulls away.

"You're scared." His voice is full of venom.

"I have no room for fear." I shake my head.

"Then why didn't you stay with me?" He takes the ring box out of his pocket and puts it on the table in front of me. "When are you gonna break your bullshit rules?"

My head is screaming, *Go! Get out. Leave.* Memories flood me of Mother flying out to LA. I had been missing Nicko, so I asked her about how she knew she loved Father, and she said, "When we first met, he swept me off my feet. Now, I love the idea of him, and the security he brings. But do I *love*, love him?" She never finished her thought, and it hung in the air long after she returned to New York.

On cue, a text message from Jade@Saks, the personal shopper, chimes through my phone: Mr. Vivien—when should we expect your guest?

Teddy never showed? I got confirmation from the driver that Teddy arrived. I realize now I don't have Teddy's cell. What if he's gone?

I sent him on his way without any real direction, while I'm here with Nicko.

Guilt tugs at my insides, my lungs feel tight.

"Nicko, I—" I don't have to negotiate this time. "I'm sorry, but I have to go."

Teddy Hughes

"Teddy Bear? What're you doing here?" The sound of Murray Whalton III's voice thrusts me backward in time one year and I'm standing outside his Tribeca loft, begging him to give our marriage another chance.

Of fucking course he looks even better than he did when last I saw him. Salt-and–golden blond pepper hair styled to the side with a crisp part, tight suit pants, and a white polo like he wandered out of some Hamptons style guide. His body has more muscle mass, too, his biceps hulking out of the sleeves of his shirt. Human boat shoe.

Act cool. "Murray! Hiya, um, hey, h-how you doing?" I fumble. My cheeks heat.

Neither of us quite know what to do. Handshake? Kiss? Hug? Some combination of the three, where we both lean in, hands out, our bodies smashing into each other ending in some *Real Housewives*–style cheek-to-cheek air-kiss.

Good, god. I want to die.

"How've you been?" Murray cocks his head and flashes his gorgeous white teeth, but it's such a pity smile I could puke.

The last time he saw me I was basically throwing myself on the concrete in a storm of snot and tears and tantrums that could rival a two-year-old. He didn't even bother showing up for our divorce proceedings. Or the pre-trial from the lawsuit his dad launched against me. He paid lawyers to stand in for him.

So, Murray, how have I been? Fan-fucking-tastic!

He puts a hand on my arm and squeezes.

"I'm great! Super good. Thriving, really," I say. "I'm actually here on an assignment." Why'd I say that? What does that even mean?

"That's wonderful," he beams. "Another window?"

I can't exactly say the truth: *I'm pretending to be a rich sex worker's boyfriend for money, you know, because the prenup you made me sign left me broke and then your dad bled me dry.*

"Babe, what do you think of—" The expired twink I saw earlier appears beside Murray. He looks me up and down a second time, his upper lip curled into a snarl. "Hi, I don't think we've met." He holds out a manicured hand. "I'm Dr. Ian Spencer." He's a forty-year-old who thinks he's twenty-five. His teeth chemically whitened, his forehead Botoxed to the gills, his body naturally thin. A weathered twunk. "And you are?"

"This is, um, Teddy," Murray says.

"As in—" Ian's eyes widen in realization. "What a surprise." He hooks his arm into Murray's, closing the gap between them quickly. "How long has it been since you two have…" He doesn't need to finish. His curled smirk tells me he knows. He's playing games. Marking his territory.

It takes me a few seconds, but when I make the connection, it takes every muscle in my body to stay upright. Murray and Ian are engaged. *To be married.*

Ian nuzzles his nose into Murray's cheek, and I remember how Murray would slip his hand out of my grasp when I'd grab it in public. How the night he took me to see the Christmas display here all those years ago, he evaded my kisses.

"Been a year." I turn to Ian. "How long have you been—?" I can't finish, motioning toward Ian's ring finger, branded in elegant diamonds.

"Thanksgiving, last year," Ian says. I do quick math—seven

months after he broke up with me. "He came with me to my family's Nantucket beach house. It was magical."

My right eye twitches. I could rip his heart out. Both their hearts, actually. I try to steady my breathing, but it's impossible.

"When's the wedding?" My mouth is dry, and I'm feeling light-headed.

"Labor Day," Ian says. "Central Park. Where we first kissed how many years ago?"

Okay, not only is he rubbing it in my face that Murray cheated on me, which I knew, he's also so damn basic; the straights aren't the only ones who co-opt national holidays. Cheating-ass gays do it, too.

"It's kind of wild," Ian says, beaming at Murray like they're in a Crest commercial, two golden retriever gays cheesing at each other with sunbeams in the background. "Remember when we met. You were a new surgery resident, and I was a new anesthesiology resident."

Quick math: he moved me to New York when he started his surgical residency. My shoulder's tense.

Murray registers the recognition on my face. "We should get moving—"

"What brings *you* here?" Ian tugs on his fiancé's arm, sizing me up.

I can't find my voice. "I—"

There's a hand on my lower back. "There you are, honey!"

Cole appears beside me, and I don't know how that's possible, but my shoulders relax. He's wearing skintight acid-washed jeans and an oversized white shirt with a subtle ribbed texture that looks worn but probably costs more than my rent. There's a personal shopper behind Cole, waiting patiently. Her name tag says "Jade." She looks like a punk rock Rihanna, short jet-black hair with eggplant-purple streaks in a sleek charcoal power suit that hugs her curves.

Murray clears his throat. "Dr. Whalton." He wriggles out of Ian's talons and extends his hand.

Cole puffs out his chest, all Henry Cavill masculine energy, says nothing.

Ian and Murray eye him curiously.

"I feel like I know you?" Ian ruminates.

"Wouldn't be surprised," Cole says. "I have one of those faces."

Ian's eyes widen in recognition. He swallows hard. He whispers something to Murray, who scrunches his smooth, beautiful, cheating bastard face.

"How do you two know each other?" Murray asks.

"He's my boyfriend." Cole presses his lips to my forehead but doesn't actually kiss me.

"Boyfriend?" Ian gives a curt, painstaking nod, like the gears in his head are working on overdrive to process this.

Murray salivates. I know that look, like a heart-eyed wolf on *Looney Tunes* who whistles at the leggy female cartoons. Whenever we would be out, whether at the beach or a restaurant or a grocery store, and saw a hot guy, he would ogle them. Not that I wouldn't, too, but I was never as obvious as Murray was; he was insatiable.

I was never enough for him. He wanted more. We used to have blow-out fights because of his cheating, so he suggested we open our marriage. I never wanted it. The thought of him fucking another guy alone ate at me, and he resented me for the ring on my finger like a collar around his neck. Maybe part of it was my fault because I never let him forget all the ways he made me feel lonely and unwanted and unattractive.

The hunger in Murray's eyes for Cole triggers the loneliness I felt when Murray looked at other men in our bed during threesomes, the way I needed him to look at me.

"And you must be the ex?" Cole asks Ian.

"No, that would be me," Murray interjects.

"Sorry about that," Cole says. "Teddy never described you. Actually, I don't know much about you at all." Cole places a hand on my chest. "Teddy is all about the here and now. I'm sure you know that. It's one of the things I adore about him. That and his passion for what he does. And the sex, *whew*!" He turns and presses his nose to my cheek. "Best I've ever had." Murray's eyes widen at Cole's revelation. "It's a shame about Plant Daddy, though. I'll never understand how divorcing couples can go for the jugular. Seems like the lowest hanging fruit, am I right?" Cole winks at Ian. "But my guy has bigger and better things in the works, don't you, babe?" he asks, and I nuzzle into him without taking my eyes off Murray's face, now drained of color. "It was great meeting you both. Our personal shopper is waiting." Cole starts walking, me and Jade in tow, her red-bottomed heels click-clacking, but stops. "And congratulations on your wedding."

I won't look back, but I hope to god Murray is watching *me* leave this time.

Cole Vivien

Teddy's body trembles.

"You okay?" I ask once we're in the clear.

His smile is dimmer than usual, and my heart pangs. The way his body shudders, he's trying so hard to keep his shoulders back and neck held high, but he's wavering, and all I want to do is hold him up.

"Hey." I place my thumb on the underside of his chin and gently stroke his cheek. He closes his eyes, but a tension pools around his lips. "What do you need right now?"

Shrugging, he looks away.

I understand. "Let's go back now."

He crinkles his brows. "But tonight?"

"What's the point of making a ton of money if I can't use it how I want," I say.

"What do you mean?"

I call Jade over. "Pull every one of your finest suits, and all the latest in men's fashion. The hottest trends. Runway. Ready to wear. Designer. Casual. We need *lewks*. We have an important dinner with a potential business partner and a wedding to attend in two days, and we need some everyday options. And shoes! Size ten. Oh, and anything from Alessandro Arcobaleno. Bring what you have to The Mark." Then I turn back to Teddy. "We'll have our own private fashion show."

I don't know what I was hoping for in his reaction, but he doesn't really have one at all, and despite myself, a tiny crack forms in my fortressed heart.

Teddy is dead quiet, staring out the window and shifting his weight uncomfortably. Though we're right next to each other, the way he plasters his body against the car door, he might as well be in New Orleans.

He says nothing as we walk back into the hotel. No sarcastic quip about the opulent feather-laced garb some older woman in the lobby dons. His eyes are glazed over, and I want to ask him a million questions about how he's feeling, about his ex and his douchey fiancé, but I have no idea where to start. I don't want to pry, but I'm curious. More than that, I want to hear his laughter again.

Once we're back in the penthouse, Teddy plods to the kitchen and straight for the wine fridge. "It's five o'clock somewhere right?" he says.

I say nothing.

"You want one?" he asks, grabbing a glass from a cabinet.

"I'm good."

He snorts as the red liquid teems into the goblet, splashing up the sides of the glass and slowly trickling down leaving nice long legs in its retreat. "Is this not okay?" he asks.

My lips tighten. "Why do you ask?"

"That look on your face," he deadpans. "Unclench, bro."

"Bro?"

He snickers. "Sorry, should I say Daddy?" Sarcasm drips from his fangs like rattlesnake venom. "Do you like that?" He's mimicking a seductive porn actress, and it comes off as incredibly fucking patronizing, causing me to shrink down to the size of a field mouse. The contents empty in one gulp. "I know you do." He pours another.

"Wow, that's unfair." I clear my throat, and the part of my heart that opened up to him, that tiny crack, fills with quick-dry cement. "I don't have time for this. I have work—"

"It's always work, isn't it, for guys like you?" He tips his glass to me, cheersing the air. "I'm just another beck-and-call girl. *You* come first. 'Sorry, babe, I'm on-call.' I understand, your career comes first! 'I can't pass up this opportunity, even though it's your thirtieth birthday!' Oh, don't worry, I can turn thirty again next weekend! 'I know it's your book release party, but this really powerful godlike attending invited me into a once in a lifetime surgery, I'll make it up to you even though I'll come home with my breath smelling like his hot salty cum.' Dinner's on the counter for you, babe!"

I feel his pain. It's raw, real, and I see how much of himself he hides behind his fun-loving exterior. I want to hug him, but this is something he needs to feel for himself, and his anger is misplaced. "This isn't about me." I start to walk away, to give him space to process, but on my way, I say, "I'm not your boyfriend." I wince because I meant to add "ex," but—

"Of course not. I'm another plaything for another rich playboy, right?" He downs another half glass of wine. "Everyone wants their cake and to eat it, too. That's all I am. Cake. Cock cake." He laughs, but it's full of sadness.

"You're not thinking clearly," I state. "You're upset."

"You don't know me." Takes a swig.

An obvious realization, but it smacks me across the face. "You're right. I don't know anything about you."

"You don't." His bottom lip quivers. He does that thing where he stares at my face, but avoids making direct eye contact. Corners of his mouth twitch like he wants to say something, but he takes a deep breath instead, nostrils flaring.

The look on his face. I recognize it as something akin to my own reflection after my last fight with Father, the way he often twisted my words. I understand the fear on Teddy's face in my bones.

But his baggage is not mine.

"And you don't know me." I reach into my pocket and pull out my money clip. I quickly count a thousand dollars in hundred-dollar bills and fling the wad on the counter, watching as it slides directly in front of him. "Seven thousand dollars for seven days, but this was barely a half day. Still, I recognize that your time is valuable, so consider it a full day's worth of pay. Wouldn't want you to feel ripped off." I turn on my heels and walk out of the kitchen, but not before saying, "You can see yourself out."

Teddy Hughes

I'm alone.

Again.

I'm not even drunk and I managed to fuck this up. I can't blame Murray. Though I most certainly do. One year, one whole plant nursery, and a new Dr. Ian Twunkybitch later and that man can still manage to fuck up my entire existence. I can't believe he's *engaged*. While I've somehow gone from horticulturist to homeless escort-to-a-rich-sex-worker.

I have a half a mind to call Murray and blast him for all the shit he and his rich-ass dad put me through. After his dad, Murray Whalton II, discovered that *his son* had moved some of their family money into my personal account using *my* information for Plant Daddy Nursery and Garden. When I opened Plant Daddy, every bill, every tax document was put in my name. I paid electric and heating, city taxes on the retail space because the business was in my name. But the retail space itself? That was in my ex-husband's name. Or so I thought. My ex had used his father's name to purchase the deed. At the time, I had no money, and he told me the lawyers would handle everything. I didn't think I needed to double-check or even understand the logistics. What would I know, anyway? I assumed Murray and I were forever, but it turned out I had about as much right to my husband as I did to my own business.

After Murray kicked me out and served me divorce papers, his father confronted me, blackmailed me, saying what he found would put me in prison. There was no proof it wasn't me; my husband had access to all my account information. His dad wanted me not to pursue spousal support *or* pull at the infidelity clause in our prenuptial agreement, which I could have easily done. But back home in Louisiana, Momma and I knew way too many people who got tangled up in the law and lost. I was terrified. So I agreed to his terms. What I didn't realize was that he never agreed not to pursue action against Plant Daddy's retail space, and so he sued me for legal rights to it, effectively bankrupting me because I chose to fight it.

His damn face and number are staring back at me. Kit changed his name in my contacts to "FUCK THAT GUY." My finger hovers over the call button.

Instead, I slam the phone down on the counter, next to the wad of hundreds Cole threw at me like I was a cheap whore.

Should I take the money and get the fuck out of here?

Counting each bill, I organize them so each is upright and facing the same direction. I tap the stack on the counter. I can't take his money. Because, realistically, all it was, was a hot night of oral sex and naked cuddles and a weird as fuck day where all he did was try to buy me some nice clothes.

My face falls into my palms as I lean against the marble

countertop. I have to get home and take a hot shower. Pack. Maybe I'll go back to Louisiana early, put this chapter to bed, see Momma and allow her to wrap me up in a warm hug.

But first, an apology is in order.

Cole Vivien

The door of the master bedroom slams shut as I let out a growl-scream from the depths of my gut. Cracking my knuckles, I pace back and forth, stomping over the whole scene in my head.

Is it my fault? Maybe I pushed too hard. Took too much control. Like Father.

It wasn't my place to wedge myself in between him and that log cabin Republican senator–looking guy, but Teddy looked ghostly white and—

No, I did what I would've wanted if I were in Teddy's shoes, and I would've expected Teddy to do the same. That's what I'm paying him for.

I stop pacing.

Was paying him for.

But that's the thing. We were both playing roles. I'm not his actual boyfriend. I was foolish to think I could pay a man to pretend to love me. There are some things you can pay for: drinks at a dive bar, clothes, jewelry, flowers, dinner at a Michelin star restaurant, sex. Love isn't one.

It's just business.

Onetwothreefour, fivesixseveneight nineteneleventwelve.

Nickolas Lund and our complicated past fills my headspace.

He loved me. Loves. Or, rather, he thinks he does. But he doesn't know me. Not really. When I became a sex worker, I found pride in showing off my body, sharing intimate parts of myself with men as a way to connect. To feel. But as much as I had connections with almost all the men I've performed with and escorted for, it's never lasted beyond those moments, even Nicko. I care about him as a person, but I don't want him as a boyfriend. He's not—

Teddy. The jolt of electricity at the bar. The warmth in my chest when I woke up next to him. New Relationship Energy? No, not a *relationship*. A connection, as authentic as it seemed, is sometimes merely a singular moment with a short expiration date.

My temples throb.

Onetwothreefour, fivesixsev—

Unmade bed, bathrobe on the floor, water glasses and knick-knacks on the nightstands including my crystals, my eyes try to find something else to focus on, to make perfect, to control, but this room is a disaster and I can't find a place to start.

—Eight, nineteeneleventwelve, onetwothree—

Perhaps yoga can center me.

Grabbing the soft rubber mat I had the front desk send up, I hear feet shuffling.

Five rhythmic knocks on the bedroom door.

I say nothing.

Two more in quick succession.

"What?" I snap.

"Can, um, I come in?" Teddy's voice is meek.

I let out a long breath and center myself. "Sure."

Teddy pushes the door open. He has one hand behind his

back. Gone is the darkness in his eyes, replaced with something softer, sadder.

I sit on the edge of the bed and wait for him to talk.

He teeters on his heels, then stumbles a bit, an aftereffect of
the wine and adrenaline. "Sorry if I was a jerk." He probably
expects me to say something, maybe, "No, you weren't," but if
he came here for that, he can leave. He corrects, "I mean, I *was*
a jerk." He takes a few hesitant steps, enough to lean against
the plush white reading chair. "Total fucking asshole move."

"Pretty much. Douchebag supreme." I look up, give him
the smallest of smiles.

"I deserve that." He looks up at the ceiling. "I really did
have a great time last night, and this morning. In another life,
if I wasn't so broken and you—" He stops himself, though I
can read the subtext: *Maybe this would be more than a business
proposition.* His hand, a closed fist, lingers on the back of the
reading chair. "I guess what I'm trying to say is that it was
wonderful to meet you." He turns around and walks out,
stopping in the door frame. "I never thanked you for what
you did earlier. Nobody but Kit has ever done something
like that for me."

I want to say, "You're welcome," but the words never come.
In another life…

Do I go after him? Is this that moment in the movies where
the main character chases after the hunky love(?) interest? Or
do I let him walk away?

It's not until the elevator dings and the doors *whoosh* shut
that I realize the wad of cash I gave him is tightly rolled on
the seat of the white reading chair.

Five
Updated Service Agreement

Teddy Hughes

I get all the way down to the damn lobby of The Mark when I realize my phone is not in my pocket.

With the doors nearly closing, I slide sideways back into the elevator and jam the penthouse button a dozen times in syncopated beats. With any luck, I'll be able to swipe my phone and get out of there without having to see him again.

My foot taps restlessly. With each passing second, I risk Cole coming out of his bedroom and finding me. How pathetic?

Tap, tap, tap. What the hell was I thinking, leaving all that cash behind? I really needed it. *Taptaptap.* I gave up seven grand! But I can't waltz back in and beg for my job.

Right?

Taptaptap.

I want to. But not for the money. *For Cole.*

Fuck. This can't be happening. I barely know him!

Come on, elevator! My chest flutters with panic as my fingers smash the penthouse button a few more times. For good measure.

My breath is terrible. Did I have garlic? Oh, god, it's the wine fermenting in my mouth. As a kid, I grew my own mint plants and chewed fresh leaves because once a cute boy in middle school told me I had bad breath. That's my villain origin story, the domino effect that led me to college for horticulture, then to Murray and New York, and the demise of Plant Daddy, which led to me making a damn fool out of myself in front of Cole.

Wow, that spiral was intense.

Breathe, Teddy. Unclench!

Ding!

The doors open and I don't look before I charge out, slamming headfirst into Cole.

"What the hell?" he yells. "Teddy?"

"Jesus shitballs!" A nervous laugh trips off my tongue. "What're you doing?"

A second is all it takes to regain his composure. He lifts his arm above his head and scratches the back of his neck in a way that makes the bottom of his shirt rise, revealing the hair dusting his stomach. His bicep flexes and holy fuck I hate him for how dumbfounded he makes me.

"Don't go," he says.

"I—what?"

"Stay. With me."

"Why? I was rude and temperamental," I say.

"Because you were rude and temperamental, and maybe I was, too. And you need a friend. Truth be told, so do I," Cole admits. He moves his hands, maybe to grab mine, but he wavers, and they fall to his side. His face contorts in confusion, like he doesn't know what to do or say next. Then, suddenly, his eyes get bright, and his head perks up. "Besides, what's the worst that can happen? You blame me for everything wrong in your life? That already happened." He smirks.

"Don't cross me," I jest.

He laughs. "Big mistake."

"Huge." I hold my hands out in front of me, measuring the air between them. "My friend Kit calls me a Sour Patch Kid. When I'm sour, I'll kick your cat—metaphorically, obviously. I love cats. But I'm mostly all gooey and sweet."

"Seems accurate." He takes my hand and holds it firmly. "So, the personal shopper from Saks is coming any minute, and I have nobody to spend an exorbitant amount of money on."

I roll my eyes. "I guess I can stay for that."

"But I have some new rules," he says.

Cole Vivien

"New rules?" Teddy repeats. "Okay, Dua Lipa, hit me. Metaphorically."

I'm still holding his hand, and the friction from our skin heats up quick.

"What's most important is that you *want* to stay. If you don't, know you're not trapped. Second: this is an equal partnership. We each get something out of it. To that end—" I count out seven thousand dollars and hand it to him. "For safekeeping. I trust you, and you can leave at any time, no questions asked."

"No, Cole, I can't—" Teddy starts, but I insist. After a few minutes of stunned staring at the wad of cash, he tucks it away, eyes teary. "Why'd you come after me?"

I shake my head, unsure what to say. I don't have a good answer beyond, "I didn't want to never see you again." But if running VERSTL has taught me anything, it's that level of vulnerability is chum in the water, and as Father might say, "the ocean is full of sharks, so you have to be a great white."

So I give him the most acceptable answer: "I could use the company this week."

He's all puppy dog eyes and sweet pouts.

"Beautiful men like you are in short supply," I add in a show of earnestness.

His cheeks turn a bright shade of pink.

The elevator dings again, and Jason's voice booms through the penthouse: "What the hell? I can't have one bottomless brunch with a bunch of bottoms without you needing me?" Jason leads an army of stylists, including Jade from Saks Fifth Avenue, straight into the foyer. His gaze falls on Teddy, who is wide-eyed, hands behind his back like a mischievous kid who did something wrong, and my heart skips. "So you're the naked guy in Cole's bed?"

"Uh—" Teddy looks to me and raises one eyebrow. "If you liked what you saw, yes. If you didn't, nope, not me."

Jason narrows his eyes at Teddy. "He'll do." For my eyes only, he mouths a discernable "for now."

"*Easy*," I mutter under my breath. Jason is a dog without boundaries.

Jason ignores me. "I'm the Nigel to Cole's Miranda Priestly."

Teddy laughs. "So infinitely more talented, kind, and constantly overlooked?"

"Don't forget double-crossed in the end," Jason adds. "Charmed."

Jason can't stop eye-fucking Teddy. Sweat trickles down my back as they do this back-and-forth dance, a series of flirtatious banter that not even touching my thumb to each of my fingers can stop my nerves from firing.

Then Jason snaps his fingers. "Cue the makeover montage!"

Charli XCX's "New Shapes," an infectious cotton candy bop, fills every corner of the penthouse as Teddy slides across the wood floor and my breath catches. The confection from his playlist captures his aura and energy much better than my playlist of classical music would.

The first look is a soft gray puppytooth wool suit, tight and tapered in the pants, his thick thighs and melon calves bulge. It's layered with a vest and jacket over a crisp white button-down and a soft yellow tie for a pop of color. He looks sexy as hell, a red-carpet leading man oozing charisma as he runs a hand through his curl crop of coppery hair. A fair, freckled James Bond with a beard, one who's a little bit gayer and ready for scotch out on the lanai overlooking the Mediterranean Sea.

Beads of sweat dot his brow. He tugs on the collar of his shirt. It's clear Teddy, as hot as he looks, is legitimately hot.

"I don't think that'll work for a summer wedding," I say.

For the next look, Teddy vogues across the room in a rich mossy green suit jacket that complements his copper hair. The larger collar and white shoes give me '70s vibes, but it's the mix of fashion eras here that I love. It's modern but vintage.

I'm staring at him, mouth agape.

"What? Too much?" Teddy asks.

"It's perfect." I feel Jason's eyes on me as Teddy disappears, changes, reemerges.

Jade narrates: "Mr. Hughes is rocking a head-to-toe light peach linen suit from a new designer in Portugal. It's lightweight with a low thread count, perfect for a summer wedding. You'll notice a faded white linen shirt underneath, with the buttons undone, and since it's a wedding, supple brown leather sneaker-style dress shoes with white soles, a bit unconventional, but perfect for an elegant outdoor affair. Straight from the Chris Hemsworth playbook, it's playful, sexy—" Hand to mouth, she gives us a chef's kiss.

All I can do is stare at Teddy, my pulse racing.

We take everything Teddy feels comfortable in, including an Alessandro Arcobaleno original for tonight—a modern take on a turtleneck with bold color blocking; paired with a pair of skinny white dress pants, brown leather boat shoes, and a light bomber jacket. Teddy will look like a perfectly worn-in catalogue boyfriend.

The problem is, I'm starting to wish all of this were real, that Teddy and I were more than a business proposition.

Teddy Hughes

Off Central Park, a streetlamp floods the tinted windows of the restaurant Per Se. My mouth is already watering, accompanying my gurgling stomach.

Cole fiddles with something in his pocket; objects clink together as he stares out the car window with a stern look on his angular face.

"Do I look okay?"

He puts a hand on my leg. "Sorry." He retracts it, but I grab his palm and squeeze it and place it right back on my thigh. His eyes widen, but then his face softens. "You look wow, I mean, you're perfect." He giggles a bit, like a little boy, and it's super fucking charming. "Before we go in, I wanted to give you something."

My face heats.

Cole pulls out a small pale pink rock. "It's a rose quartz. I'm big into crystals, and energy, and being one with the earth. I know it's very LA, but I really think they work." We palm the stone together. With my free hand, I feel his chest, his heart beating so fast, the *thumpthumpthump* quickening as I touch him. "Rose quartz is meant to restore trust and harmony."

"What do I do with it?"

"Channel its energy when you hold it." Cole takes another out of his pocket. It's bright yellow, more like a diamond. "I'm carrying a citrine. It's meant to bring about prosperity and abundance." He squeezes his hand around it.

"I have a good feeling about tonight," I say. "Thank you."

Cole licks his lips.

I pull out a small tube of ChapStick and hand it to him.

"I always have one handy, in case of emergencies." He un-caps it and rolls it across his lips, and I joke that, "This means we've kissed now."

His grin fills me with music, and I could dance on the balls of his cheeks. "I also had Jade bring something I thought would suit you." Under the lamplight, in the darkness of the car, his eyes change colors from brown to yellow to green, the way leaves change from green to yellow to brown, but in reverse, each stage more beautiful than the last. From inside his suit jacket, he pulls a deep purple velvet jewelry box. "I saw this collection and was taken by its uniqueness. It's exquisite. To-tally different. Not right for my aesthetic, but you—" He opens the box, and inside is a matching necklace and bracelet. It's a crocheted tangle of different sterling silver and 24-karat gold chains, twisted around and woven into each other. It's mascu-line, strong, and it sparkles when the light hits. It almost re-minds me of ivory vines wound together.

"It's beautiful." My mouth is dry.

"It's yours," he says.

"I can't accept it, you've already done enough." I pull at the sleeve of my shirt, but he takes my hand and lays it in his lap. He removes the bracelet from the box and tenderly works it around my wrist, clasping the metal hook. His fin-gers, cold to the touch, linger on my skin, sending a bolt of electricity up my arm.

He motions toward the necklace. "May I?"

Turning my back to him, he reaches around my neck, sweeping his arm and accidentally tugging me to his chest. His cool minty breath on my neck, his nose against my ear,

I tilt my head back, arch my neck, giving him more surface area, if he wants it.

The air between us is thick, and I want to straddle him, but resist the urge. He chuckles and I wonder if he can read my energy.

His touch remains on the nape of my neck.

I shudder as he clasps the necklace.

It lies perfectly on top of my ridiculously expensive shirt, contrasting its crisp design with the jewelry's jagged metal vines, and I love the contradiction.

I crack my knuckles, admiring the bracelet. My fingers feel naked. "I wish I brought my rings! I didn't think they fit the look, but with these pieces!"

Cole reaches into his other pocket and pulls out my rings, but they're no longer tarnished or worn. He had them polished.

"What else you got in there, Mary Poppins?" I ask, my fingers like sparklers as he slowly puts each of my rings back. On the wrong fingers of course, but I'll fix that later.

"I'd give you more if I had anything." He pats his empty pockets.

For a moment, maybe longer, we say nothing.

The silence is heavy, and I swear I catch him staring at my lips.

Then he says, "Shall we?"

The inside of the restaurant is a *Mad Men* set piece melded with vintage Hollywood glamour, yet somehow minimalist at the same time. I feel instantly uncomfortable. I'd rather do a walking food tour of the East Village: A slice of artichoke pizza, some pierogis from Veselka, a custom mac and cheese from S'MAC. No wonder I'm still carrying holiday weight from six holidays ago.

Cole holds my hand, his palms sweaty, as the hostess takes us on a journey that weaves around two tops on dates, men in suits talking business, and women with too much plastic surgery, all of whom stop and stare at us—no, *Cole*—until we reach the back and she Vanna White's us to a large round table. Directly in the center is a beautiful olive-skinned white man with blue eyes and long, windswept brown hair that looks effortlessly like a TRESemmé commercial. He even has a full, thick dark beard. A sexy Italian Jesus.

Flanked on his right is a model-gorgeous dark-skinned Black man with a jawline that could cut glass, buzzed bleach blond hair, a gold hoop septum piercing, and thick crystal-rimmed eyeglasses. He looks up from his phone and his mouth drops, recognizing Cole. His back straightens and he taps Sexy Italian Jesus's bare, hairy arm below his rolled-up sleeves.

Who are these guys? What kind of business dinner is this? Oh my god, is this, like, something Cole does before he films a scene? Are these guys *scene partners*, and he wants me here to round out the cast? Mouth dry, my heart pounds against my rib cage. My mind wanders and I'm on a porn set, where a naked and glistening Cole is taking turns pounding them both, and one at a time, they look my way, waiting for me to join. I pull on the collar of my shirt as beads of sweat trickle down to the small of my back.

"Signore Vivien!" Sexy Italian Jesus rises to his feet, his date following suit, to extend a gracious hand. I admire the rings on his fingers, like antique museum pieces. "A pleasure." His Italian accent is thick, and it pulls me in like a lullaby.

"Alessandro," Cole says. "The pleasure is truly mine." They shake hands, and Cole is so strong, his biceps bulging, but more than that, his demeanor is fortified with confidence, a skyscraper of impenetrable metals.

"This is my partner, Max," Alessandro says. "He's a big fan of your work."

I'm fairly certain that means Max enjoys watching my fake boyfriend fuck. The idea twists my stomach a bit in jealousy. Which is odd because I have nothing to be jealous of, technically. I never gave much thought to dating a sex worker before; post-Murray, I dated a few who told me it was hard to date because their partners had to be understanding that sex for them, even when it looks hot and intimate and loving, is a job, no different than an exchange of goods, like a single, anonymous Grindr hookup in the bathroom of The Eagle: no feelings, only release. But is it that simple? Can sex work and monogamy go hand in hand? Maybe. With a healthy dose of trust. *Maybe.* Open relationships and non-monogamy *are* more common in queer relationships than monogamy, but given my history with Murray, I don't *think* it's something I want again.

What am I saying? Cole and I are not in a real relationship. So I shouldn't be jealous. Or thinking about this at all.

I'm doing the thing Kit warned me against: imagining a fairy tale in my head.

Cole says, "This is my boyfriend, Teddy."

"Cute couple," Alessandro says. "*Bellisimo!* Have a seat, have a seat!" Okay, this guy is like a super enthusiastic, handsome orchestra conductor talking with his hands and showing all his pearly white teeth.

After Cole orders both of us martinis—I'd prefer a beer

in a frosty mug—I let him and Alessandro talk, exchanging pleasantries and talking about New York in the way that trans-plants do, complaining about the tourists who don't know what the "real New York" is all about. My cue to tune out. I name plant genus and species in my head because I have no idea what this dinner is even for, and I don't want to acci-dentally stick my foot in my mouth. Still, I laugh when they laugh, nod when Cole does.

Somewhere along the way, Cole grabs my thigh under the table.

Alessandro says my name.

"Hmm?" Fuck. I wasn't listening and he caught me. Max snickers.

"I said, I love your shirt, where did you get it?" Alessandro asks.

I look down. "Oh, yeah, I love it. It's super nice and, to be honest, I'm afraid to drink this martini or eat because I don't wanna ruin it!"

Cole's lips are stretched into a thin, painted-on smile.

"Do you not like it? Is not com-for-ta-bull?" He backflips over the word "comfortable," enunciating each syllable. "You can be honest here. You are among friends. I see you squirm, a little bit."

"Honestly? It looks sick. I love it. And it is comfy," I start. "But, you know, I'm more of a Target guy. I feel weird in expensive clothes, like they don't really belong on my body."

"Teddy—" Cole mutters, shifting in his seat.

"What do you mean?" Alessandro asks.

Max puts his phone down and leans forward like I'm spill-ing some tea he desperately needs to quench his thirst.

"Teddy, I," Cole stammers. "Alessandro—"

"No, no," Alessandro says, motioning for Cole to sit back. "I want to hear what this handsome copper-headed man has to say. Go on."

Swig the martini, try not to pucker. "Well, designer clothes tend to be shaped for certain body types. I'm pretty curvy, and this definitely feels a bit tight in places because I don't have that V-shape torso. I love the design, but I prefer comfort. That's not very gay of me, but…"

Cole buries his head in his hands. At some point, he had let go of my thigh.

"You know Alessandro designed that, right?" Max says with an eye roll.

If I could dissolve into a puddle, I would. "Oh, fuck."

"No, no, this is good," Alessandro insists. "You are enchanting, real." He looks to Cole. "Honestly, I half expected you to show up with a rent boy on your arm."

Yikes. This dude holds no punches. Cole peeks through his fingers, then slowly lets his hands drop to his side.

"I like that you have this man by your side who represents the everyday gay man," Alessandro says. "I had this discussion with Max earlier. I want my clothes to speak to everyone, and maybe the designs do, but the construction, price point, and the accessibility. Maybe not so much. This is what happens when you're featured in Italian *Vogue*, then American *Vogue*, and suddenly you're designing for Billy Porter, Lil Nas X, Lena Waithe, Elliot Page." He lists queer celebrities like items on a grocery list. "Your demand goes up, and then you're in this stratosphere most people cannot reach."

Through all the noise and chatter and resounding screams

inside my head telling me I fucked up Cole's meeting, I remember something Cole said to me last night as we cuddled naked in his bed, in that gorgeous penthouse that felt so luxurious, like a dream. He stroked my hair and something about the way he looked at me, the relaxed way his cheeks sat beneath a violent storm in his eyes, as I asked him, "Are you happy?"

"I own my own company at twenty-nine. I'm able to stay at the penthouse of The Mark without worry. Live a lifestyle I grew up accustomed to, but on my own terms," Cole said, cupping the side of my face in his hand. "What's not to be happy about?"

"I heard a lot of material things, but nothing about happiness," I said.

"Right now? In this moment, I am happy." Cole looked away.

I stroked his face this time. "What will make you happy when this moment ends?"

"I'd love to have my own line one day. Design clothes. Maybe one day."

I'd love to have my own line one day. Cole's words repeat in my head, and now it makes sense. His business meeting with the most prominent emerging gay fashion designer isn't about some fuck session, it's about Cole getting into the fashion world, and I want Alessandro to understand Cole's heart and drive the way I'm coming to.

Alessandro continues, "That's why I'm looking for a *good* partnership, to reach the masses of our community."

"Actually," I interrupt, but he seems to welcome it, grabbing his drink and taking a sip. "VERSTL is a great avenue. What better place to reach a queer audience than an app designed by a queer sex-positive creative?" Cole sucks in a breath. "Unlike its competitors, VERSTL performers span the entire community and they make sure to elevate body diversity— lesbian, non-binary, trans performers, performers of color, Black performers, not just cis gay white male models, which is crucial and trailblazing."

"I won't lie, I do worry about the association with sex work," Alessandro says.

"That's pretty sex negative," I say, and Alessandro mutters something in Italian to Max. Cole pinches my leg, but I can't help myself. "As a member of the queer community, you should know how sex-phobic the straights can be when it comes to us. They think all we do is fuck and give each other HIV and STDs, and not only is that painfully wrong, it's harmful and reductive." I'm fired up now. "The VERSTL brand is more than a 'sexperience.' It's community. Making connections. Opportunity. It's in the name: *Versatility*. It can adapt, top, bottom, side to side. Cole *is* a versatile man."

For a few seconds, nobody says anything. Then Alessandro leans over and reaches for something on the floor. He pulls up a portfolio and spreads it out on the table. Inside are the most exquisite sketches of a gender ambiguous clothing line.

"I was hesitant to meet with you, Mr. Vivien," Alessandro says. "I wasn't sure how the Arcobaleno brand could meld with VERSTL and still maintain its dignity, even with your design ideas, which have merit and a certain spark. I think I could bring out your vision. Your branding—*Switch Positions*— the emphasis on comfort and accessibility, not gender, I love. But your beautiful boyfriend here shows me that you share my vision. The way he looks at you—" He says something in Italian that sounds like a symphony. His gaze bounces between me and Cole. "This!" He brings his hands to his mouth like a nonna watching her grandchildren taste her homemade sauce. "*Bellisimo, bravo!*

"I'm heading to LA in a few weeks. Let's set aside a weekend. A retreat. The four of us can escape to wine country. We can come up with a more solid design for the line while our better halves enjoy all Napa has to offer." He holds out his hand for Cole.

Cole licks his dry lips. I reach into my pocket for the ChapStick and feel the rose quartz he gave me. I give it a quick rub for harmony's sake.

"Does this mean—" Cole starts.

"Welcome to the Arcobaleno family," Alessandro says, grabbing Cole's hand. "Now, let's eat! I am, how you say it in America? *Hangry?*"

Cole Vivien

"That was fucking incredible!" I spin Teddy around the penthouse like a ballerina, the world in centrifugal force around me, and with each rotation, my eyes fixate on Teddy.

My center of gravity.

I wobble a bit when I stop, but it's only because I have to move toward him. My legs, under some sort of spell, trip before I reach him. But he catches me.

Strong forearms hold me up, muscles strain through his shirt. He laughs. I lean into it, *him*, and look up and into his eyes.

It might be the martinis—I had five or six, and the mixologist at the restaurant must've been a magician because they were pure liquor yet tasted like candy—but my limbs go dead and I forget what to do next. This never happens. All my moves are always at the ready, a Rolodex of intuition rendered useless.

"Jesus, Cole," he grunts. "I carried your ass to bed last night—how are you this heavy right now?" His knees buckle and my mind wanders to the middle of the night when he grinded into me, his naked torso bathed in moonlight from the skylights. My leg was wedged into the pillows, and the weight of his body was pressing me further into the skeleton of the couch, so I suggested we go upstairs to the master. Without hesitation, he hopped off, bent down, and I wrapped my legs around him. He lifted me in the air and walked us to the bed.

His eyes are blue and green amethysts, or a topaz and an emerald, side by side, connecting our minds, bodies, and souls. I stabilize, find my balance, and say, "I want you." My breathing is ragged. "Is that okay?"

"Why wouldn't it be?" His voice is low, husky.

Last night, the foreplay wasn't planned. Sex, for me, has become something staged to a degree that removes spontaneity. Do I even remember what it's like to get lost in a moment? To forget about time and schedules and camera angles and editing and what my subscribers want, and instead focus on what I and *my partner* need?

Teddy places a hand over my heart. "Your heart." His gaze dips downward to the spot on my chest, and I place my hand over his. I'm breathing so hard and fast it's like my body is weightless, the room around us dissolving until all I see is Teddy.

We both look up at once, our eyes locking, noses grazing.

His breath against my lips.

We move closer, our lips hovering, getting closer and closer until I can feel the warmth of his skin. I hold my breath, willing myself to forget my one rule, but I can't, so I swerve, diving for his neck, kissing him there, making up for what I can't give him.

Peeling back the high collar of his shirt, I kiss and lick my way as far down as I can before it's clear that his shirt must come off.

Up and over his head, I whip his shirt to the floor and he growls.

"I want you," I repeat. "Badly."

"Say it again," he grunts.

"I need you," I pant, hungrily kissing down his hairy chest, across his pecs and down to his belly. I grip the waist of his pants, and if they weren't so damn expensive, I'd rip them off him. The buttons are complicated, and I fumble—fucking expensive pants! The friction of my hand against his hardening dick makes him buck. So I rub him over the fabric. "You're so fucking hot."

"What do you want to do to me?" he asks, grabbing my chin with such force that my eyes roll and I whimper. I bite my lip and he moves his fingers to wrap around my neck, his grip tightening. "Tell me."

What I really want, I can't say out loud. Not in English. Maybe not in any language, none I know yet, anyway. I look up at him. "*Je veux faire l'amour avec vous.*"

"Fuck," he groans, his lips puckered as air escapes him. "You really are French?"

I shrug as he guides me to my feet, my hand still on his

dick. He gets close again, and I wonder if he'll try to kiss me, even though he knows my boundaries. I wonder if I'll let him. My heart is beating faster now, and I have to remember how to breathe.

His lips caress my chin softly and he pecks along the edges until he reaches my ear. "You know what I want?" he asks, and I whimper for him to tell me. "Fuck me like I'm one of your cam sluts. Don't hold back." He grabs my chin. "And when you're done, I'm going to unload inside you."

With great force, he whirls my body around until my ass is against his dick. His hands explore under my shirt, grab at my chest, as he sloppily tongues my earlobe.

"Come on, treat me like you're about to throw me away," he begs. "Be rough. Choke me. Do what you want to me."

I can't allow myself to process what he's asking. It conflicts with what I really want. I take a deep breath. *Get it together, Cole! This is what you do.* So I force my instincts to kick in, and I power up, do what I was designed to do, and I duck out from under him, whirl back around and take control.

Hand on his throat.

Push him up against the wall.

"You like that?"

His eyes roll. "Yes, Daddy."

"Don't call me Daddy, call me sir."

"Yes, sir," he obeys.

"Good boy." I push him to his knees. "What do you want?"

"Your cock," he mumbles as he mashes his face into my crotch, lapping at the material until I'm so hard that if I don't unleash soon I might bust through.

Slowly, he unzips, reaching inside until his warm hand

wraps around me, stroking harder and harder. His thumb slides across the head, and I shudder. "Fuck, you're so wet. I bet your audience loves that." He uses my precum as lube.

I try not to think about the act of performing, so I concentrate on how hot he looks admiring my dick.

His tongue runs along the shaft and my head falls back as he engulfs me, right down to the base.

My hips buck, faster, faster, faster, until I hit the back of his throat.

I hold him there, and he works his tongue.

"Good boy," I say when he doesn't gag.

I release him, and he gulps down air like water on a hot day.

"Fuck," he cries, panting as he moves to stand. "You have, um, you know?" He intimates. He's wobbly on his feet.

"Of course. In the master bathroom, under the sink. Unused bulbs and solution," I say, stepping out of character.

As I wait, I strip completely naked and stroke myself on the couch thinking about Teddy, his full lips, his amethyst eyes, his curly red-blond hair, the fur on his chest and belly and legs, the way he laughs, how he defended VERSTL and my character earlier with Alessandro even though he didn't need to, and that brings me to the brink of eruption.

Teddy returns, fully naked, water dripping down his body as he towels himself.

"Don't," I command.

I get on all fours in front of him. Beads of water trickle down the musculature of his legs, leaving a wet trail through the forest of hair like a river I want to swim.

Slowly, I lick the water drops off his body, starting from the top of his feet to his shins, crawling around back of him to reach his grapefruit calves, and up the back of his thighs to the underside of his bubbly, hairy ass, until he's bending forward.

Soon he's on his knees, too, stomach pressed to the floor, ass in the air, making it easy to explore him with my tongue.

He's moaning as I penetrate him, spelling my name with my tongue over and over and over again, marking my territory the way he wants me to. He grips his cheeks and spreads himself open to me, and I kiss him and lick him over and over until he arches his back and lets out a moan that drives me wild. I grunt, going faster, getting sloppier, making him wetter and wetter until he's so relaxed that I can feel the changes in his body.

I pick up my head to check on him.

He turns to look at me. "Fuck me, sir."

Teddy Hughes

When I beg, all the blood rushes to Cole's throbbing dick.

"Please, sir. I need to feel you inside me."

A devilish grin takes over his face as he presses against me, teasing.

"I'll be right back," he says. "Condom."

"Wait." I need to feel him inside me, without anything between us. "I was tested three months ago. Neg across the board. Haven't been with anyone in five months. Also on PrEP. Except I didn't take it today because I haven't been home." I grimace.

"I have extra pills," he says. "I'm negative across the board. DDF."

"Same. No condoms." No hesitation.

"You sure?"

My back arches and I press back into him. "I wanna feel you deep inside me."

"PrEP first. I'll be right back." He races out of the room.

Like a good boy, I stay in the same position until he comes back with two glasses of water and a bottle of Truvada.

"A lifesaver and a gentleman," I say.

"You say that to all your tops," he responds.

"Wait until I top you. The things that'll come out of my mouth."

"Fuck." He's stroking his thick, hard cock, and it looks like the greatest work of art I've ever seen. I need to feel him, all of him, inside me.

"Please," I beg, puckering for him.

The second he pushes into me, I breathe out steadily, centering my mind in order to feel every inch of him, the weight of his body on top of mine, the way he presses his hand down on my back.

When he's all the way in, his mushroom head expands and I contract my hole, suctioning to his cock. I exhale slowly, feeling every inch as he holds steady.

I start to gyrate on him, grinding and twerking until he's successfully hypnotized by my hips. Makes him easy to control.

Without stopping, I begin the rise to my knees with him still inside me; it's my go-to move. Cole stops thrusting, holding steady, and I back into him as I straighten my back until his chest presses against it. I reach behind me and grab his ass, goose bumps erupting across his skin.

He wraps one arm around my torso while the other holds tight to my hips.

I rest the back of my head against his collarbone. His lips and tongue lap at the side of my face.

"Choke me," I beg, bucking into him.

The hand on my hips slides up my side and over to my neck until his fingers wrap around my throat.

"Harder," I plead, and he obliges, my eyes rolling as the pressure builds, builds, builds and I gasp, not for air, but for release.

Suddenly, he's in control, and his hip thrusts overtake my own.

The penthouse around us melts away and all I see and feel is Cole, Cole, Cole.

He slows down, shifts his weight, and the reposition is so slight that it's almost negligible, until I feel his dick massage my prostate.

"Fuck," I shout, whine, beg, plead.

I need more of him, all of him.

He picks up the pace and I'm screaming, sweat dripping down the side of my face, flinging off my chin.

Pleasure, pain, sweet, sweet pain.

I can't get enough.

"Fuck—" Cole shouts. "I'm gonna—"

"Cum inside me," I command.

He grunts so loudly the island of Manhattan quakes and he feels even bigger inside me as he grips tight to my body, his own body jerking and jolting, his cock pulsating as he fills me, which is all it takes to push me over the edge and I shoot rope after rope, my body convulsing like I'm tripping on some sort of hallucinogenic drug.

Panting, I fold over and he collapses onto my back.

"Did...you...cum...hands-free?" He gasps for breath.

All I can do is nod because I'm floating somewhere between heaven and hell, where orgasms are apples on the Tree of Knowledge and I've bitten every single last fucking one.

"So hot," he gasps, and he slips out of me, leaving me feeling empty.

"My turn?" I ask.

"Damn, already?" He breathes out hard and looks to the floor before standing up, places his hands on his hips and sighs.

"You okay?"

He waits a few seconds. "Absolutely, handsome. You want to fuck me?" The question, like his expression, is forced. He climbs onto the couch long ways, smooth ass in the air, turns like a female porn star from the '80s and puckers his lips, and the realization washes over me. He said something in French earlier when I asked him what he wanted to do to me, and I don't speak a lick of the language, but I did recognize one word: *l'amour*. Love. Meanwhile I told him to fuck me like a whore. To degrade me. To slip into VERSTL mode, be @TheColeVivien. That seems to be the exact opposite of what Cole wants, or needs.

I stand up and walk over to the couch, sit beside him, right in front of his head.

He scans my face, my naked body, slick with sweat.

I reach for him and gently run my fingers through his hair. His eyes close and he leans into my hand the way a puppy might when being pet. When he looks up at me, I say, "Would you mind if maybe I held you instead?"

His body relaxes, all pretenses gone.

And I pull him onto my lap and stroke his hair as we lie together in silence.

★ ★ ★

At some point, we make our way upstairs and into the master bed. This time, I snuggle into his side, and he plays with my earlobe.

"How are you?" he asks.

"So great," I say.

"You sure, because I know you wanted to fuck me—"

I cut him off; he shouldn't have to feel obligated. He must carry so many people's expectations. How much do folks take from him? Want him to perform, to be a sexual machination instead of a person? "Only if you want to."

He moves to say something, but stops and sighs. "I definitely want you to. No question. But. Is it okay if it's not tonight?"

"Never apologize," I say, holding tighter to him.

"Thanks for understanding," he says. "I'm not used to that."

"Can I ask you something?" I sit up. "And if I'm being too nosy or forward, please feel free to swat me like a fly."

"Like a Venus fly trap?"

"Nice." I chuckle. "Is it hard to perform the way you do? You know, sexually, for an audience." I wince. "I don't know if this is coming off right or if I sound like an ignorant shitbag."

He clears his throat. "I wouldn't say it's hard. But it is a lot of emotional labor."

I sit up, straightening my back, and he moves his arm so I can get comfortable shoulder to shoulder. "Emotional labor? I'd never thought of sex work as emotional labor. Physical, absolutely. Mental, sure."

He grabs my hand and intertwines his fingers with mine. "The biggest part of my job is nurturing other people, making sure that I'm fully present for them, giving them what they want. If it's another performer, I need to make sure that they're comfortable, which, obviously, when you're having sex is always important, but there's an additional layer of their comfort level on camera. If I'm interacting with subscribers, I have to manage their expectations in real time, react to them like they're the center of my world because they pay for me to be the center of theirs. And when I escort, most of the time I get hired by folks who want me to pretend to be their boyfriend." He massages each of my fingers methodically, one at a time, circling back in groups of four. I've noticed that he does something similar with his own fingers, counting them when he's lost in thought or nervous. "The physical stuff, fucking, that's easy. So many people want intimacy. For someone to care about them."

"Is that what you want?" I say, softly.

He shrugs, turns away. "The after part, for me, when the realization kicks in that you have less than what you had when you started because you gave and don't always get back. That's hard." His voice is thick as he avoids answering my question. Cole is so used to providing, to giving of himself, that he wanted to buy what he is used to giving. What he said when he thought I was sleeping last night, about wanting the ability to fly away and find a place he belonged. He bought me because he wanted to feel something, and I've been incredibly selfish, acting like a complete ass because of Murray when all Cole wanted to do was drop a mini fortune on clothes for me, almost leaving him, telling him how *I* wanted to get fucked.

"I'm sorry," I say.

"For what?" He crinkles his nose.

I try to explain my thoughts, my selfishness, without centering his actions, but they're a tangled mess, so it comes out as, "I made you fuck me after I almost left!"

He chuckles, steadies me by grabbing hold of my hand, and squeezing in a rhythm, beats of four at a time. "Did you have a great time? Be honest."

"Best sex I've ever had. No joke. The way you smashed my prostate to pieces. To quote Sexy Italian Jesus, Alessandro: *Bellisimo!*"

"Then I'm happy," Cole says. "That's what I wanted. For you to enjoy yourself."

Even now, he's concerned about my feelings. Who does this for him?

"What about you?" I ask. "Be honest."

"This," he says, lifting our hands. "I'm grateful for this."

In some weird way, I understand what he means. After my entire life unraveled, it's comforting to know that this, right now with Cole, even though it's contained and contractual, can still exist somewhere: a simple gesture from a man of great versatility.

Cole Vivien

Teddy's chest rises and falls as I stroke his upper arm. How he looks when he sleeps, the buoyancy of his full cheeks, the softness of his eyelids, the way his lips turn slightly upward as if his dreams are providing for him what waking life can't, makes it impossible for me to look away.

Briefly, his eyes flutter open.

"You awake?" The LED alarm clock on the bedside flashes 4:04 a.m.

"Nope," he grumbles. He fights back a yawn, stretching to reach around my midsection and hug me. "What's up?"

"Nothing."

"Liar."

"I don't lie!"

"Mmm-hmm," he coos as his hand runs down my chest, stopping at the plume of groomed hair above my soft dick. His thumb grazes the shaft, and a shiver shoots up my back, eliciting an unexpected moan. The way he touches me, with such grace and care, is unlike anything I've ever felt.

Carving around the base, his hand wedges itself beneath my balls and he slowly but confidently cups them. With a tug, my back arches.

He kisses up my neck, closer and closer to my mouth, and it feels dangerous. My heart is racing as he reaches the ledge of my chin. He tugs on my balls more, harder, until my toes curl and writhe under him.

Just beneath my lower lip, he stops, holds his breath, waiting.

For a second, I consider it, but as quick as the thought enters my brain, it's replaced by my business alter ego screaming, "DON'T!" So I turn my head until our faces are out of alignment, and he quietly understands.

Not wanting him to stop, my legs part for him, and, releasing my balls, he continues his exploration further and further south until the pad of his index finger presses against my taint.

"Fuck, Teddy, don't stop."

My balls contract as he moves down to my hole, pressing both buttons at once.

"Fuck, Cole, you're so tight," he growls as he toils with entering me.

I lick my dry lips and grab my hard, throbbing member with one hand while reaching for his with my other hand. "I want you inside of me."

"I like it when *you* beg." He releases me so he can climb on top of me.

When we're stomach to stomach, dick to dick, I grab hold of both cocks at the same time and start pumping. He throws his head back and thrusts over and over, grunting breathlessly until he explodes, shooting his load across my chest and reaching up and onto my face.

He collapses to the side, tossing an arm over me and burrowing his head into my sticky chest. I lick him off my lips.

The back of his hand reaches upward and gently caresses my cheek. I lean into it and purr, and it coaxes the unfiltered thoughts from my mind. "You're so beautiful. How could your ex let you go?"

Air flaps through his lips in a trill.

"Sorry, shit, that was out of order!" Embarrassed, my cheeks heat.

He shakes his head into my chest before moving to sit upright.

"I shouldn't pry," I say. "*La curiosité a tué le chat.*"

He looks at me with mix of hunger and confusion. Like when you're starving at a restaurant and the waiter brings over another table's food. "I don't speak French, baby. Parlay voo eng-lays."

I burst out laughing. "I said, 'Curiosity killed the cat.'"

"Sure, *voulez vous coucher avec moi*, Creole Lady Marma-lade," Teddy says, pushing his pecs together like breasts and imitating Christina Aguilera with wild gesticulating hands. I can't breathe from laughing.

Then, out of nowhere he gets quiet.

"You don't have to tell me anything."

"I trust you." He takes my hand and places it on his hairy pec; his heart beats so fast I'm worried he's having a heart attack. His eyes are unmistakably glassy in the moonlight. "You meet someone and you think it's forever. The years go by, you shape your lives around each other, but somewhere along the way, that insatiable attraction you felt for each other, the need to rip each other's clothes off and swallow each other's loads lessens and lessens until one day, it's been six months since you even touched each other. Then a year. I'll never forget the night Murray got out of the shower, water dripping down his body, and he walked to the edge of the bed, and a primal urge I hadn't felt for him in ages overcame me. I crawled toward him, untied his towel, and started to lick him. I didn't register it at first, but he flinched. I started sucking his dick, but it stayed limp. Chubby, but not hard. And after a while, the lust left my body, and I stared up at him and he had his eyes closed. But not like, in pleasure. They were squeezed tight. His fists were clenched at his side. I asked him what was wrong." Teddy is fiddling with his fingers, pulling at them nervously. He nibbles at the skin on his lips.

There's so much left unsaid, and I want to give him the chance, the courage, to finish his story without interjecting.

Finally, Teddy speaks again. "That's when he told me, 'I'm no longer sexually attracted to you.'" His lips quiver, his voice breaks. "He hadn't been for a *long* time. He said I actively turned him off, that I wasn't the strong, confident man I was when he fell in love with me. I'd let myself go. He didn't find me sexy. That's why he wanted an open relationship, why he never touched me, why some nights I felt invisible as he stared at his fucking phone, knowing he was on Grindr and Scruff talking to other guys he desired for hours on end." A tear falls down his cheek and I pull him closer, but he wrestles away. "He always acted like I wasn't even in the room. He would whip out his hard dick and snap pictures to men, touch himself and say their names on video and if I said anything, tried to jump in on the action, he would say no, yell at me to go to sleep."

I can't imagine being with someone for years, loving them, knowing them inside and out and then being told that they're turned off by you. It's expected that, over time, people in a long-term, committed relationship will lose attraction to each other; one person can't be all things to another. Attraction waxes and wanes. It's normal to be attracted to other people, and sometimes less so to your partner. I get that, in theory. But to be told so blatantly is cruel.

"Teddy—" I want to tell him his ex was wrong, show him he's beautiful, more than beautiful, he's the kind of breathtaking that only exists in great literature.

"The worst part is that the day he broke up with me, he was so sweet. Attentive. We went out for brunch, held hands through the West Village after. We walked along The High Line and he stopped and hugged, held me for a little while. I should've known something was up, he wasn't usually affectionate in public, but I craved that."

I move closer before I say anything, and when he doesn't

pull away, I wrap my arm around him. "That must have been impossibly hard for you."

Teddy leans his head on my shoulder. "I always told Plant Daddy customers to be careful not to overwater their plant babies because their leaves would thin and start to wilt. Green leaves become yellowed and develop bacterial infections. I gave and gave and gave until my soil became waterlogged and I was drowning. And I guess so was he, and he started to openly resent me until he stopped wanting to fuck me. To him, I'd become a leech, reliant on him like a potted plant needing human care to survive." He laughs, but its sticky, full of tears. "I'm a potted plant in need of love. Men like Murray aren't confined to one planter."

When he says that, something inside me breaks. I wouldn't have used a plant analogy, but in so many ways, it resonates. I grew up in a verdant garden with the best "care," but I never took root. Anywhere, really.

I hold tighter to him so he knows I see him, hear him, understand him more than I can process right now. All that comes out is, "Thank you for trusting me with that."

"Thank you for listening."

He hugs me, the way a boyfriend hugs his person, arms tight around my whole body, head a perfect puzzle piece fitting into the side of my neck, chin resting on my shoulder. At first, I'm not sure what to do because out of everything we've done, this feels the most intimate and line crossing.

But I do what my body tells me is right. I squeeze him back and he sighs in relief.

When he peels back, and we're face-to-face, our noses graze. Synapses firing between us, our lips magnets, we don't break eye contact. His irises, a star map of his entire universe, everywhere he's been, study mine.

"Truth time?" His voice is shallow. "Why don't you kiss?"

"Someone once told me that *kissing me was liking falling in love.*"

"How dare they!"

Then the raw confession spills out: "I don't know how to be in love. Because of that, kissing always made me feel worse when I inevitably ended up alone."

"Not kissing on the lips is your way of protecting yourself." The sadness in his eyes tell me he gets it. "Will you kiss…" I drown in the green and blue whirlpool of his irises. I feel his breath on my chin as he whispers, "Again?"

I hold him there, my body and mind negotiating, resisting the pull forward.

Teddy Hughes

Need. Coffee.

An iced oat milk latte, quadruple shot of espresso, topped with cold foam, to be exact. And Cole's penthouse hotel room has many things, but not a working barista. Cole is passed out, and he looks so damn peaceful that I don't want to wake him up, so I decide to go for an early morning run, then stop at the nearest coffee shop and get us both caffeine. I'm sure he'll appreciate the boost.

The thought of him being surprised by the gesture warms me.

I grab a pair of loose workout trunks from Cole's dresser

that fit my meaty thighs like compression shorts. Lacing up some new kicks Cole bought me, I'm down the elevator and through the lobby in a flash. I have to go shirtless since Cole is too lean for me to pilfer his closet, and I don't have anything I feel comfortable coating in sweat, so it's a relief that the lobby is empty. Not even that judgy queen Frank is working.

The city is still sleeping, and there's a briskness to the air that'll surely be gone in a few hours, replaced with an unrelenting heat. But right now, it's perfect.

Running has always been a way for me to escape my head. After deep leg stretches against the side of the building and a set of side lunges, I take off.

Pounding pavement, I push myself, weaving around traffic cones, construction zones, the odd passerby. At this time of day, when all that's in front of me is open city air and endless combinations of streets and avenues, I can clear my head— turn everything off, all the chatter in my mind, the sadness and failure and second-guessing. Feel the burn in my chest, the soothing kind that reminds me I'm alive. The cooling sensation of the breeze against my sweaty torso. The fire in my calves propelling me forward.

Freedom.

I don't know how long I've been running, but by the time I reach the nearest Starbucks, order a tray of four different espresso-based options—two iced, two hot because I have no idea what Cole drinks and it's the least I could do for him—a blanket of humidity has already starting encroaching on the city.

As I cross Madison Avenue on 77th, I spot Jason, Cole's manager, on the corner. He looks to be arguing with an extremely delicious, tall blond man covered in tattoos. I don't want him to see me, so I hug the other side of the building and listen.

"I'm not doing this anymore. I'm done!" Tattooed Blond demands.

"You're done when I tell you you're done," Jason says.

"This isn't right, playing with Vivièn like this."

"Don't act like you're not getting anything out of this, Nicko."

"It's killing me." Tattooed Blond—Nicko's voice is thick with emotion. Tears.

"He needs this push. The company needs the PR. Trust me, he'll thank us both for all of this when we go public," Jason states.

"We?" Nicko questions sharply. "What are you getting out of this?"

"Don't worry about me. I always get what I want."

A chill creeps down my back as condensation from the iced coffees drips down my hands.

"Well," Nicko says. "I want out. I never should have let you talk me into any of this. All it did was bring up the pain of the past, and I want to focus on the future."

"Babe," Jason's voice gets low, almost sensual. "I do too. I have a few minor obstacles, but—" I can't make out the rest of what Jason says because it's getting farther away, but I definitely hear a "it'll all be over soon."

Intuition has my chest in a vice grip.

Cole's manager is up to something, and I have a feeling Cole is at the center.

But what, exactly?

And do I tell Cole, or keep it to myself? I don't exactly have specifics. I don't even know who the blond, Nicko, is, and nothing concrete was said.

I have to say something. Even if it's nothing, Cole deserves that much.

I peek round the corner of 77th and Madison Avenue to make sure the coast is clear before making my way back to the hotel, looking over my shoulder every step of the way.

Cole Vivien

Golden hour sunlight illuminates the kitchen, casting yellow beams onto the white marble. Reaching into the refrigerator, I grab a leftover platter from the VERSTL party. A shadowy figure emerges from the patio, making me scream and nearly drop the tray.

"Jason, what the fuck?" I shout.

He snickers and grabs a hunk of cheese from me. "My bad, dude. Couldn't sleep. Not all of us were invited to very important business dinners with a certain Italian fashion designer." His words are tacky like glue.

"Come on, Jason, you understand," I say.

Moonlight paints jealousy across his face. "Of course, boss. How'd it go?"

"He wants to collaborate."

As he listens to me recount last night's dinner and what Teddy did for the company, he furiously pops cheese into his mouth like a subway rat.

"I heard you two," he says. "You're not quiet."

"Jesus, Jace. Eavesdrop much?" When we shared a tiny apartment, we had zero boundaries. And I mean none. There's little Jason hasn't seen or heard of *me*, and vice versa. I was comfortable with him knowing everything from my morning bathroom rituals to how much cheese I "secretly" consumed at midnight when I couldn't sleep. But this? Listening in on *Teddy* feels like a boundary, crossed. A boundary that isn't mine to allow Jason to invade.

"I don't trust this Teddy guy," Jason adds.

"Jace, come on, he's harmless."

"He's a rent boy." He pulls out his phone, taps, and I hear a ping on my phone. He's airdropping a folder. "I did some digging on him. He's an 'author.'" The way he says *author*, with pomp and circumstance, makes Teddy sound like he describes himself as a magical wizard.

"Yes, and?" I don't hit Accept, but I stare at the label: *Ginger Grifter.*

"I had my PI do me a favor. There's a lot you don't know about this guy. Some shifty shit that got buried in the press. I think he's running a con. I've pushed my return to LA. I'm going to your sister's wedding," he says. "Someone needs to keep an eye on him. And you." He grabs more cheese and a glass that looks like whiskey, and starts to walk out. "Read the file. For your sake, and VERSTL's."

"I don't need to. From everything I've seen of Teddy so far, he's been nothing but genuine. Maybe a bit too genuine, too open. How could he run a con when I'm the one who propositioned *him*?"

"Never underestimate a mark." Jason has never been anything but a loyal friend and manager, but this is going too far. Right?

But something stopped me from kissing Teddy last night.

Maybe it was a sign, the universe telling me that Teddy is not the person to break my one rule for, that I needed to continue protecting myself against him because the last time I broke my rule, even though it was someone I'd kissed thousands of times before, it clouded my judgment and I'm still bracing for the fallout.

Count to twelve on my fingers, once, twice, three times.

Hesitantly, I hit Accept on my phone, and the file downloads.

Unexpectedly, Teddy enters the kitchen, shirtless and sweaty, startling me. He's all smiles, a tray of coffees in hand. "Pick-me-up?"

Six

DOWNLOADING: Beta Boyfriend

Teddy Hughes

Leaving the city is like transplanting old roots to a new bed, a fresh plot of nutrient-rich soil with enough room to finally bloom. The greenery is vibrant, lush, out here in the burbs. Not quite rural, but there are farms with sunflower stalks and maypoles, wood barns that look like Pinterest photos, and cherry blossoms in bloom. Everything is spaced out, and there are dirt and gravel roads tucked into thick woods, verdant and full of life.

Maybe moving out of the city wouldn't be the worst thing in the world. Thoughts of using the money from being Cole's fake boyfriend to start a new nursery fill my head.

The sun bakes into my cells, and I absorb its rays. Cole lets me keep the windows down so I can stick my face out and feel the warm wind whip past. I make a tongue-in-cheek joke about wagging my tongue like a good boy, hoping he'd remember when I made that bougie-ass older couple uncomfortable, but either he didn't hear or find it funny because he doesn't react.

"You okay?" I ask, sticking my head back inside. My hair is frizzy, so I pat it down with my hand.

"Huh?" He grips the wheel of the rental, a white Mercedes-Benz with a light tan leather interior, white-knuckled, at ten and two. "No, I'm good."

"You sure about that, sparky?"

He taps his fingers restlessly. "Nervous about seeing my family." He adjusts the rearview mirror, and I follow his line of sight to the gray Mercedes Zipcar rental behind him. Jason is behind the wheel. I haven't had the chance to talk to Cole yet. Truth be told, I have no idea how to broach the subject, so I'm biding my time, waiting for a good moment.

"When was the last time you saw them?"

"My sister, a couple days ago. Her fiancé, Mikey, a year ago when they came to visit LA. He proposed to her on a secluded beach in Malibu. I helped him organize it."

"That's so romantic!" My heart melts.

"Mikey's one of those model straight ally dudebros. Very 'I love my gay brother-in-law,' wears glitter at Pride, and isn't uncomfortable when a guy hits on him. I actually think he likes it. He went back to school—the Culinary Institute, much to Father's chagrin. He'd probably prefer she marry within her class."

I *humph* and squirm thinking about the clothes I wore the night I met him, wondering what he'd think of my tiny studio with Kit or the small apartment I grew up in on the out-skirts of New Orleans.

He glances quickly to me. "Yeah, so you'd think he'd be one of those romantic chef boyfriends. But he's not exactly one for *l'amour*. He told me he wanted to propose on a Ferris wheel with a damn flash mob."

"How 2013 of him."

"Very that. I told him I'd take care of it. I had it arranged where the beach was littered with rose petals and those battery-operated candles that look like real flames. There was an open-top cabana with fluffy white pillows and rosé champagne and a violinist dressed in white cotton." He looks over and his eyes widen at the sight of me leaning on the armrest, googly-eyed and basically drooling. "Are *you* okay?"

"I didn't realize you were such a Casanova."

I remind myself this is a temporary gig. Cole is not *mine*.

My pocket vibrates. I slide in and pull out my phone. "Kit's FaceTiming. I'll send her to voicemail."

"No, answer. She's your bestie."

Kit's face explodes on the screen. "Hey, bitch! Oh my god, hey, Mercedes!"

Cole laughs. "How'd she know?" he whispers.

"It's one of my lesbian car enthusiast powers, Frenchy!" Kit moves her head around the screen, as if that will allow her a better view inside the car.

Flustered, I mute her.

He shoots me a concerned look. "How *much* does she know?"

"I tell her everything. I hope that's not a problem."

Checking the rearview mirror again, he utters a cold, "Of course not."

He's been so weird and cagey since I came back this morning.

When we checked out of the hotel, and I stepped out with new threads, Frank the doorman dropped his jaw to the marble floors and nodded in approval.

"See you around, Frankie," I said to him.

Exasperated, he shook his head and actually cracked a smile. I figured it was best not to push my luck—little victories and all—so I tipped a nonexistent hat to him. With a dramatic flair, I burst through the double doors, and I think Frank said something to effect of, "Well done." Jason chimed in with a, "Cole is quite generous, isn't he?" and all Cole said to that was, "It's good business."

Good business? I brushed it off at the time, but given Cole's odd behavior, something is up.

"Sorry, I'll be quick." I take Kit off mute.

"Bitch, did you mute me? How dare!"

"Sorry, Cole had to take a call."

"He's a professional daddy," she says with a wink, which makes Cole stir. "So where are you headed? And will you be back before your move-out date?"

A large wood sign with "Welcome to Garrison" carved into its face, painted dull gold, whizzes by.

Cole turns onto a private road surrounded by thick pines. In the distance, an ornate gate that cuts the road in half swings open as we approach. An engraved copper plaque on a stone pillar reads "Château Deplantier." Why do all rich folks name their houses?

He clears his throat, a sign for me to get off the phone. We must be close.

"Gotta go, Kit. Talk more later love you, bye!"

Her brows furrow and she starts to yell something, but I click off before anything damaging comes out of her mouth.

The driveway winds through the woods until suddenly it opens to a lush green and manicured lawn at the foreground. In the distance, a sprawling field of wildflowers, red poppies and white and yellow daisies and soft purple forget-me-nots.

We brake in front of a massive sunny yellow Victorian with ornate moldings from the 1800s accented in dark greens and rust reds and golds. It's surrounded by large looming oak trees. The pathway to the front door is outlined in strawberry pink hydrangeas and lavender bushes, with perfectly pruned tall grasses interspersed throughout. Some of the windows on the left are open, so the wind rushes through in a cross-breeze, letting the white curtains inside wave to us. There's a French flag jutting out from the patio, and right below it, a trans-inclusive pride flag. It's beautiful, but I have to be honest, I was expecting something grander.

"This is your parent's house?"

Cole snorts. "Oh, no. This is my sister's house. Used to be the caretaker's, but once Mallory started working for the company, Father wanted her close by. It's considered an historic house, so he couldn't knock it down and build something else."

"Who would tear *this* down?" I ask, slightly horrified at the prospect. "This is serious home goals."

He points beyond the Victorian, down the winding driveway where, in the distance, is a massive French château with a white stone exterior and black iron lining large picture windows, sweeping roofs with peaks and valleys, ivy vines crawling up the stone face. A weeping willow stretches its flowy, dreamy tendrils across one side of the house, and there are blooming apple and almond trees beyond that. On the other side of the house is a porte cochere that houses what looks like a white Bugatti.

My mouth hangs open and Cole gently places his fingers on the underside of my chin and pushes up, a sign for me to close it.

He rolls his eyes. "Everyone has that reaction. It's the—"

"Extreme wealth?" I mutter. "Got it."

A powder blue VW Bug convertible sits on the side of the house.

"Now, *that* is super cute!" And more my speed. Or at least within the realm of potential affordability.

"That's Mal's daytime car. She keeps the Rolls Royce at our parents'," Cole says. "We're not staying on the family compound, by the way. I like to keep my life separate from the family. We have an Airbnb outside Cold Spring, away from prying eyes."

Good business. "So what do I need to know about you and the family, so I make sure I'm on my game?" I ask. My phone buzzes in my hand.

"Right," he says. "Well, she's going to assume you live in LA."

I grimace as my phone keeps vibrating. I know exactly nothing about LA.

"Maybe you moved there recently?" he asks, though it's more like a decision because he asks, "Where'd we meet?"

"Oh, that restaurant from that trash reality show!" I snap my fingers, trying to remember the name.

Frustration pools in his jaw. "Jesus, how about I say we met on the corner of Hollywood Boulevard?"

"Way to make me feel cheap."

"That's not what I meant. There's a good restaurant I love there. Cicada. My sister *died* when we went. The escargot is divine."

"Mmm, snails. Yum. Good save, by the way. Let's just play our cards gay and say we met on a dating app and ate at Cicada. How long have we been seeing each other?"

"Two months," Cole says.

"Wow, that's ten years in straight world," I quip.

This elicits a laugh. "Mother studied film in Paris, Father grew up outside the city. Old money." He peers at me through his periphery. "They met on the Champs-Élysées while she was eating a croissant and he was on his way to a meeting. Very *Eat, Pray, Love*. She loves movies and Hollywood and the idea of me having a boyfriend, so you'll do perfect with her."

"And your dad?"

He makes a sound like rusty gears that need to be oiled. "He's demanding and still carries a grudge because I walked away from the family business, and his money. He doesn't like what he can't control. It's best to stay away entirely. Definitely don't mention anything Marie Antoinette–related."

"Why would I—"

"Mal's friend once said she loved that Kirsten Dunst movie, and my dad lost it. Something about an American bastardized version of reality." He massages his temples. "I don't know. And don't mention anything about VERSTL. As far as Mother and Father know, I work in social media. Mallory knows everything, so you're good there."

The front door swings open, and a girl who looks supermodel gorgeous, like Cole, flies out, waving her hands and screaming.

Cole flings open the car door and runs toward her. She jumps into his arms.

I look down at my phone to five separate text bubbles from Kit:

RUDE!

Where are you? Are you okay? Is he holding you hostage? Blink once for yes, twice for YES!

WHAT'S THE SAFE WORD?

Saw your location on Find My. Cold Spring, huh? Bougie. Me and the girls might have to take a road trip.

Lesbi-intuition. Don't argue with me.

I flap my lips as I exhale. I can't tell Cole, he'll flip. He's waving me over. Mallory's eyes are hungry to meet me. Here goes nothing.

Cole Vivien

You know what "they" say? That thing about not being able to go home?

Yeah. This all feels weird. An unsettling time warp. And the funny thing is, I'm not even at the house I should be calling "home." The one up the hill, Château Deplantier, is technically where I slept, but this Victorian is where I *lived*. The caretaker, Miss Molly, a sweet woman who lost her only son when he was five years old in a car accident, cared for me and Mallory, and she stayed here, so we spent our days as kids here. When Miss Molly moved to Florida, Father gave the house to Mallory.

Everything is exactly as I remember it: the porch swing, the treehouse Father's workers built for us twenty years ago still nestled in the branches off to the side of the house. Even the wild blueberry bushes in the center of the yard, so lush and green with unripened berries, which were always my favorite to pick because they were crispy and tasted like sour candies when they popped in my mouth.

The last time I lived in this small, sleepy town with one short Main Street, I was a tall pimply kid who went away to boarding school where everyone made fun of my name and only had "friends" because of my family's money.

So much has changed in a decade; all the old Victorian houses in the surrounding areas have been restored. New money changed the landscape. When Father and Mother first moved to Cold Spring, it was largely unpopulated, with massive plots of gorgeous wooded land ripe for building a secluded French château hidden from prying eyes, Father's dream. Growing up, he had a penthouse on the Upper West Side in the city and we still have the family home in France, but Father wanted the illusion of mystique, hence a permanent residence in quiet suburbia. I wonder if the heart of the town still remains.

When I see Mallory, all my worries melt and I'm running

into her arms the way we did when we were kids. Almost immediately, she pulls back and squints at the car, waving him over. "Is *that* your man? I'm shocked."

"Shocked?"

"I always pictured you with a pretty boy," she says. "He's got this rugged thing going. What do you call it? Beefy bear?"

I burst out laughing. "Two different descriptors, but yes. Teddy is a bear-in-training. A bit thicker than an otter."

"Otters, and bears, and tigers, oh my!" Mal jokes. "What is with the gays and your animal names?" I love the way straight women refer to the entire queer community as simply, "The Gays." She continues, "Questions I will never get answers to, much like 'are bottoms allowed to attend bottomless brunch?'"

I purse my lips. "You stole that joke from me."

She shrugs and says, "But I made it funny." She beckons Teddy over hurriedly. "Are you nervous, having a boyfriend home? Be honest!"

Honestly, Teddy is setting my teeth on edge. Jason wormed into my brain, and all I thought about the entire car ride was that damn mystery folder he sent me on Teddy that I haven't opened. On one hand, Jason is right. I don't really know Teddy. I've only spent two nights and a single day with him. He could be a con artist. But I look over at him, goofy grinning and my intuition is telling me I'm overreacting.

Watching him walk over, looking so damn handsome, my worries vanish with each step he takes.

She whispers loudly enough for him to hear, "He is gorgeous. Like that guy in *Game of Thrones*. All hail the King in the North!" Mallory curtsies in front of Teddy, whose cheeks get so red he must turn away.

"I would make a Red Wedding joke, but that feels like bad form," Teddy says.

She. Loses. It. Doubles over in backbreaking, stomach-pained kind of laughter.

Teddy leans in. "It wasn't that funny, was it?"

"Nope." I place a hand on her shoulder. "Have you cracked, *sœur*?"

She looks up, teary-eyed, but still laughing. "I needed a good joke about a disaster wedding!" Regaining her composure, hands gripping the sides of her stomach, she says, "Good one, new guy. Though, if anything goes wrong tomorrow, I'm blaming you."

Teddy throws his hands up. "Fair."

Mallory hooks her arm into Teddy's. "He's a keeper, this one." Shock strikes her. "Oh my god, you have two different color eyes!"

"Heterochromia," Teddy says.

"God bless you," Mal says.

He chuckles. "*Merci*." The French, though he pronounces it incorrectly, impresses her. "It's called heterochromia, two different color eyes. It's hereditary. The only hetero I'll ever be, amiright, babe?" I wink at Cole.

Mal's beaming, glancing between us. "Mother is gonna cry when she sees you two dancing tomorrow night."

"You and Mikey too," I assure her.

"We both know that's a lie," Mal says. "Speaking of, she and Mikey are meeting us at Castle Rock. Mother insisted we have a car drive us, but I knew you would want to drive yourself."

"Thank you," I praise.

"We should get going." She points to the car behind mine. "Who is that?"

"Jason." He's been in the car on the phone yelling at someone since we pulled in.

Mal rolls her eyes. "*Jason* is here?"

"I have some work I need to do while I'm here and he's helping out," I lie. "He won't be around much. He's staying at that boutique hotel on the water in Cold Spring. He's not coming to Castle Rock."

Mal exhales in relief and tosses her hair. "Praise. I really don't love him. But you know that." She waved the thought of Jason away. I never quite understood the disdain she has for him. He's been nothing but a loyal friend when I had nobody. "Anyway, you guys been together for how long?"

"Two months," we answer at the same time, not at all sounding rehearsed.

She eyes me suspiciously, then returns to Teddy. "You must see Jason all the time. What do you think of him?"

Teddy shrugs. "He's nice enough."

"Nice *enough*," Mallory repeats. "I don't like how clingy he got after you guys hooked up."

My cheeks heat.

Teddy's eyes widen, and my heart drops. "You and Jason?"

"Oops," Mallory says, her face pained as she avoids eye contact with me.

Thanks, Mal! I scramble to think of an explanation because despite Jason's intense reservations and warnings, Mal's ill-timed tea-spilling puts Teddy's feelings front and center for me. "It w-wasn't anything, Teddy." I fumble over my words and work quick to steady my voice. "I should've told you—but it wasn't a romantic thing."

Teddy gingerly grabs my upper arm. "Tale as old as gay time. Friends fucking friends."

I exhale in relief. "See, Mal. Gay friends can hook up and still be just friends. And Jason wasn't clingy. Just territorial over our friendship. Definitely nothing unrequited."

She squeezes her eyes shut. "Does not compute," she says robotically. "Either way, I'm protective over my baby brother."

"As you should be," Teddy adds.

"I get a really lovely energy from you, Teddy," Mallory finishes.

Sister test: passed.

Teddy Hughes

Mallory is absolutely everything. And I take every opportunity to tell her as much.

She gives me the grand tour of Garrison from the back seat as we drive to the wedding venue. I wanted her to take the front seat, but she insisted Cole and I sit next to each other. Mallory points out her favorite antique shop and the niche wine shop where they special order cases of fabulously cheap rosé branded by some former contestant of *The Bachelorette*.

Cole takes my hand in his and massages my palm and plays with my fingers.

The road up to Castle Rock is long and narrow and winds up a heavily wooded mountain, through a state-owned nature preserve. We pass by clusters of parked cars with hikers and bird watchers; according to Mal, there are a few bald eagle nests around the castle and on a clear day like today, you can see them flying overhead and along the Hudson. A rusted no-trespassing sign whizzes past.

"What's the deal with this place?" I ask.

"Mal's been in love with it since we were kids," Cole says.

"It looks closed to the public," I say.

"Technically, yes," Cole responds. "It's a private state preserve. Father has pull with the governor, though."

"But not for *inside* the castle." Mal's voice is high enough to shatter glass.

"It'll be gorgeous," Cole says, doing his best to soothe her. "Either way."

"I am calm. I am peace. I am serenity," Mal chants like a prayer, breathing steadily.

Cole reaches into his pocket and pulls out a smooth, shiny blue stone with waves of different hues on its surface. A perfect river rock. He hands it to her.

"Lifesaver!" She paws at it like a raccoon in a dumpster and immediately rubs it all over her cheeks.

Cole leans in. "Blue lace agate. Meant to calm the mind and heal broken emotions."

"You're a regular crystal shop." I can't help but smile at Cole's thoughtful gesture. I study his face, the concern he has for his sister, and all I want to do is kiss him. Alas—

Mal is still anxious, but now she looks certifiable, frantically sliding it across her forehead and down the side of her face.

"Is she okay?"

"It's a crystal, not a miracle worker," he whispers.

"I can hear you!" Her voice is stoic. "By the way, we must go to the new apothecary in town!"

"There's an apothecary?" Cole asks.

"Two now! The mass exodus out of Brooklyn during the pandemic brought all the anti-corporate heritage hipsters to our parts, and their apothecaries with them! I might've used some of my inheritance to help fund one, for fun," Mal explains. "Look, guys, there's it is!" She squeals pointing toward the castle.

Built in the late 1800s, its rough-cut stone exterior looms over treetops. Like something ripped from an old Disney film with its tall exaggerated, angular magnificence and unobstructed views of the entire Hudson Valley, it evokes magic and mystery. And a coldness. The closer we get to it, the more it looks in need of some TLC, the grounds around the castle are cracked from time, moss and weeds and vines sprouting up through stone and suffocating concrete; nature bending man to its will. A piled stone wall surrounds the property like some sort of medieval barrier against whatever lurked in the maples and saps beyond. The grass in front, a wide-open space, is vibrant and green, and a team of people and landscapers work diligently to arrange seating in front of a vine-covered distressed wood arbor that has the castle in its background. Off to the side and out of sight of where the ceremony is set to take place is an insulated white tent.

We pull up alongside a white Lexus SUV. A fabulous woman who looks exactly like Cole and Mallory, add twenty-ish years, Botox, and a good face-lift, waves excitedly.

Mallory slaps my and Cole's still-clasped hands. "Brace

yourself. Gird your loins. *Je vous salue Marie!*" She does the sign of the cross, kissing the crystal in her hand.

Cole stops me before we get out. "One last thing. My name isn't Cole Vivien."

"Excuse me?"

"It's Vivièn DuBois-Deplantier. My parents don't know me as Cole, even though I did legally change it a few years back." He really sells that last one, *De-plon-tee-yay*. I can see why he changed it. @TheViviènDuBoisDeplantier is a mouthful. "I realized on the drive I hadn't told you."

"I wondered why your estate was named Château Deplantier."

He corrects my pronunciation. "I hope you're not mad—I don't tell anyone my previous name."

"Not at all." What else can I say? Thanks for not trusting me?

"Oh, and Mother likes to be referred to as *Ms.* DuBois. She doesn't use the Deplantier name, which is a whole feud I won't start right now."

"Got it."

"She's the most perceptive person I've ever met. It's a feat I've managed to evade her questioning about what I do for a living."

"I'm great with moms, they lo—"

The door opens. Ms. DuBois stands at attention, expectantly waiting for me to rise up and greet her like the Queen Mother. When I do a small curtsy, she lets out a cackle and pulls me into a hug before sizing me up. She smells like rose perfume and money. Brown tortoise sunnies take up half her face, and when she whips them off, I get a good look at her.

"He looks healthy, Mal!" She grips my shoulders and squeezes, her voice buttery soft yet crisp like a freshly baked croissant. She's fabulous, serving Marion Cotillard realness, her hair effortless, her makeup so light and flawless. She's wearing a navy blue linen pantsuit with a flowy pale yellow blouse underneath that ties into a loose bow under her neck.

"Hello, Ms. DuBois!" I'm cheesing hard, laying it on thick. "It's so nice to finally meet you! Vivièn told me so much about you."

She scrunches her nose the way Cole does, except she makes it look devious. "I wish I could say the same. And please, call me Brigitte, or *Mom*."

"*Mom?*" Cole asks in confusion.

With a wink, she turns to Cole and beckons him the way she would a well-trained dog. "Come here! You're looking thin, are you eating?"

"I've gained fifteen pounds, Mother," Cole says.

"Maybe in your ass!" She smacks his perfectly round butt and stifles a laugh. "My god, what are you feeding that thing?"

"Squats." Cole slides away gracefully and blushes.

"So listen, excuse my French, Teddy," she says to me, but is looking only at her son. "But the bitch who runs the place won't talk to anybody but your father for some godforsaken reason, and he's currently occupied." She rolls her eyes. "Maybe she'll talk to you. I swear she's making me want a cigarette so bad. I almost had Driver take me to the gas station. Or run her over." She's talking with her hands, reminding me of my momma. There's something safe about that, and I'm drawn to her. I've always been drawn to strong, take-no-shit women, and Brigitte DuBois is their queen.

"I'll speak with her, Mother." Cole is so confident it lights a fire in my chest. He and Mal start off toward the chaos in front of the castle, but Brigitte grabs me.

Flinging her sunglasses back on, she says, "Come, handsome, take a walk with an older, more distinguished woman, won't you?"

We head toward the right side of the castle. Yellow and purple wildflowers dot its stone walls like an impressionist painting. So many of the stones have cracks, worn down by the years, but it's resilient. Breathtaking. It reminds me of Cole.

Meanwhile, Brigitte examines every square inch of me. "When my little Vivièn and Mallory were young, they would ride their bikes up here with Miss Molly, the château caretaker, and sneak onto the property. It's usually closed to the public, you know. They were small enough to wriggle into boarded-up windows and scale the once-grand staircases and not get caught. Mallory loved the idea of being a princess and climbing towers. Vivièn, on the other hand, always stayed on the ground."

"I see that hesitation in him," I say.

Brigitte coos. "Vivièn wanted a *different* life, away from expectations. Like my husband, he keeps himself guarded. For protection." I see a lot of Cole in Brigitte, the complexity in how she holds herself, so poised, contrasting with the pain in her eyes and the wisdom in her voice. "All I ever wanted was for him to believe there was more out there for him. Love, most of all."

We reach a landing with unobstructed views of the Hudson River, blue skies reflected in its waves.

"Do you bird?" she asks.

Bird? "Excuse me?"

She chuckles and points to a bald eagle gliding a tailwind of a warm breeze. "I love bird-watching. They're so beautiful, free. Did Vivièn tell you I was an actress, once upon a time?"

"Tell me everything." I'm perched, ready to absorb.

"That's how I met my husband. I was cast in a French film, very low-budget. I had wanted to get out of regional theater here in the States and the opportunity to move to Paris came and I grabbed at it." She tells me about the film, a black-and-white sexual noir without any dialogue. "It was the eighties, and very avant-garde."

"I'm obsessed."

She laughs. "I have a copy somewhere. But you'll have to keep it from my husband. He doesn't like it so much." She waves the thought away like a buzzing bee. "Anyway, Vivièn and I watched movies together. It was our 'thing.' Old black-and-whites. French and Italian films. *La Dolce Vita.* Silly Disney musicals. I wanted Vivièn to dream. I was in love with love, while he deconstructed and poked holes in their love stories. I tried everything to break through. We only get a few great adventures in this life." She looks to me, knowing I'm hanging on her every word. "Take every one."

My breath catches on her words, and they tumble around my head for a while.

"I saw how unhappy he was at home, how the fighting between me and my husband impacted him. He had too many pressures to follow in his father's footsteps. He never felt at home here as a gay man, either. I can't blame him for fleeing to Los Angeles." Clicking her tongue in disgust, she continues. "I worry that instead of inspiring him to dream, we made him afraid."

I stare at her, unsure of what to say.

"He pretends he doesn't need anyone, but that's nonsense. Everyone needs someone. Wouldn't you agree?"

Last night, as Cole held me and traced the outline of my arm with his soft fingertips, I had never felt safer. Murray never did that for me. Cole's breathing fell into rhythm with mine, and I drifted off into a deep sleep. I dreamed about meeting him under different circumstances, where he was just a guy in a bar, not a rich sex worker visiting my city, and I wasn't falling apart at the seams. He took me on a proper date to Joe's Pizza and we walked along the Hudson on the West Side at sunset and we kept walking until the sun rose up and over the skyline.

She studies me carefully. "I am fiercely protective of my son. He and my daughter are the two good things I ever did in this life, and I saw the way he looked at you. He looks happy for the first time in years. Forgive me for being skeptical."

"I haven't known your son for very long, but in all the time I've spent with him, what I do know is that he has a massive heart. He's afraid to show it, but I see it. And it's beautiful." I squeeze her hand on my arm.

Acknowledging it, satisfied, she continues. "So tell me about you, since my son doesn't feel the need to fill me in on important life details. He's never had a boyfriend before. Unless you count Nicko. Which I don't, because they were never official."

My breath catches. That's the name I heard this morning,

the tattooed blond man arguing with Jason, who he called "babe." Breathlessly, I ask, "What happened?"

"Nickolas was a mess," she says, waving away his aura. "Clingy and manipulative. Wanted more than my Vivièn could give, and resented him for that. Take it from an old woman who learned a long time ago that the greatest gift you can offer someone, if you love them, is grace."

Murray floats into my mind the way a bee lands on the filament of a flower.

"How long have you been together?" she quizzes.

"Two months," I say. "About."

"Honeymoon glow, I see," she says.

"He's made me happy," I say, surprising myself. It's not a lie. I've been happier and felt more alive over the past few days than I have in years. But as I tell his fabulous mom this, the reality of what she said about Cole hits me. I have to be careful. Tread lightly. Cole doesn't deserve something that isn't real, and I don't want either of us to feel empty when he says goodbye to me. The line between fact and fiction can blur easily when you're in someone else's dreams. I'm not even sure there is a line anymore.

She flicks an imaginary speck of dust off her blouse. "So what do you do, Theodore? I assume Teddy is short for Theodore."

Improv 101: Tell the truth. I took a random improvisation class in college to fulfill some ridiculous elective requirement, and it's come in handy more than any other class that wasn't in my major. "I wish. Theodore is so distinguished. Edward is my given name. I'm an author and horticulturalist."

"An *author*?" Her voice piques. "Anything I've read?"

I shake my head. "Do you like gardening?"

"Do I look like I get my hands dirty." Brigitte shows off her pearly white skin, soft as a baby's ass, without so much as a single wrinkle.

"I write about plants. Research. Gardening tips. How I started my successful nursery and became one of the most sought-after horticulturalists in the city. With fun stories along the way."

"Fascinating," she says. "There's a quaint indie bookstore in Cold Spring. I wonder if they have your books. Maybe Mal can take you there to have a look."

"I highly doubt they have it, but I'd love to go!"

"So do you still own your nursery?"

"No. I, um—" *Think quick, Teddy!* I babble my way through nonsense.

She takes the reins. "You should come here. We need something like that in our little town. You'd do well. A lot of affluent people who spend money on frivolities."

Not a fan of her calling plants *frivolities*, seeing as, you know, they literally provide the oxygen we breathe, but I don't feel like throwing down with Brigitte.

"Plus, I would be a very happy mother if you could convince my Vivièn to move back to New York."

"This area *is* beautiful," I say.

"I agree, Theodore," she says. "I hope you don't mind, I think Theodore suits you much better than Edward. *Local writer and horticulturalist Theodore—*"

God, I love her. "Hughes," I say.

"*Theodore Hughes.* Has a nice ring to it. Theodore DuBois-Deplantier does too."

My mouth goes dry. How do I answer that? Cole is going to have to pay me extra for a fake marriage.

"Deplantier means *of the trees*," she says. "And what better place to be among the trees than here." She gestures all around us. "Much better than acrid LA."

"I've never been to LA, but I'd have to agree."

Silence.

She eyes me closely, like I said something that doesn't fit, and now I'm panicking, though I don't know what I said. Her grip loosens, if only for a second. *What did I do?*

Grabbing me harder, she swings us around and we saunter toward the castle.

"I appreciate you indulging the mother of the bride." She pats my chest. "I have a feeling about you. *Don't* disappoint."

Cole Vivien

Teddy belly flops onto the bed of the Airbnb, a beautiful old stone house built directly into a hillside, flanked by trees and a lush garden that he drooled over the second we pulled in. Most of the house is underground except for the foyer and a loft where the master bedroom is that we have to climb a gorgeous wrought iron spiral staircase to reach. It's a carefully curated artist's retreat that's massive and open on the inside, despite the landscape around it. Teddy says it reminds him of the Hobbit houses in the Shire, whatever the hell that means. There's a placard on the butcher block countertop in the white, newly renovated kitchen that says the stones that make up the face of the house were imported from Greece and

Italy, and it was renovated by a famous artist who calls themselves Anonym(h)ous(e). I kind of love it. Never thought I'd
say that about being home. *Home*, the word tumbles around
my head on low.

Could I move back to New York? Run VERSTL from
here? I moved to LA to escape Father and make it on my own.
As my trajectory with VERSTL changes, LA seems less like
a sensible place to rest my head.

Teddy is shirtless, rubbing his hairy belly, his legs dangling
off the edge of the bed, and my breath catches. He picks up
his head and flashes his goofy smile. "Hey, Vivièn DuBois-
Deplantier!"

"Edward." I bow.

"Oof, yeah, that name makes me sound like a stuffy old
Brit with yellow teeth."

"Rubbish," I apply my best British accent. "I do believe me
mum fancies you quite a bit." I move to stand between his
legs. "I'm chuffed to bits."

"Fucking hell, so sexy." He grabs his crotch, massaging it
roughly as he stares up at me, never losing eye contact. His
fingers slip beneath the waistband of his jeans and he closes his
eyes, begging me to imagine how his dick feels in his hand.
My own dick strains against the fabric of my pants, begging
to be let free. "You got me chubbed up, babe." The way he
says *babe* now with a fire in his voice, yet so comfortably, like
we've been doing this for a long time, hits me and a lust I
can't control overwhelms me.

Lowering myself to my knees, I hook my fingers into the
fabric of his pants. "I did, huh?" I remove his hand and dive
in, pressing my nose and lips to him.

Kissing through the material, I feel how hard he is for me, until his hips buck from being so constrained.

My hands travel up the side of his body to his nipples, and I tweak and tug and they immediately firm up and he lets out an incredible moan that shakes the bed.

He grabs my arms and squeezes.

I stand up. "We gotta go. We're meeting Mal and Mikey to walk around town before the rehearsal dinner tonight."

"Oh, fuck," he cries. "Tease!"

Checking my watch, I calculate the time. "We have a good twenty-five minutes. Shower with me?" I hold out a hand.

He grabs hold and I hoist him to his feet, his chest crashing into mine.

Our eyes lock, his lips slightly part, and he moves closer as if he's going to kiss me.

Then he turns his head, grabs my bulge with his free hand, and grips it. He's leading the way now, pushing forward forcing me to walk backward. He guides me into the bathroom and turns the faucet on.

Slowly, he undresses me, our eye contact never breaking.

Water rains down from the waterfall showerhead, and he guides me inside. My legs are his legs, his hands are my hands as he reaches for the individually wrapped locally handcrafted bar soap, unwraps it, and gently washes my body.

Suds spread across my chest, under my arms, down my side, to the small of my back where he rests his hands above my butt.

My breathing is slow, drawn out in pleasure. I close my eyes and feel so safe in the palm of his worshipping hands; delicate like clay or porcelain, something to treasure and treat with the utmost care. Though he's shorter than me, I feel small in his large hands. Protected, admired.

Soft kisses travel across my neck and I feel him tremble, warms lips on cold skin as hot water cascades over us, causing an eruption of goose bumps.

The way he bathes me, never once allowing his lust to overtake the action, is the most intimate act I've ever experienced. When he grabs my penis and gently washes it, adjusting his hands as it grows, or the way he holds my balls, he does so tenderly.

Nobody has ever done this for me before.

I want to thank him, but the right words haven't been invented yet.

Hot water cascades over me, washing away his careful work. With my eyes closed, I try to breathe, but my lungs can't keep up with my beating heart, especially when he touches either side of my hips.

I've never felt so naked.

I reach for him, pull him under, our wet bodies pressed together. And I start washing him now, wanting to return the favor, starting at his back as he presses his forehead into my chest and exhales.

Under the water, we stay in each other's arms. He looks into my eyes, and me into his. His beautiful amethysts, one green, one blue.

Logically, I know this is part of an arrangement, a deal brokered, but it feels real.

Maybe I can't stay here forever, but I can be here, now.

Teddy Hughes

All the buildings that line Main Street in quaint, Dicken-sian Cold Spring are fortified with old red brick and thick chunky brown molding. Six blocks of storefronts—a small but delightfully stinky fromagerie, a specialty olive oil store with tastings, quite a few antique shops ranging from "grandma's mothball-infused tchotchkes" to high-end consignment to care-fully curated "lifestyle" stores with pieces from local artists—and we end up in Eudemonia Wellness & Apothecary. Cole is in heaven, perusing crystals and incense and soaps on shelves that are deliberately sparse in a space that feels much more like a Brooklyn spa. I tail him as he browses while we wait for Mallory and her fiancé.

A text buzzes from inside my pocket: **In front of Eudemonia.**

Then, a selfie of Kit and her partners, Naomi and Tara.

I pinch-zoom to find Cole in the background, smelling a handcrafted beeswax candle. I frantically search through the storefront window, but I can't see her.

Cole is wrapped up in conversation with a worker about hand cream infused with black tourmaline crystals, so I slip out the door.

Kit, Naomi, and Tara are off to the side, in front of a store that sells an awful lot of flannel. I want to make a joke about lesbians and flannel, but I'm too pissed.

"What the hell, Kit?"

"I told you I was coming." She's unfazed. Her loyalty is unmatched. Unhinged, but I'm glad I have her in my corner.

"I know, but I didn't really believe you," I say and Naomi and Tara both laugh.

"Have you met her?" Tara's arms are folded over her chest.

"A woman on a mission," Naomi says. She's a light-skinned former runway model–turned journalist with vitiligo who indulges Kit's fancies far too much. She carries herself with such poise and drama that Kerry Washington would be jealous.

"She's been a nervous wreck," Tara says, always the voice of reason. She's an elementary school art teacher at a charter school. A meek white woman with skin like snow who loves wearing paint-smeared smocks non-ironically. "Please tell her you're okay."

"Do I look not okay?" I ask.

"Actually, you look horrible." Kit grabs the sleeve of my expensive Ralph Lauren shirt. "What is *this*?"

"Ralph Lauren, love," Naomi says. "You look chic, Teddy. Don't listen to her."

"Thank you, Queen." I hail her.

Kit glares at her. "I have a right to be concerned." She turns her ire to me. "You got picked up at a bar and—"

"On your insistence, let's not forget," I cut her off.

Her hand buzzes around her head as if she's swatting away a bee. "Neither here nor there. I thought you'd get dicked down for a night, not disappear for a week?" She's so loud she draws attention from strangers across the street, so she takes a second to compose herself. "You have a pattern, Teddy."

Tara steps between us, meekly.

"People are looking," Naomi adds, shooing away their judgmental stares and telling them to "keep it moving."

Embarrassment clouds my vision.

"I'm not his prisoner, Kit, and I'm not repeating the past," I assure her. "He's a wonderful, sweet, beautiful guy and I'm getting paid for a job. Nothing more." My chest pangs because this isn't the truth, it's a piss-poor reduction.

"You have a tendency to get lost in men, and let them dictate your life until you have nothing," she says, evoking Murray's memory. "Don't make me say his name."

Knife to the chest. "That's not fair, Kit. This isn't the same."

"Isn't it?"

"I can't have feelings for Cole. This isn't like that." My bottom lip quivers, but I power through resolutely. "It's a business transaction. A paycheck. *Fiction*. It'll make a great book, that's for sure."

"Is that what this is about?" she asks, her body relaxing but her face still twisted in confusion and anger. "Your writing?"

Shrugging, I say, "I don't know," because it's the only veritable "out loud" answer. I haven't given my writing career a solitary thought in ages. The truth is that for the first time in years, I feel alive, more like myself with Cole than I ever was with Murray, and I don't want it to end. Is it too much to ask to stay in this bubble a little while longer?

Kit shakes her head, and walks alone to the corner of the block, head down.

I turn to Naomi and Tara. "What's really going on with her?" I usually know every one of Kit's emotions, but I'm having trouble reading her.

Naomi gives it to me straight, her face absent sympathy. "She's sad, dumbass."

The obvious truth smacks me across the face.

Naomi rolls her eyes as Tara soothingly touches my arm.

"You're moving out. Kit wanted to spend your last week together. She had activities planned."

"Really?" My heart dissolves, leaves my body. I'm a hollow log, crumbling and covered in moss. "She never said she had anything specifically planned."

"She wanted it to be a surprise." Tara tousles her wavy bottle-red hair.

"I *am* a dumbass."

"Seems that way," I hear from behind me. The voice turns me to stone.

Jason.

My blood runs cold.

How much did he hear?

Kit turns around, her danger antennae perking.

"Teddy!" Mallory shouts from down the block. She's arm in arm with a walking Abercrombie & Fitch ad of a fiancé. He's a total golden retriever of a man. Curly blond hair, scruffy, cheek dimples, and muscles the Hubble Space Telescope can spot.

Cole steps out of the apothecary. "There you are, T—" He stops, his gaze bouncing from me to Mallory, then landing on Kit. His nostrils flare and the rigidity returns to his body. "What's going on?"

Cole Vivien

Mallory flings her arms around Teddy, and slowly peels off him when she notices Kit and the two people I'm guessing are Kit's partners, from what Teddy has told me about them. Her eyebrows arch as she asks, "What's going on, guys?"

My eyes plead with both Teddy *and* Kit, who, right on cue, comes over to hug me as if we're old friends.

"Kit," she says to Mal. "Teddy and I went to school together. I'm here on a little getaway with my girlfriends and I saw him in the window and almost had a heart attack! I haven't seen him in so long. We were besties, *once*." She purses her lips.

"*Quelle surprise!*" Of course Mallory is genuinely excited. "I'm obsessed with Teddy! Can I have a hug? I'm a hugger!" She doesn't wait for Kit to answer, pulling her into a hug. Kit introduces her partners, Naomi, whose eyes are owl-wide from Mal's sudden physical contact, and Tara who welcomes Mal's warmth like a child.

Jason steps into the circle.

Teddy's chest heaves as he eyes Jason. Did Teddy bring Kit here purposely to sabotage my ruse? Was Jason right about him? The sound of my heart thrashing against my ribcage like rhythmic drumming drowns out everything, and I don't hear Mallory or Teddy or Kit. What doesn't add up is how he acted in the shower earlier; if he had some sort of agenda, he'd have to be a damn good actor to pull that off.

Jason slaps my back. "You okay, bud?"

The drums simmer, but my head is throbbing from the reverb.

"He's fine," Mallory says. "Jason."

"Mal." He gives her an air-kiss on each cheek. She feigns pleasantries, but irritation pulls at the corners of her lips like needles pulling thread. "So good to see you, big sis!"

Ignoring him, Mal says, "Hate to be that girl, but we have to get to the rehearsal dinner." Her eyes widen. "Oh! We have the entire restaurant to ourselves." She turns to Kit and her girlfriends. "You all should come, if you don't have plans. We have more than enough food, and it's not a formal sit-down thing."

Kit looks to me. "I don't know."

"It's right at the water's edge. The Foundry." Mallory points down the street, but it's hard to see the water. There's a train station that cuts through the bottom of Main Street, and the lower portion of the street, where the restaurant sits, is obstructed by the brick structure. "It's *so* gorgeous down there, if you haven't been. It's an old metal casting factory converted into the most gorgeous space, right on the river."

"You should come," I say, measured. Having them there might blow my cover, but not having them there means I can't poke around for intel on Teddy.

Jason zeroes in on us, eyes unwavering on Teddy.

On the quick walk to The Foundry, Teddy sidles up next to me. "Cole, I swear I had no idea." I ignore him, but he continues, "She was tracking me. She was worried."

"I can understand *that*." I slow my pace until the group gets a bit farther ahead. "But why didn't you tell me?" Jason's voice swirls inside my head; it's faraway, but then it morphs into Father's, calling me naive.

He stares blankly, explains Kit's sudden selfie and says, "She thinks every guy is like my ex, and that I'm going to get hurt." I recall what he said the other night about getting involved with men who come from money: *They stick to their kind, they'll never let someone like you in.* Then he admits, "I handled that poorly." He grabs both of my hands, and our fingers intertwine. "I know how important this is to you. And believe me, I'm not rationalizing anything, but she loves me and she'd never wreck anything important to me." Words unsaid hang on the tip of his tongue. "I'll ask her to leave."

"No, it's okay," I say, and he starts to protest, but I add, "You said it yourself. She won't do anything to ruin something important to you." I look down at our hands. "It's a gamble, but isn't everything?"

He licks his lips and my chest flutters. "You look like you want to say something."

"Me?" How does he do that? It's like he's taking a peek inside my head, unearthing thoughts I didn't know were buried there. His question is a seed that sprouts in my chest and flowers.

"You don't have to hide from me." His voice is low.

He takes a step forward, it's treacherous and my heartbeat quickens.

I want more than anything to kiss him, but that's a line that, once I cross, I don't think it's possible to come back from. My mind takes me into the future, to that place where I have to say goodbye to him and fly back to my life in LA, and he'll be in Louisiana, and we'll be nothing more than memories to each other.

I don't have to tell him this. He pulls me into the biggest, warmest bear hug and the rest of Main Street, the world, disappears.

Wrapping my arms around him, my nose nuzzles into his neck.

I inhale him: sandalwood, vanilla, sweat.

Teddy's heart is racing, racing, racing.

Gravity pushes and pulls us closer; I didn't think it was possible to be this close to someone and still be clothed. It's a different kind of closeness, one of comfort, like being wrapped in a fleece blanket in the middle of the snowstorm as a fire crackles at your feet. His fingers gently soothe my back, rubbing in circular motions.

I hum and he hardens against me, and I grow to meet him.

This is way better than catastrophizing the future, more intimate than a kiss, the kind of sensory memory that imprints and lingers, and I want to hold on to this for as long as possible.

Then he says, "Cole, I have to tell you something."

"Aw, isn't this *cute?*" Jason shouts, cutting Teddy off. "Hate to break this up, but you're holding up the party." He wedges between us and drapes his arms around both of us, glancing between us. "Tonight's gonna be fun, eh, boss?!"

The Foundry sits at the end of Main Street at the riverfront overlooking a cute gazebo surrounded by lush greenery and red flowers. It's so clear this evening that, in the southern distance, it's easy to see West Point Academy, it's lights glittering against the water as the neon orange sun hangs low overhead, slowly dipping behind the mountains opposite us. Couples holding hands pass by with ice cream cones, and families dash toward the water's edge to watch the last bit of sunset. I look down at my hands, and I feel Teddy's phantom grip.

Though Mallory insisted on a small rehearsal dinner, Father still bought out the entire restaurant. The party might be small, however we're loud enough to make passersby stare as we mingle and laugh and toast.

All the food is family style, platters scattered on each table, so guests can come and go as they please, without place settings. Maryland-style jumbo lump crab cakes with a tangy remoulade. Yellowfin tuna sashimi, fresh oysters, burrata with sautéed peaches and crostini with a thick balsamic glaze, cold mini New England lobster rolls and hot mini Connecticut lobster rolls—because Mallory is a people pleaser and could never force a mayonnaise-or-butter-type decision on her guests—swirls of house-made lemon fettucini in small cups with lemon zest, thinly sliced filet mignon with rosemary.

Any second, Father will show up—late from business meetings, of course—and I'll have to face him.

Jason pounds back extra dirty martinis, while Mother chats demurely with Tara, Naomi, and Kit. Teddy captivates me, distracting from my paranoia because even with his friends here, he's mingling with family like he's one of us, fitting better than I ever could. For a second, I allow my body to relax.

A mistake.

"How are you finding our family, Theodore?" Mother's voice is sharp.

"Y'all are fabulous! It was just me and Momma growing up, no siblings, no extended family, and definitely no dinners like this."

Mother looks bemused before turning to Kit. "So Mallory tells me these two beautiful women are your girlfriends."

"We're a triad, yeah," Kit says, her body tensing.

"That's lovely," Mother says. "I was in a triad or two myself in my younger years."

"Mother!" I shout.

"Oh, unclench, baby, it was the '80s! I was living in France. François and Isabelle. It felt like the moment. That was before I met your father, of course." She says it so nonchalantly that it nearly knocks me off my feet.

"Does Father know?" Mallory asks.

"Of course, he does!" She waves Mallory's judgment away with a flourish. "And our Theodore here is your friend, is that right?"

"Best friend." Kit offers a toothy grin, like someone showing off their most prized possession. "We've known each other since, what, fourth grade?"

"Fifth. She pulled my hair on the playground," Teddy says. "She later told me she had a crush on me."

"Obviously a lie," Kit says. "I was drawn to his energy."

"He has great energy," Mallory says, and my heart beats faster with pride against my chest.

Teddy blushes. "Excuse me, I have to use the restroom."

"And you grew up where?" Mother continues with Kit as Teddy takes leave.

"Louisiana suburbs, outside Nawlins," Kit answers.

"Is that where you live now?" Mother asks in a lightning round of questions that make me sweat.

"No, I moved to New York City about ten years ago." Kit braces herself on the table, clearly aware of the third degree.

Mother: "Is that how long you three have been together?"

Kit: "We've been together two years now."

Mother: "That's a long time. And what happened to you and Teddy's relationship when you moved states?"

Kit: "We stayed in touch until he moved to the city, too."

Mother: "Why did he move to the city?"

Kit: "To start his business. A nursery."

Mother: "And would you say you're still close after all these years?"

Kit: "With Teddy? He's my brother."

My mouth goes dry. I didn't think to ask Teddy if he told Kit to lie about where Teddy lives. Because if he lives in New York, and I live in LA, how could we be dating for the last two months?

Fuck, fuck, fuck.

No amount of crystals or counting to twelve is going to get Kit out of a skilled Brigitte DuBois cross-examination.

Kit's voice is scratchy: "We talk every day." Her answer is slower this time, and at least she knew enough not to say that they're still roommates.

Mother: "And he still lives in New York City?"

Kit nods and my heart stops beating. "We're roommates."

I'm dead.

Mother: "What a coincidence it is, then, that you all were in Cold Spring, of all places, today! *And* that he didn't tell you he would be here. Or you didn't tell him you would be here. Very curious." She sits back, pleased with her detective skills, and I swear if she had a cigarette, she would light it.

Mallory eyes me. The cogs are already turning. I can only hope the wine works its magic on everyone, dulling their collective sharpness.

I don't have time to interfere because Father steps onto the porch and all my brainpower and anxiety goes toward keeping myself upright. The room sucks in a collective breath. Everyone might as well feed his ego more and bow like he's the fucking King of Garrison. Like a good king, he shakes the hands of his royal subjects, but keeps his eyes trained on me.

Onetwothreefour, fivesixseveneight, nineteneleventwelve.

"Vivièn." He grabs my face and kisses both cheeks. "My boy." Smiles crinkle his eyes, and eight years of no contact melts away as he tells me in French how wonderful it is to see me before turning his attention to Teddy, who appears at my side.

Teddy whispers, "I got you," before turning on his charm for Father. "It's a pleasure to meet you, sir."

"Gerard Deplantier," Father says, taking Teddy's hand. "*Mains rugueuses.*"

"Bless you," Teddy jokes, and Father examines him curiously. "Sorry, I don't speak French." Father is still holding strong to Teddy's hand, an intimidation tactic he practically invented.

"He said you have rough hands," I interject, and the second I speak, I realize I'd been holding back and my body finally relaxes. Seeing Father wasn't the earth-shattering drama I expected. Though a big part of me still feels trapped in the back seat of his car, him dangling my inheritance in front of me like a golden carrot. If I told Father about VERSTL here, now? Would he be proud? Or would he scoff, call it *un passe-temps*, a pet project. Or worse, disown me again.

"I like that," Father says. "You work construction, my boy?"

"No, with plants."

"A gardener?" Father examines him thoroughly the way he would a contract or blueprints, studying his foundation looking for cracks or stress fractures. He lets go of Teddy's hand. "Come, have a cigar with me."

Father turns to Mallory, grabs her hand, and kisses it five times. That was always his way of saying "I love you" without uttering the words. I don't think I've ever actually heard him say it to either of us. When I was a small child, Mallory and I were playing outside at night, catching fireflies and trapping them in jars to create night-lights, while Mother and Miss Molly would be indulging in a glass of wine outside. I heard Mother say, "I wish he would say, *je t'aime, mon chéri*, the way he used to when we first met." It never made sense to me why he never said "I love you" to either of us.

"Let's have a toast!" Jason booms, breaking me out of my head. He's clearly had a few too many martinis—his eyes are hazy, the lids drooping. Back home, Jason is known as the "sloppy bottom drunk of WeHo." A term of endearment, to some.

"Who is this?" Father booms.

"Jason, sir," he answers. "Cole's best friend, right-hand man-*ager*."

Crickets.

"Who is Cole?" My father waves him away.

Everybody looks around, confused. Whispers break out.

Jason stands up and the chair skids back against the wood decking, nearly toppling, but Mallory's fiancé, Mikey, catches its back. What the hell is he doing?

Mallory buries face in her hands. "Vivièn!"

"*Vivièn!*" Jason makes a scrunchy face like he's going to sneeze, but fights it off.

Instinctively, I stand up. "Jace, why don't you come with me."

"My friend." He tips his martini glass to me. "I'm so happy you found lurv." He bursts out laughing so loudly it echoes out to the street. "You and Nicko make such a beautiful couple. I mean Teddy."

Teddy's eyes go wide, and he looks at me. So does Mother, her jaw pulsating.

Jason turns to Teddy. "Aren't they the most *perfect* couple? Almost *too* perfect."

A tightness in my chest untangles. Teddy isn't trying to sabotage me, and Jason isn't being protective over me—he's jealous.

"Jace, *enough*." Embarrassment drips from my lips.

He stumbles toward me and lands in my arms. His hand strokes my chest. "I love you, you know that. I'm looking out for our best interests."

Our? "Leave now and get your shit together," I say, as calmly as possible, but my nerves are frying. "You have an early flight home in the morning."

Jason's nostrils flare. "Boss, you don't mean that."

Through gritted teeth, I utter, "Leave."

Teddy grabs Jason's other arm, who bucks and yanks it away.

"Get off me, grifter!" Jason shoves Teddy backward into another table who knocks down half-drunk wineglasses and a pitcher of water that sloshes into a plate of lobster rolls.

Kit is at Teddy's side fast. Mal and Mikey position themselves ready to pounce.

Jason brushes himself off as if he actually got into a scuffle. He looks to me for some sort of absolution, but he gets nothing from me. And in a moment of clear sobriety, he says, "You'll thank me." He winks, grabs a random glass of wine off a table, downs it, and marches out of The Foundry.

"Well, that certainly was cinematic," Mother says, clacking her nails. "Hopefully tomorrow's festivities provide a little less physical comedy."

"What is wrong with you?" Father asks me.

"Me?" Blood rushes to my head. A thudding in my ears

makes everything seem far away. I count to twelve on my fingers.

"The company you keep could've ruined your sister's wedding." He curses at me in French. "The embarrassment!"

"Father," Mallory speaks for me. "Nothing's ruined."

"I don't want to hear any of it." Father throws his hands up. "I've bitten my tongue and sat back and waited for him to be an adult for too long." He glares at Mother, shakes his head in disappointment. "Waited and waited and *this* is how you come back to the family?" He curses in French under his breath, and walks away.

Father will never accept me. All I'll ever be to him is the foolish boy who walked away from the path he paved for me. It doesn't matter who I am or what I do. My bottom lip trembles and I fight back tears.

Teddy's hand is on my back. "You okay?"

If Father taught me one thing, it's not to show weakness. I'm starting to crack.

Teddy Hughes

I find Cole at the riverfront, alone beneath the Milky Way. It's a cool night in a sleepy town. We're the only ones out now.

Obsidian waters with moonlight reflecting in the waves. Yellow lights dot the shoreline. The night sky is so bright, without a cloud in the sky, and the stars are so vibrant out here.

Cole leans his back against the railing overlooking the river, and I rest my stomach against it as I stare at the current, watching it race by. There's a steady rhythm to the way the water moves, ripples, splashes up against the rocks. It's loud and quiet all at once.

I want to reach out, touch him, hold him, provide some sort of comfort. The hurt he's feeling is palpable. "I wish I could make everything better." The words tumble out.

His eyes reflect the moon. "You do a good job of that."

He grabs my hand, intertwines his fingers with mine.

"What Jason said in there," I start. "About us being too perfect. I know this is all supposed to be an act, but I need you to know I'm not acting, Cole. Everything I do and say when we're alone, even when we're not—" I almost say more, but fear grips me.

His head tilts softly. My gaze is fixated on the mountain of rock directly opposite us. Even in the dark, it glitters from the sky glow.

"What?" His voice is low, almost a whisper. "I know you want to say something."

"How do you know that?"

"You do this thing where your forehead crinkles and you bite the inside of your cheek. And you have that faraway look in your eyes like you're somewhere else."

His baby-soft thumb gingerly rubs the underside of my palm. "You came after me. To find me."

"Of course," I say. "I'm right here."

"You don't have to be." He continues to stroke my hand.

I sigh. "Can I ask you something? This started as a one-night stand. Then it became a job. But it was never either, was it?"

He looks away. "I suppose not."

"Tell me this isn't a bad idea," I say, delicately grabbing his face and urging him to look at me.

"What?" Cole moves closer to me.

"Feeling what I feel for you." I'm unable to breathe as I ramble: "I know we just met, but when you smile my heart fucking stops, like, I need paddles and the entire surgical staff of New York-Pres to revive me and when you hold me at night, I've never felt safer and I'm obsessed with your family and the way you count to twelve when you're anxious, and you laugh at my ridiculous jokes and don't take my bullshit, which means you qualify for the Nobel Peace Prize or something but I historically don't fit into this world so—"

He stops me by kissing me.

I pull away because I can't stop my brain. "Your rule?"

"Shut up." He commands me with his lips. Grabs my face in his hands and pulls me to him, to his lips, and they're so soft that all the tension in my body melts away.

His *lips*.

His beautiful, full, soft life-giving lips.

They're so tender. He kisses like he's afraid to let go, like opening the cage to a bird that might fly away.

I kiss him back with everything I have.

I wrap my arms around him, running my fingers through his hair, rubbing his back, pulling at him because I can't possibly be closer to him, but I want to be. I crave it.

Our tongues dance a slow waltz, and time stands still, the earth stops rotating on its axis, and the only two living organisms left in the universe are me and Cole. It's Macy's fireworks at the Fourth of July, and every childhood Christmas morning, and the first time I had mind-blowing, backbreaking sex, and the day my agent sold my book, and the first time I fell in love, the pride from the first bloom from the first flower in the first garden I ever planted, and reaching the highest peak on the tallest roller coaster, and eating a fresh Krispie Kreme right off the conveyor belt all at once. No, it's better.

I could spend every minute for the rest of my life kissing him.

Hours or days or decades later, when our lips are chapped, we pull apart.

A single tear runs down Cole's cheek.

That night, we lie in bed together, him hovering on top of me naked as I slowly enter him, our bodies breathing as one. As he rides me, in full control of how deep and fast I explore him in new ways, he brings me to the point of no return, and I explode inside him as he kisses me and kisses me and kisses me until he collapses to the side. He wraps his arm around me and I pull him close. Moments later, light snoring tells me he's fallen asleep.

Before I slip into REM, I hear him whisper something.

At first, I don't say anything, but he mumbles again.

"Cole?"

Nothing.

Then he groans and says, "I love you."

Seven
Swipe Right for Love?

Cole Vivien

Eyes blinking open, my body stirs naturally; I feel alive.

I can't remember the last time I slept soundly and woke up rested. Teddy's bare feet are locked into mine, but otherwise, we've managed to peacefully disconnect over the course of the night. Still, knowing he was there by his touch was like a magic sleeping pill. I could lie here, side by side with him, forever.

Beams of sunlight through the windows blind me, and a sharp realization hits:

I broke my one rule. Over and over and over.

When Teddy came to find me outside the restaurant last night, my breath caught in my throat. Nobody has ever cared enough to chase after me, to find me in the dark. My body ached for him, and it brought me back to what it felt like as a gay kid in New York who liked to wander empty streets at night, hoping to stumble upon something that would help me make sense of the life I wanted.

Seeing him felt like I suddenly made sense. Leaving here for Los Angeles, the mess with Nicko, starting VERSTL, coming back home after years away—everything in my life brought me back to that moment by the Hudson River with Teddy.

It isn't logical that I feel this way after only a few days with Teddy.

But his lips were like slipping into a well-worn hoodie.

Teddy rouses, his eyes slits as he peers at me, smiling like a doofus, his copper hair plastered to his forehead. "Morning, gorgeous." His voice is froggy, and I can't help myself, I pull him toward me and break my rule again and again.

Until, breathless, I pull away and ask him, "What if you came to LA with me?"

"If by LA you mean Louisiana," he jokes. "Are you serious?"

I shrug and purse my lips playfully. "Why not?" I don't know what's come over me, but I'm reaching out for something I don't want to slip away.

Before he can answer, I kiss him again, three pecks on his lips, then move down his body, tracing the hair on his abdomen down to his hard cock, swallowing it whole.

Teddy's soft dick is still deep in my mouth long after he came. I swallowed every drop of his load, but I can't get enough. His body twitches, writhes from oversensitivity, and he starts laughing, begging me to stop.

My tongue runs along his plump shaft. "Can't get enough of you."

He grins and it's so goofy and sweet and sexy that I growl.

"You drive me crazy," I admit.

"Likewise." His fingers grab at mine, interlocking us as the alarm on my phone blares throughout our room.

"I don't wanna goooooooo." I oscillate between groaning and whining.

"Wow," he says, a hint of judgment in his voice. "This is a new side of you."

"I'm multifaceted. There's only one solution!" I dive straight into the crook of his arm, burying my face into his pits. Euphoria takes over my body as I breathe in his musk.

"What's on the agenda for you, pig, on Mal's big day?" he asks.

Oinking, I say, "As her man of honor, my bridal duties include keeping her from fully breaking down, and holding her hand during hair and makeup. She has a massive team for everything else."

"Moral support," Teddy sums.

"Exactly." Ever since I broke my rule, all I want to do is kiss him.

So I do. His tongue, the way it dances with mine. His pillowy soft lips. I never want to stop. He nibbles my bottom lip before pushing me off him.

"Go before I have no choice but to ride you," Teddy says. "But, um, make sure you use some mouthwash. Your breath smells like cum."

"You're a bitch." I playfully push him this time, and he grabs me and pins me to the mattress, his sturdy, hairy body holding me in place. If we had time, I would break out some of my assless wrestling singlets and we could spend the day role-playing until we're both covered in sweat and cum.

"Says the man full of *my* loads." We're both laughing as we wrestle around on the bed, limbs and fleshy appendages flapping. He's clearly stronger than me, and I only have one way out. My hand shoots straight back into his armpits and I tickle the hell out of him, which works so beautifully because it renders him completely useless.

His grip relents, limbs go numb, before he flops like a fish out of water and shouts, "I GIVE, I GIVE!"

I pry myself off him. "Yes, you do." I stick my tongue out at him before making my way to the bathroom.

As I start brushing, I hear him ask, "What are you gonna do about Jason?"

I groan. "I don't know. I booked him a flight for later this afternoon, earliest I could get. Sent him the itinerary last night. All I know is, I'm not dealing with him today, of all days." I'll sit down with him and talk once I'm back in LA, but honestly, I'm not sure I can continue working with him. He's broken my trust, ruined my entrée back home, and for what? I need to understand his motives, but I don't need to ruin Mal's wedding day.

Teddy's silence pulls me back into the room, toothbrush dangling from my lips. Suds drip down and land with a plop on the head of my penis. This elicits a strained laugh from him.

"You okay?"

"I—" The way the corners of his mouth twitch, he looks like he wants to say something. His head bobs like he's negotiating silently with himself. I know that look well, it's one I wear often. "Never mind. It's not my place."

I quickly dash back to the sink to spit out the rest of the minty foam. "Now you have to tell me," I shout so he can hear me from the other room.

Silence. Then, "Do you remember what you said to me last night?"

My chest tightens. I brace myself on the sink. What did I say?

"I didn't know if you were sleeping or not. I think you were. Never mind."

My heart is beating so fast as something like a dream returns to me. The words *I love you* flood my ears like a memory I can't escape. But the thing is, I don't dream. Never have. I stop breathing when I realize that I actually said those words to Teddy. They slipped out. I was so relaxed, so comfortable, my guard not only down, but completely obliterated, that I allowed my unfiltered thoughts to escape.

I remember exactly how I felt in that moment. It was honest, raw, real. For once, my brain wasn't thinking five steps ahead and overprocessing, and the phrase I let out is the heaviest one I've ever uttered.

"Do you talk in your sleep?" he asks.

I croak out a painful, "Yeah. I've been told I babble. Nonsense." I pepper in a nervous laugh.

"Oh." More silence. "That's what I figured."

Kissing isn't the only rule I broke.

Teddy Hughes

Cole drops me off at the cutest rustic brunch spot in the center of Cold Spring to meet Kit, Naomi, and Tara. Overflowing plates of eggs Benedict, lemon berry ricotta pancakes,

French toast, and sides of bacon, sausage, and biscuits with gravy are devoured ravenously by all of us.

"So what's the verdict?" I ask as Tara returns from the restroom, bathing her hands in rose-scented hand cream.

"As if you need our opinions," Kit says.

"Y'know those three old hags from Greek mythology, The Fates, who share an eyeball and see the future? That's y'all," I say with a laugh. "Except y'all are gorgeous and share a brain."

"I rebuke that," Kit says.

"Yeah, that's reductive and heterosexist," Tara chimes in.

"I see you living in a place like this, Teddy," Naomi says, ignoring her girlfriends.

"I meant about Cole. Everything that happened last night."

In tandem, Naomi and Tara say, "Love Cole."

I wait for Kit. "What about you?"

Air shoots out of her nose like a stubborn bull. She stamps her feet a bit. "He's...*fine*. I love Mal. She's my girl. Did I tell you that after you guys disappeared last night, the three of us and her and her fiancé, Mikey, stayed up for hours drinking and laughing? They invited us to the wedding. I'm...almost tempted." Which in Kit-chat means she's absolutely going because she'd never pass up an opportunity to crash a fancy party. Bonus points for keeping her eyes on me; she's always been my protective shepherd, ever since we were young, dumb kids. This is no exception, and I love her for it. Though it makes me feel like an ass because I haven't been present with everything I've been going through; I could be a better friend. I know I can be grating, especially lately, but we've taken turns doing the heavy lifting for each other over the years.

I exhale in relief, and motion for us to leave once we pay the check. "I'd love to have y'all there."

"I have literally nothing to wear to a rich person's wedding," Kit says.

"I scoped out a cute dress boutique in town," Naomi says as we walk out. "Any excuse to shop. Then we'll head back to the city tonight, after."

I check the time. I have to get back to the Airbnb; Cole said he'd meet me there so we could go to Castle Rock together, so I can be with him as he takes pictures with the bridal party. My role: loving background boyfriend. Cole left the gorgeous peach linen suit from that fancy Portuguese designer draped over the chaise lounge in the bedroom, the brown leather shoes with white soles on the floor, shiny and ready to be worn. He instructed me to wear a nude jock, and the thought gets me chubbed now. Maybe I'll surprise him and be douched and on all fours, ass up, when he comes for me.

Standing on the corner outside the busy brunch spot, everyone stares at Kit, who's a denim-and-neon-clad comic book character from the '80s, fanny pack and all.

Kit asks, "It's settled then. But, are you really okay, Teddy?"

"Why do you think I'm not?"

"Because." She grabs my hand. "I was with you through the whole Murray aftermath. And I'm not saying Cole is a Murray, but I also don't know that he isn't."

My heartbeat thuds in my ears. "He's not."

"I see the way you two look at each other, and let me tell you, that's not a boss-employee situation. I wouldn't give a fuck if it was purely transactional. Get your bussy destroyed, not your heart. But there's more here, isn't there? That's why I'm worried."

There's nowhere to hide. Not from Kit.

Naomi and Tara slowly step back and amble away.

I shake my head. Slowly, like air leaking from balloon, I tell her about Cole's rules, and everything that's transpired between us, backbreaking sex and all. And the kissing. The incredible earth-shattering kissing. "Then last night, he was sleeping, dead asleep I think, and he said 'I love you.'"

If Kit's eyes could get wider, she'd be a cartoon character and they'd pop out of their sockets. "It's been three days!" But the tension in her shoulders melts away and she follows it up with a soft, "But I see it in your eyes. You love him too."

I don't know how it's possible because I don't think I have the strength or resolve to say those words out loud, partly because, like Kit said, it's been three fucking days and I'm a fully grown man who should have more self-awareness than to fall for someone in such a short time, but also because I never loved anyone but Murray. And this feels different. Where I never fully felt like myself with Murray, I feel at home with Cole.

"You don't have to say anything, T," she says. "But I have to tell you, I don't like what went down with his manager friend last night. So I looked up Cole's VERSTL profile, and I might have subscribed so I could see his content—"

"You what?" Where are Cole's damn crystals because I need to calm the fuck down. "Why would you do that?"

"Because I wanted to find out whatever I could about this guy. And let me tell you, he lays it on pretty thick. He's got that whole 'Prince Charming' thing down. His whole brand is making people fall in 'love' with him." She pulls up the app on her phone and shows me the screen.

"That doesn't matter." I shove the phone back to her. "I know what Cole does."

"His whole shtick is faking intimacy," Kit says, and before I can rebut, she continues, "And while he's busy kissing you, he's posting sus content while making you feel like this is all some fairy tale. I don't know, it feels like a game." She makes me look into her eyes. "And what happens at the end of this? This isn't about money or writing a book...for *you*."

I don't have an answer for her, and a pressure builds in my head, a disembodied fear, anxiety like hands around my neck, like the one I felt merely days ago as I said goodbye to Plant Daddy. "I—" I begin, but my words trail off as I spot Jason on the opposite side of the road, walking hand in hand with that tattooed blond, Nicko.

"Shit."

Kit follows my line of sight to Jason at the exact moment he turns to see us.

There's nowhere to hide.

Kit sidles up close to me and whispers, "I know that guy."

"Uh, that's Jason. You met him last night. Remember the fiasco?"

She hisses like a cat. "Not Jason, the dumb-looking beef-cake."

Jason lets go of Nicko's hand like the guy's suddenly diseased, takes a deep breath, straightens out the hem of his polo shirt, and crosses the street toward us. The smell of his cologne is so strong it chokes me, like fingers around my throat.

Cole Vivien

Mallory scrunches her nose like she smells the sex on my breath. "You look different."

"Uh—" I step in front of Mal's hairstylist's mirror to examine the state of my face. If anything, "I look fresh."

She motions for me to move "You do. You usually have this sunken-eye thing going on. Dark circles. Like you never sleep."

"Please continue, I *love* compliments."

A burst of laughter explodes from her. "And you're funny today. Like, was that a *joke, petit frère*?!"

"I joke all the time!"

"I must have missed those," she says with a wink. She's right. Teddy's hands have been an escape rope from the dark I didn't realize I'd been trapped in. His lips breathed oxygen into my aching lungs.

"You love him, don't you?" she says, matter-of-factly.

"Excuse me? I don't—I—"

"You can't hide from me. It's okay to love someone. *Him*." She touches my arm lovingly. "I know you don't allow yourself to feel that kind of stuff."

"It's not that," I begin.

But she already knows. "You feel *everything*."

"*Précisément*." The near-confession almost takes me out. To have Mal feel what I feel is like coming up for air after being underwater for so long. I gulp in a breath. "It's too soon, though."

"Is it?" she asks. "When I met Mikey, he took me for culinary donuts in Beacon and then on a three-mile hike up a fucking mountain. Me! Never met this guy and only swiped right 'cause I thought he was a total smokeshow whose profile said 'adventurous.' Five hours and a head of frizzy hair and sweat later, I knew I'd marry him."

"Gross."

She shrugs. "Mikey and Teddy, they're not like us. They didn't grow up like we did. They're *human*. I knew I loved Mikey when we met. Not *love*, loved him, but I felt something I couldn't yet place." She flashes the diamond engagement ring she paid for. "You can take your time saying it out loud."

"I think said it last night."

She nearly falls forward in her chair. "And?"

"I don't know—"

"What's not to know, Cole?" she asks. "Everyone loves him. Even Father seemed to. We're all thankful he's not Jason. Or Nicko." She twitches her lips curiously.

The wedding planner, who has been running in and out of the bridal suite all morning, comes rushing in. "Quick run of show! Limo will be here in four hours to take the wedding party to Castle Rock. Pictures *before* guests arrive by charter bus. There's an air-conditioned tent for the bridal party to relax in before it's all—" She starts singing, "Here comes the bride, ceremony, ceremony, ceremony, then reception." She turns to me. "Man of honor, is your speech ready?"

I slide the handwritten copy from my pocket. "I've had it written since I was five."

"Do *not* make me cry!" Mal says. "Can I read it?"

Before I can answer, the wedding planner snatches it from my hands. "You'll *hear* it yourself later. The rest of your brides-maids are here. I already gave them the spiel outside."

Mallory looks overwhelmed.

I hold out my hand for her and drop a celestite crystal neck-lace into her hand.

She covets it; holds it to her chest. "Everything will be perfect today, right?"

I've never been happier. For her. And maybe today can be the day I finally take a chance for myself. "Beyond perfect."

"Good," she says. "And I don't want to make a big deal about this, but I can't keep it from you. You know how I told you I would look into April Fitzgerald's story on VERSTL at the *New York Times*?"

I knew even a sliver of bliss was too good to be true.

"My contacts did some digging, and I know how she got your given name." Mal hands me her phone, an email open from April with quoted text in the body of an email address I immediately recognize: **Jason Meyer**. There's an attachment of the certified copy of name change document that only I have access to. But Jason knows where I keep those files at home. Because he's my best friend, and I trusted him.

My heart races so fast I feel as if I might pass out. The edges of my vision are fuzzy.

"Cole, you look pale." Mal snaps her fingers and the wed-ding planner races over with a glass of ice water. "Drink!"

Sitting down, my mind is whirring. How could Jason do this?

"There's more—" Mal says, scrolling down to an audio file, a recording of my voice. Her finger hovers over it, but then retracts and motions for everyone in the room to leave. "I couldn't kill the story. You have to tell Mother and Father. *And Teddy*, if this ends up in her reporting."

Teddy Hughes

Kit's Zipcar swerves round corners like she's Vin Freaking Diesel in a *Fast & Furious* movie. Naomi and Tara's bodies smash against the left side of the back seat as she slams on the gas pedal and the engine revs. I'm white-knuckled on the handle above the passenger door, a mix of nerves and nausea.

"I'm gonna vom," Naomi says.

"Yeah, Kit, baby, I think you can slow down now," Tara adds, calmly, though I can hear the escalation in her voice. "We're not being followed."

Before Jason could cross the street, Kit pulled me away toward her rental car, calling for Naomi and Tara in that high-pitched shrill she has that signals danger. She peeled off and he watched us drive away, not moving.

Actually, looking back at the last five minutes, it's all very anticlimactic.

I place a hand on Kit's knee, and she takes a deep breath. "Sorry, loves. That guy gave me the creeps. I didn't like the way he was looking at you," she says to me.

"What exactly happened?" Naomi asks. "Was he, like, threatening you?"

"I'm not even sure," I say, looking at the girls in the rear-view mirror. They're clutching each other as if Kit's driving could launch them through the windshield any second. "But no, he's douchey, not evil."

Kit inflates her cheeks like a puffer fish.

"Spit it out, babe," I say.

"Okay so you know how I told you I subscribed to Cole's VERSTL profile? That guy who was with Jason, I figured

out where I saw him as Jason was walking toward us." Her
eyes are wet as she hands over her phone, the VERSTL app
open. It's a series of video diaries dated last night, and I immediately recognize the guy Cole is pictured with: Nicko,
the tattooed blond. His full name: Nickolas Lund. A quick
bio reveals he's the most popular gay porn star today. But it's
the title of the video diaries that catches my attention; it's the
most liked, most commented on, and most viewed video,
with nearly half a million views since it was uploaded hours
ago: **Soulmates.**

The description: **Love blooms again for two old flames!
Can't wait to see you again, my love @TheOnlyNicko! Watch
to the end!**

Against my better judgment, I click play on the video. Cole
is lying on top of Nicko, both of them naked, and they're…

Kissing.

My chest tightens.

I fast-forward to the last few seconds and turn up the vol-
ume. The night vision on the camera catches his arm wrapping around Cole as they spoon, the mic picking up a faint,
"I love you," and the car might as well crash.

We drive around aimlessly for a while in silence.

I don't want to talk about Cole or his latest video post with
the girls because I'm still processing the reveal myself. My
stomach is knotted, and a potent cocktail of anger and confusion bubbles deep inside me. Something isn't quite adding up.

How could he kiss me, say all the things he's said, ask me
to move to the fucking West Coast with him, only to post
something like that? And why was Nicko arguing with Jason

yesterday morning outside The Mark about not wanting to do something? And if Cole and this tattooed god of a man are together, why am I here?

Love blooms again for two old flames!

I think I'm going to be sick.

Especially when I look at the digital clock on the dashboard and realize it's dangerously close to the time Cole told me to be ready for him.

"I need to get back," I say. "And you all need to get clothes for the wedding."

"You're still going?" Kit asks. "Why?"

"I made a promise. And I'm going to get to the bottom of this mess."

"You gonna get messy?" Naomi asks.

"Not one bit," I say. "I need to know who the real Cole Vivien is."

Kit insists on walking me inside, but I tell her to leave. I don't want any of them around when Cole comes to pick me up. I need to talk to him myself, without distractions.

When his car tires roll atop gravel, I brace myself on the lounge chair in the living room, right in front of the door like some sort of Godfather dude, hands folded carefully on my lap, impossible to miss, and the image elicits a chuckle.

My chest flutters in panic. I have no clue what to say to him.

Then I start to second-guess my whole approach. Maybe I'm blowing everything out of proportion.

A knock at the door startles me. Cole wouldn't knock.

The doorknob jiggles.

Creaks open.

I'm frozen.

Especially because it's not Cole who walks through the door.

It's Nickolas Lund carrying a small velvet box, sized for a ring. "Where's Cole?"

Cole Vivien

Jason has already checked out of his hotel when I get there, looking for him.

His flight isn't for a few hours, and I was hoping to talk to him, ask him why he went behind my back with April Fitzgerald, and sent a sound bite I can't get out of my head: "The matchmaking service is in beta testing now. VERSTL Romance. It's an easy sell, and with this content it's a modern love story." At the end, is bit of added, extracted hot mic audio of Nicko telling me he loved me the weekend we stayed in Palm Springs.

Ça me fait chier, that was a *much* larger conversation between me and my app developer. Why would Jason manipulate the audio? What's his game? Our meetings are always recorded, and Jason has access to everything. He'd been wanting to formally join the ranks of the company, and I'd already granted him access to our files while the paperwork processed to make him CFO. I feel like an absolute idiot.

I'm gutted. Jason, my best friend, took advantage of me. But why?

As I drive, my assistant back in LA sends me the full audio of the staff meeting so I play it back through the car speakers:

"I understand that the matchmaking service is in beta testing now. I think it's premature, and may muddy the brand, which has been legitimizing and supporting sex work, supplying intimacy, and I don't want to sell the idea that people can expect to fall in love. That's powerful stuff. I'm not saying never, but not right now. And I especially don't want to push a false narrative of me and Nickolas Lund as some VERSTL romance. It's an easy sell, sure, but at what cost? It twists something real and private Nicko felt for me, and exploits it. It's not a modern love story, it's unrequited, and quite painful to relive as I don't reciprocate those feelings, and I refuse to deceive him *or* subscribers."

How does Nicko factor into all of this? Jason suggested Nicko join the *Times* interview because it was good PR, but it devolved into a near-proposal stunt show. Was Jason behind that, too? Tears form in the corners of my eyes, but their presence quickly ignites my rage. A rage I haven't felt since Father rejected me, all those years ago.

I ask my assistant to forward the full audio to April's email, but it's too late.

A Google Alert for both "Cole Vivien" and "Vivièn DuBois-Deplantier" buzz and pop across on my phone screen, both from the *New York Times*.

April Fitzgerald's article is live.

The New York Times

Commodifying Love and Selling Intimacy

How VERSTL Became the Most Successful, Groundbreaking Sex Work App

By April Fitzgerald

May 27, 2024 at 11:00 a.m. ET

EXCERPT: "A man in his fifties who lost his husband the year before reached out to me not too long ago. He had been mourning and didn't know how to put himself out there, so he reached out, hoping he could experience intimacy and connection. He wanted to feel safe and protected, so I arranged to spend the weekend with him, and I held him. He asked me to help him enjoy sex, so I went slow with him, making sure he knew what he wanted. It was a beautiful thing to be part of because I got to see him feel confident and secure again. That's what we're selling. It's real, even if it's temporary." Vivien noted how, until recently sex workers were relegated to parks after dark, illegal bath houses, and seedy hotels without any protections. This despite sex work being an important pillar of a functioning society, a "base need." VERSTL, founded by Vivien, whose real name is Vivièn DuBois-Deplantier, son of the construction titan Gerard Deplantier and actress Brigitte DuBois, seeks to combine sex work, creator content, and high-end escort services with employee protections, all in the pursuit of commodifying intimacy for those who need it most.

And if all goes as planned, VERSTL seems to be getting into the love game with a potential dating app in the works. Vivien aims to sell a version of love in a venture tentatively called "Love Potion. Look, loneliness is a powerful motivator and tool of isolation. VERSTL, through its innovative, personalized matching system, seeks to partner sex workers with clients who need what I call 'love simulators.' Everyone knows what they're paying for, there are no tricks, there are clear contracts and stipulations, and every employed, fully vetted sex worker sets their own firm boundaries; so then as escorts, we offer clients a hyper-idealized version of love. Sure, it lasts for a night, or a weekend, or in rare cases, a couple weeks, but it expires. Like any other business venture, Love Potion is a product. It's good business."

Nickolas Lund, the app's highest-grossing and most successful performer, details his romantic history with the CEO, saying, "For all of Cole's talk about the performative aspects, he's a bleeding heart." The two star-crossed lovers, who have been on again, off again for the better part of a decade, have some surprises up their sleeves, posting a steamy love scene on Vivien's page, setting up a behind-the-scenes fairy-tale romance. At the VERSTL party, Lund reportedly proposed to Vivien, who did not respond to further requests for interviews.

Teddy Hughes

I'm numb. My head buzzes, busy with the white noise of information overload as I try to wrap my thoughts around what Nicko just told me about Cole. It's hard enough concentrating in front of a Swedish god, a brick shithouse of solid muscle wrapped in tattoos that make zero cohesive sense—lots of tribal designs and gay iconography like Dolly Parton next to Princess Peach from *Super Mario* and a ripped merman with a large trident that says "Daddy" in a font straight men pair with "Mom" heart tattoos. How can I compete with Nicko? The realization sinks and so does my heart.

Moving on. Here's what I now know:

Ten years ago, Cole met Nicko when they were both in college at NYU. They hooked up once, but Cole wasn't interested in more. Two years later, their paths crossed and Cole, having just graduated from college, ignited a relationship with Nicko, which only lasted a summer before Cole moved to LA. Years later, after Cole started VERSTL, he reconnected with Nicko, who had become one of the most sought-after sex performers. Nicko never stopped carrying a torch for Cole, and when they got together to perform last year, his heart got the better of him, and he told Cole he loved him.

"So you still love him?" My question shakes as it leaves my lips.

"I do," Nicko says, his words daggers to my heart.

"So that video—" I begin, but he cuts me off.

"Is real, yes." He looks away, crosses his arms and almost folds in on himself. Even with all that muscle mass, he looks fragile.

"But only on my end. Cole doesn't do love. He likes it as a concept, but doesn't believe he can have it. He holds himself back."

Not sure what hurts more, knowing this beautiful man loves Cole, or hearing him say that Cole doesn't allow himself to fall for anyone.

"Why tell me this?"

He shrugs. "Because of Jason." He rocks back and forth on his heels. "He has it out for Cole, and he used me. I didn't understand what he was doing until I realized he wouldn't stop until he destroyed Cole and the people around him to get what he wanted, including you. And I don't even know who you are, but clearly you're important enough to be around his family, which I didn't even have, besides Mallory."

Again, "I don't get it." My temples throb. I need to sit.

He peers out the window nervously and checks the time on his phone. "After Palm Springs last year, I started getting all these emails from Cole. Love letters, telling me how much he wanted to be with me, but he was scared. Sometimes I would go weeks or months without hearing from him, but then I'd get something from him, and it gave me hope that one day he'd come back to me. Then his assistant called me and told me he was coming to New York and wanted to get dinner. I thought that was it, he was finally ready to commit. But all he wanted was to ask me to do that *Times* interview."

Right. *That* article. Kit sent it to me right as Nicko came in and she screenshotted the part about Cole's potential engagement to Nicko. I didn't get to read the whole thing, but it knocked the fucking wind out of me.

"Where does Jason come in?" I have to stop myself from saying something snarky like, "Land your plane."

He scratches his head. "At the same time that all this was going on, I had also been in contact with Jason. He was telling me how much Cole wanted to be with me, blah blah blah. And one night, when Jason was in New York on business a few months ago, we met up for dinner and he got plastered, let his guard down, and I found out he was working hard with potential investors to create the narrative that VERSTL was transitioning to a matchmaking service. Turns out, he brokered a deal with a high-powered investor who would invest if VERSTL moved into the dating app market. But they wanted Cole out. Part of Jason's deal was that they would make him majority owner and CEO. I guess it wasn't enough that Cole was already bringing Jason in as CFO. He wanted it all, friendship be damned."

Anger pools in my fists. "Fucking scumbag." My brows furrow. "But wait, all that time you loved Cole and you didn't think to warn him."

He holds out his hands, begging for more time to explain. "Jason manipulated me too. He told me that if they could create this narrative that we were in a loving relationship, they would keep Cole on as CEO. And I'd get the man of my dreams." His lips quiver. "He was the one who posted that video diary to Cole's account. He sent a car to bring me here from the city and told me I needed to do some grand romantic gesture at the wedding to generate press, but when I refused, saying it had gone too far and that I wouldn't embarrass myself again, he told me the pieces were already in motion. If the *Times* article was proven false, it would tank VERSTL's brand, and Cole along with it. I told him he could go fuck himself. But he was drunk..." His voice trails off.

I lean forward, studying him, the way he winces, the sweat beading his brow, the dark circles around his eyes. How could something so beautiful look so broken?

"What happened?" I ask.

"He grabbed my face and said, 'Listen, you're a plaything. Nothing more. A wet hole to slide into.' He told me he was the one sending all those love letters to me, not Cole, as he reached down and squeezed my junk, hard. He fucking kissed me, like I was nothing. His lips were like sandpaper." He shudders.

"Nicko, you don't have to—"

"I have to tell someone. I still feel him on me, like I'm not in my body anymore, I'm floating somewhere outside of myself, seeing it all happen, and trying to scream but nothing comes out. He threw me backward, slamming me into the wall. He told me Cole would never love someone like me as he slid his hands inside my jeans." He goes silent, and I want to get up and hug him, but I don't want to trigger him by moving or invading his space, so I remain still and listen. "I tried to fight him off, and I should have, I'm so much fucking bigger than he is, you know?" He's crying now, tears streaming down his cheeks, and my heart cracks open for this beautiful man I met minutes earlier.

I say the only thing that comes to mind. "Thank you for trusting me. I'm so sorry that happened to you. I'm here, if you need a friend."

He looks up at me, tears magnifying his irises; he looks like a terrified boy. But he blinks them away. "Look at what he did to me!" Now he's shouting, jumping to his feet and ripping off his shirt. Across his abs is a deep purple bruise.

That's an older bruise. Jason has done this before. Not just last night.

"I should have fought him off." He starts to pace, but frustration takes him over and he swipes at a lamp, sending it flying off an end table and shattering on the floor. He doubles over in pain from the realization of what happened.

I rise to my feet, slowly, as to not trigger him. "It's okay. It's only a lamp." I move toward him, place a comforting hand on his back, his skin hot like fire. "You did everything you could. That should never have happened in the first place, and you need to know it's not your fault."

Tires scrap across the gravel lot and he sucks in a frantic breath. "I have to get out of here."

"Nicko, wait for Cole—"

The door pushes open, and Cole glares at us from the door frame. "What the hell?"

Cole Vivien

Blind. Breathless. *Rage.*

As Teddy tells me everything that happened between Nicko and Jason, I'm unable to focus on anything.

White-hot fury pools in the pit of my stomach and bubbles up my body, flowing through my veins like lava. I'm a volcano at its eruption point. I want to take Nicko in my arms, but I don't have the right to, not after everything that happened to him. I wish I had the chance to beat the shit out of Jason, the man I thought was my best friend in the world. My would-be business partner.

Then there's Teddy, who Jason also tried to turn me against with that investigative folder bullshit, calling Teddy a con artist. Guess Jason was talking about himself.

I could strangle him. I call him over and over, send him text after text to call me back, but nothing.

He's off the grid now.

Nicko begs me not to call the police. "Sex workers and the criminal justice system don't mix. Nobody would believe me over Jason. Olivia Benson doesn't exist in real life."

I hate that he's right. That no matter how far we've come, because of what we do, we wouldn't be believed.

Balling my fists, I wind up, envision Jason's face like a bull's-eye and punch a hole directly into a barren section of the wall, and my bones crack! I bark in pain as blood drips on the hard-wood floor. Chips and flecks of drywall peel away, revealing cement.

Nicko whimpers, curled into himself on the couch. "Cole, please, stop."

Teddy wraps an arm around me. "He's not worth the extra Airbnb charge."

I laugh, despite myself. "How could he do this to you," I say to Nicko, my lips quivering. For everything I thought Nicko put me through, all he ever did was love me. Guilt arrests me because I was never able to love him. If I had talked to him after Palm Springs, instead of ignoring him, none of this would have ever happened.

Teddy urges me to go to him, to sit with him, comfort him.

For a while, all three of us sit in silence.

Teddy never leaves my side, and though my hand holds

Nicko's, my heart is tucked safely inside Teddy's chest. Word-lessly, he understands this too.

Then my phone goes off.

Mallory. "Fuck, I'm late!" I don't want to leave Nicko alone. Not here, not now. I look to Teddy for permission, but don't get it. I know it's unfair to him, but I can't turn my back on Nicko. "Hey, bud, you in the mood for a wedding?"

Eight
Diamond-Tier Member Access

Teddy Hughes

Castle Rock is pristine, its surface scrubbed and sparkling like a European palace in its prime. I float through the backdrop of bridal party photographs like a ghost, a smiling afterimage of the castle's long-deceased residents.

It's an otherwise gorgeous day, the kind of vibrant, cloudless blue skies and emerald grasses you'd see in a movie, with a golden sun and a soundtrack of bees buzzing, birds chirping, and leaves rustling in the breeze.

For a little while, I forget what happened with Nicko and Jason and Cole. The tangled web of lies and deception and abuse, all woven by Jason in the pursuit of money and power and status. It's the same kind of shit Murray Whalton and his family engaged in, the same fuel that fired up Murray's father to come after me and Plant Daddy.

When Nicko arrives with the first of the guests after photos, Brigitte sidles up to me instantly, as if she knows I need the comfort. I understand why Cole invited him, but I wish he hadn't. She hooks her arm in mine and side-hugs me, talking my ear off about different plants, misnaming every single one in the most endearing way.

"Nickolas Lund, I see?" Brigitte coos curiously. "I assume you knew Vivièn invited him?" When I ask her if she knew details, she says, "He told me something terrible happened and the poor boy needed a friend, but he did not go into specifics."

Cole and I briefly discussed the *Times* article drop on the drive over, and he's certain it'll be idle gossip soon enough now that his given name is out there. But he asked me not to bring it up until he has a chance to talk to his parents. He said, "With any luck, they'll be too busy today to read headlines."

But the way Brigitte looks at me, pity and sadness and confusion in her eyes, makes me think she's already seen it. If she has, though, she says nothing and holds tight to me, commenting about the weather and that Cole and I make a beautiful couple. Eventually, Gerard joins us and doesn't stop complaining about how hot it is, constantly wiping the sweat off his forehead with a handkerchief. Eventually, they both bid me adieu as they join the bridal party for the procession.

I look over my shoulders, study each person who walks by, and hold my breath when I see the bride.

Mallory looks like a vintage Barbie in a lacey mermaid dress with embroidered butterflies. Her hair is flowy and wavy, like a 1960s flower child, with white French hyacinths sewn in. Her makeup is so natural and subdued that all I see is the striking cut of her face, like a rare gemstone. In her hands, a whimsical bouquet of lily of the valleys. Castle behind her, she truly looks like a quirky princess next to her cookie-cutter blond prince.

But it's Cole I can't keep my eyes off; he looks every bit as breathtaking sauntering down the aisle as he did the night I saw him in the bar, his swagger oozing off him in spades. Except now when I look at him, I also feel a twinge of longing.

Could I ever be enough for him?

Fill the void in his heart?

Fit in with this world? The same world that destroyed Nicko and shunned Cole and stole Plant Daddy?

I want to walk up to Cole and fall into his arms, tell him that I love him, too. That maybe I love him too much, and that it's too soon to feel the kind of love I have for him.

Because when I think about it, I can't compete with the history between Cole and Nicko, and even if I could separate the two, can Cole?

Tears fill my eyes.

He catches my gaze and smiles, and it's so alluring, so full of hope and guilt.

I bow my head and look at Nicko, who can't take his eyes off the love of *his* life.

The Teddy who said yes impulsively to a stranger can't be the Teddy who says yes to more until I figure out my life. Cole can't save me, and I don't want him to try. I owe myself—and Cole—that much.

Can anybody love a premise so flawed from its conception?

Reaching into my pocket, I palm the crystal Cole gave me

the other night. *"Rose quartz is meant to restore trust and harmony,"* he said. I could use that right now.

Kit, Naomi, and Tara, dressed in the finest vintage sundresses they could find in town, sidestep into the row and sit next to me.

"Everything okay?" Kit asks as the string quartet begins to play.

"Why wouldn't it be?"

She places her hand on my knee, steadying my restless leg.

"You have room in your car tonight?" I ask.

She doesn't ask me why, or what happened. All she says is, "Always."

Mallory floats down the aisle flanked by Gerard and Brigitte on either side, and the string quartet starts playing an instrumental of Taylor Swift's "Begin Again," which I immediately recognize because I listened to this song on repeat after Murray left me, wishing we could start over. That it would be easy to rekindle. Now I understand the song isn't about that at all; it's about experiencing that spark of love after a broken heart left you devastated.

The pastor asks Mallory and Mikey, "Do you take this person, to have and to hold, in sickness and in health, until death parts you?"

As they take turns saying "I do," Cole's eyes well, and my heart breaks open.

Cole Vivien

Mallory is the perfect bride. Ethereal. Mikey is the pinnacle of handsome. They look like a dream. I understand now why people describe couples on their wedding day as "glowing." A pang of jealousy in my chest twists as I watch them after the ceremony.

Before this weekend, I never wanted anything close to marriage, but...could I?

Leaning against one of the tent poles, I stare out at the cerulean blue skies beyond the castle, watching two small birds flit around each other. I can't look away, and suddenly I'm imagining all the possibilities of their story: Two birds meet, both a little bit lost, a little broken by their lives, one more hardened and guarded than the other, who is a beautiful bleeding heart. And they do this dance with each other, fluttering toward and away, their wings flapping as they try to find a solid place to land.

"Daydreaming?" Mallory's voice cuts through my thoughts.

"I don't—"

She rolls her eyes. "It's okay to dream, *petit frère*."

"You don't know me."

"I wanted to check on you before Mikey and I head into the castle for private time."

"Christening the castle?"

Shock splashes across her face. "Ew. Gross. No. Not in this dress, perv." She knocks into me. "They're graciously letting us in for pictures and a breather."

"I don't want to pull focus from your day at all." Guilt tugs at me. "But has Mother or Father said anything about the *Times* article?"

"As far as I know, no. You know Father, he would be pulling me off the altar for an emergency board meeting if he saw the contents of that piece," she says. "It's only a matter of time. But for now, try to enjoy my day. Celebrate me." She leans in and kisses my cheek softly.

"You look beautiful, you know," I say as she walks back toward Mikey.

"I know." She winks, sticking out her tongue.

Though she's not gone long, my heart starts to ache in her wake.

Loneliness.

Sure, I've felt this before, but it's always been rather dull, easy to ignore. If I focused on work, building VERSTL, going out in WeHo and getting drunk, fucking random men, I was usually able to bury it, make it feel like it never existed.

Why, then, does it feel so strong right now?

Being home with Mal and Mother has made me feel whole. Even Father.

Including being here with *Teddy*. When I think of him and how I feel when we're together, that familiar loneliness evaporates.

I search for those two small birds, but they're no longer in flight, and I can only spot one on the ledge of a nearby tower. Where'd his partner go? My heart starts to race until I see him, his tiny wings flapping as he lands with something in his beak, a twig or a worm, for his love.

Don't I deserve what Mallory and Mikey have? What these two beautiful birds have? I never believed it was possible before, but the only way to find out is to find Teddy.

"You looked gorgeous up there," Nicko says, appearing in front of me, slowing me down. "I wasn't the only one who couldn't take my eyes off you."

"Thanks, Nicko. How are you feeling?"

He shrugs. "This is a nice distraction." Reaching out for me, he runs his fingers down the arm of my suit jacket.

My body tenses. I don't want to reject him right now after everything he's been through, but all that floods me is how damn cyclical this is. I show him a little affection and he runs with it.

"I never thanked you for understanding," he says. "Or apologized."

"Apology not needed," I say. "We have a long history, and we've changed a lot."

He takes a step forward. "When I'm around you, I feel like I'm twenty again."

In a swift move, he leans in toward my lips, nearly catching them as I swerve my head away.

Taking a step back, I tell him, "We're not twenty anymore, Nicko."

Tears form in his eyes, but never fall. "I'll never be enough for you, will I? Ever since that night we first met." His words tremble on his tongue. "I thought maybe what we had was real."

My chest aches for him. "We had one night followed by one summer, and one week in Palm Springs. I *do* care for you. And I *do* love you." The words pour out. "Not in *that* way, only as a friend. I cherish the memories we share. But—" I let that word stay suspended in the air.

Silence presses into my chest cavity.

"You love him, don't you?" he asks, eyelids heavy with sadness. "Teddy. I can see it on both of your faces. You look at him the way I wish you looked at me."

When I don't say anything, he continues. "I know you've

spent so much of your life running from the idea of love, not thinking you're worthy. I hope you realize that's the furthest thing from the truth."

Relief washes over me. "Thank you, Nicko. You too. You deserve someone who loves you back the way you need them, too." My anxiety kicks in. I have to find Teddy. Tell him everything I've been too afraid to say. "I, um, have to go."

"Me too, Vivièn."

As I walk away, something tells me this is the last time I'll ever see Nickolas Lund.

Teddy Hughes

Cole grabs hold of my hand as we make our way into the palatial wedding tent on the great lawn. It's actually not a tent at all, not what I would consider a tent, anyway. It's a clear-roof marquee, with firefly lights, and a lush garland is strung around beams that pool at the center where a large white crystal chandelier hangs down over the biggest dance floor I've ever seen.

Hanging bouquets of flowers with hints of golds and pinks, complete with small glass baubles are suspended over all the tables. At the center of each table is a collection of drippy candles of varying heights on diamond platforms surrounded by white flowers. Cole excuses himself to speak with guests I don't know, leaving me alone.

Brigitte walks over and gracefully sits down next to me. She's holding something behind her back. "Darling, remember when I told you about that adorable little bookshop in town?

Gerard stopped in this morning and look what he found." On the table, she lays, *Plant Daddy: How to Embrace Your Inner Horticulturist* and *Plant Daddy in the City*. "Would you do me the great honor of signing these for me?" She pulls out a swanky, engraved pen.

"It would be an honor." I scribble my name on the title pages.

When she takes them back, she also grabs my hand. "My Vivièn, he's a good boy, and he means well, doesn't he?" She studies my face, watching for recognition, but I'm not sure how she wants me to react. "Sometimes, people can get lost. No matter how hard we try to run from the monsters, they always find us." She stands up, and I rise to meet her out of respect. She hugs me earnestly.

"Can I tell you something?" I ask, and she tilts her head, giving permission. "Your son is the greatest adventure I've ever had."

Breath catches in her throat, and she sighs. "It's not easy to make love work, and it won't always look the way you thought it might. In our line of work, loving the men we love, it rarely does."

She takes her leave as Cole walks up, kissing him on the cheek as she goes.

He holds out his hand. "Would you like to dance with me?"

Brigitte's words echo in my head, so I take it. "Of course."

Adele's "Chasing Pavements" plays over the speakers, and people flee the dance floor until all that's left are a few older couples, and Kit, Naomi, and Tara, who sway in a tight circle.

Cole holds me tight. We move enough to keep in time with the tempo of the song.

Resting my head on his shoulders, I nuzzle into his neck. He's so warm and safe, and he pulls me close. He smells like teakwood and lavender and sweat, and it reminds me of the nights we spent in each other's arms, naked and cuddled together.

"I don't want to go," I whisper, knowing he'll hear me but hoping he doesn't. I turn my head and rest my cheek on him.

"Then don't," he whispers back, so quiet it almost fades into the song. "Stay with me." He bows his head and buries his chin in the crook of my neck. "We can figure everything out together." He pulls me tighter. "Because I do love you, Teddy Hughes, and I think you heard me say it last night, but I didn't mean for it to come out. I mean, it's not that I didn't mean to say it, I did, I *do*, *now*, but not in *that* way. Fuck, I'm messing this up big-time, aren't I?"

I chuckle because I'm usually the rambling mess. I hug him back, fiercely, until we're no longer dancing, but bear-hugging.

We sway for a few silent seconds. "I want to say it back." I do, but—

"Only if you mean it," he requests. "Because this isn't pretend for me."

"Our lives are messy. Mine is a shambles. And yours." I'm unable to look at him. "It looks perfect, but all that shit with Jason. The article. VERSTL." I don't mean to add his company to the mix, but how can I not? It's been the source of so much chaos and drama and I don't know how to separate the two.

"It's not—"

"But it is, Cole. Look around you. Your sister got married at a literal castle. You have more money than you know what to do with." I point to myself as if I'm a designer handbag or gold watch. "And despite what you think, you have a family who loves you. Might not be how you want them to love you, but they do. And I'm—I don't fit, and I don't want to be a burden, or a scapegoat." I think of Murray and all the horrible things he put me through.

"You do fit, Teddy. With *me*." Cole brushes his hand beneath my chin.

I want to believe that's true, yet every single time I've allowed my heart to open, a seed planted, I end up unrooted.

Our lips are magnets drawn together, and it's all I can do to stop him as he bends forward and I launch myself on my tiptoes to meet him.

It's so soft, tender, sweet.

The world stops. Revolves around us. Centripetal motion pulls us inward, convincing me I could stay here with him, only to fling us apart.

Mallory taps my shoulder. "Do you mind if I dance with my brother, gorgeous?"

"Anything for the bride."

Before I go, Cole kisses the tip of my nose and my cheeks heat.

What I never expected was to turn around and see Brigitte and Gerard talking to my ex-husband's father, Murray Whalton II.

Cole Vivien

As soon as Teddy walks away, Mallory's bright smile shifts into disappointment mode. She bites her lips and holds tight to the crystal around her neck. "Did you pay Teddy to be your boyfriend?" On her phone screen is a video of Teddy standing in front of the apothecary shop in town. I lean forward to better hear the audio. Teddy very clearly says: "*I can't have feelings for Cole. This isn't like that. It's a business transaction. A paycheck. Fiction.*" Pause. "*It'll make a great book, that's for sure.*"

Everything stops moving. Including our bodies.

I'm paralyzed by his betrayal.

The flippant way in which he said those hurtful, awful things.

Reducing me to an employer, a paycheck disbursement.

How could he say something like that?

Then again, maybe I'm the idiot for thinking it could be more.

A tear falls down my cheek and she wipes it away.

"I don't know Teddy, but you should talk to him. I got this video from—"

"No," I spit, not listening to her, blind with rage. There's a reason why I've spent so much of my life guarded. Why I never want to let anyone in. My thoughts shift to the folder of information on Teddy. *Was Jason right?* My temples throb, drowning everything out. Jason might have been a duplicitous backstabber, but Teddy saying all of this hurts more.

I take out my phone, quickly tap on the folder. Inside are sealed legal documents from the Whalton Estate. A lawsuit against Edward Hughes and Plant Daddy. A settlement. Bankruptcy documents. And even a financial history of Teddy's mother, who never managed to live above the poverty line, and has been married four times in the last decade. Teddy was always so evasive about what happened to his nursery and

Jason *did* say Teddy was a grifter. Seems like he had a modus operandi the whole time.

"Vivièn." Mallory's face falls.

"I should never have let my guard down for him." Letting go of Mal's hand, I turn my body like a soldier at Buckingham Palace, smooth out the folds of my shirt, and fix the lapel of my jacket, all while zeroing in on Teddy. "Trust me when I say I won't make that mistake again."

Teddy Hughes

All rich people know each other.

Turns out, my ex-father-in-law, Murray Whalton II, is a long-term investor in the Deplantier Corporation. Go figure.

My ex-father-in-law doesn't say a single word to me. It's almost as if we're strangers. I tried to shake his hand, to hold my own, but he doesn't reciprocate. Probably for the best because I can't stop trembling.

"Murray was telling us some interesting information," Brigitte says to me as Cole walks over. "About you, my dear."

"Teddy embezzled family money to start his business. Until recently, he'd been squatting in a storefront rightfully owned by me," Murray says.

"That's not true," I say, but my voice is meek and goes unheard.

Brigitte doesn't react, her poker face fortifying her resolve.

Gerard, on the other hand, throws his hands in the air. "What the hell is this, Murray? What are you on about?"

"He targeted our family," Murray adds. "Took my son for

a ride. I thought, given our long history, I would warn you."
Before he walks away, he turns to Gerard and adds something
else neither I nor Cole was expecting. "Speaking of, members
of my board contacted me this afternoon about your son's…
business endeavor."

"Pardon?" Gerard says.

"The *Times* piece." Murray's face scrunches as if he's smelling shit. I know that face, the judgment. It's how he looked
at me for years around his golden boy. "They're urging me
to reconsider our ties with Deplantier."

"What article?" Gerard puffs his chest.

Brigitte moves swiftly to her husband's side. "This is my
daughter's wedding. Gentlemen, let's take this to the cigar
room, discuss this with civility."

Cole's face is stark white. He grabs for his mom's hand, but
she shoos him away.

I turn to Cole. "I'm so sorry." I don't even know what I'm
apologizing for, but that exchange between Murray and Gerard had to have gutted Cole. His parents clearly didn't know
about the *Times* article. But I have to tell him that what Murray said wasn't true.

"Save it," he says, hearing none of it. He presses Play on
a video.

A lump forms in my throat. It's the lie I told Kit to get her
off my back. "That's not what it sounds like—"

He cuts me off. "I guess being a writer primed you to be
a great actor because you fooled me into thinking we had
something real. But it seems you have a pattern. Was I always
a target?" He keeps his voice lowered, but people at neigh-

boring tables, including his parents, are staring intently like we're animals in a zoo.

"You know that's not true." I'm so stunned, it's all I can think to say.

Cole takes out his wallet and counts out a few hundred dollars. "Consider it a tip for your superb acting. It's time for you to go." He points toward the exit of the tent. "Cinderella's carriage is about to turn into a pumpkin."

How ironic that he treats me like a whore, after all the game he talks.

All the lies.

All the Big Feels and declarations; he's nothing more than a scared little boy.

I would feel bad for him if my heart weren't shattered.

Kit was right.

"Vivièn," Mallory pleads, looking between us like she wants to reach out, say something to me, maybe even reason with him, but Cole is her brother.

There's nothing more to say.

No point in me pleading my case. He's made up his mind about me.

This time, he walks away from *me*.

Kit chases me through the parking area. I don't even know where I'm running to because I don't have a fucking car.

"Slow down, Teddy!" Kit shouts. "What the hell happened in there?"

"He's a fucking asshole." My chest is heaving and I don't realize I'm crying until I stop moving and a tear drops off my chin. I wipe the snot from my face and feel the money in my breast pocket. "I don't even want his money." I take it out and start screaming, "I DON'T WANT YOUR FUCKING MONEY!" and toss it to the ground.

"Look, I know you're upset, but—" Kit bends down, grabs the cash, and says, "But this is good money." Naomi and Tara come up behind her.

Nothing is registering. I'm starting to panic. I have to leave.

"I'm a fucking fool for falling in love." My stomach caves in as I start to understand why Cole swore off the idea for most of his life. Maybe it's easier to turn off emotions than feel every single fucking one so acutely. "I'm hopeless."

"Stop! Right now." Naomi dips to my side and tries to hold me up.

Tara drapes her arms around my side. "Don't say that about yourself."

"Who falls in love with a sex worker?"

"Uh," Naomi starts. "Actually, quite a few people. You should really come to the dyke bar sometime. Point is, love is not easy. It's complicated as fuck. Add sex work to the mix, and messy rich white colonizers—" Tara nudges her. "What? Prove me wrong. Anyway, all I'm saying is I saw y'all on the dance floor. Hugging on the street yesterday. Holding hands at dinner last night. The way he looked at you all day today. Gross heterosexual-like displays of public affection."

"It doesn't matter now. Real or not, it's done," I whisper.

The three of them huddle around me in the middle of the dark parking lot, lit only by nearby streetlamps and moonlight.

When I can't cry anymore, they hoist me to my feet.

"You ready to go home?" Kit asks.

I turn back toward the barn, hoping Cole might come after me.

But he doesn't.

Defeated, I say, "There's nothing here for me."

Cole Vivien

Outside, at the far side of the castle, it's pitch-black, deserted.

No windows, lights, or Teddy, just silence. This place, this town, my chest, feel empty without him, the way it used to all those years ago, growing up detached from Father and a legacy I never wanted.

I bummed a cigarette and a lighter off one of my aunts on the way—I haven't smoked since I was fifteen and in my rebel phase—but now's a good a time as any to ignite old habits.

"There you are!" Mallory's voice pierces the darkness. She sniffs the air. "What is that smell?"

I lift my hand to my lips and suck in a drag off a cigarette; the end embers burn bright in the shadows.

"Vivièn DuBois-Deplantier!" She snatches it from my hand and stomps it into the ground. "I swear if I burn my dress because of you, I'll kill you."

I crouch down and bury my face in my hands. "Tell me, how disappointed are our lovely parents?"

She shrugs. "I don't know."

"What do you mean, you don't know? They had to have seen the article by now, after Murray Whalton's big fucking mouth."

"I'm not their babysitter," she says. "And they were going

to see it eventually. I'm surprised we made it this far into the day. Plus, we're Parisian. Sex work is in our blood. Our history. And you know how Father feels about French history and culture." She jabs me with her elbow and laughs. "I am concerned about you, though." She curtsies beside me, careful not to rip her dress.

"Why did you pay Teddy to be your boyfriend?"

"Because I thought having him here would take all the focus off me. The last month leading up to this was so nerve-racking, thinking of seeing Father, having to deal with his perpetual disappointment. I wanted to distract him. And Mother. Give her something to fawn over. Besides you, blushing bride."

"Girl, please. You're her baby. We all know she likes you more. It's fine." She stares up into the night sky. "So you decided to fake a relationship? Sound decision-making."

I laugh. "Terrible idea, huh?"

"Monumentally," she says. "But I will say, you picked one hell of a man to fall in love with."

My eyes sting with tears, and I sniffle.

"Why didn't you give him a chance to explain himself?"

"What's there to explain?"

"Everything!" she shouts. "And nothing! You didn't even give him a chance!"

"He—"

She cuts me off. "Said something really insensitive to his best friend so that she'd stop worrying about him. I saw Kit after you threw Teddy out. He's a wreck. Did you ever ask Teddy about the context of what he said?"

"You're the one who showed me that video!"

"Because I'm a good sister, and Smarmy Hammer is a fucking shithead for sending me that video and trying to start shit. Among everything else your former manager and best friend did."

I laugh because "Smarmy Hammer" sounds like something Teddy would say. If she only knew what happened between Jason and Nicko. *Wait.* "Jason sent that video to you?"

"If you would've listened to me, I would have told you that. But you didn't even give me a chance to talk to you about it before you reacted and stormed off. Like Father does."

Fuck. "I'm the world's biggest asshole. I'm worse than Father." I pause, hoping she'll tell me I'm wrong. When she doesn't, I add, "But it's not even that, it's—"

"Please don't tell me Murray Whalton II is what did you in?"

"What do you mean?"

"He has a nickname in our world. The Murraly Corrupt Whalton." She blinks like she's waiting for me to laugh. "Get it, *Morally, Murray.*"

"Terribly punny." My stomach winces. "Did I make a mistake?"

"If you didn't hear him out," she says. "You failed, *petit frère.*"

"Fuck." I tell Mallory what happened between Jason and Nicko, and she gasps, clasps her hand to her mouth, and cries. "Are you kidding me, Cole? Your 'best friend' assaulted your ex-pseudo boyfriend-person and not only does Teddy not run away screaming, he stays with you and you can't even manage to hear him out?" She smacks me upside the head. "You kinda suck."

Her words are a bullet to the chest. Right to the heart. Kill shot.

"Oh, god." The realization hits me, suddenly it's like I'm suffocating.

Hyperventilating.

Unable.

To.

Breathe.

I bang my chest.

Dry heave.

Mallory keeps me on my feet, but all the blood rushes to my head and I nearly topple over, which causes me to panic more.

"Breathe." She rips her celestite necklace off and places it in my hands, wraps my fingers around it, and squeezes tight so that I can feel its power.

"I fucked everything up." Deep breath in. "Now he's gone." Deep breath out.

I try to count to twelve on my fingertips, but I keep messing up and having to start over, and the more I mess up, the worse my anxiety gets.

"Maybe you can still catch him." She nudges.

I look up. "You think?"

"There's always a chance."

"What would I say to him?"

"You can start with an apology," she says. "Go."

With all this adrenaline, I take off, nearly propelling myself off the wall of the tent and ricocheting off the grass like I'm superhuman, dodging rogue family and weaving in between wedding guests dancing to some god-awful dance craze music from the '90s. The table with our name cards is empty, and Teddy is nowhere to be found. But why would he be here? He left so long ago. With any luck, he went back to the Airbnb to grab his clothes, and maybe I can intercept him there.

As I dash through the reception, fly out the door, and into the lot where the cars are parked, I run directly into Mother.

"Vivièn, my god," she shouts, brushing imaginary wrinkles out of her dress.

"Sorry, Mother," I say, my back stiffening. I have no idea what she's going to do or say, but I don't have time to find out. "I really want to talk to you, and I'm sure you're upset with me, but I—"

"Theodore left, you know," she says. "I watched them all leave. I doubt you'll catch them. They looked in quite a hurry."

Panting, I nearly collapse. I've spent so long running from this place, trying my best to be impenetrable, to never let anyone see me crack, especially my parents, that my knees buckle under the weight of my own expectations.

"I read that article," she says. "I think it's best we wait for cooler heads before we discuss it. All I'll say is that I love you."

I start sobbing as if I came out to her, all over again.

"And I'm proud of you, though I do wish I taught you better than to tell us important life information through the news media." She shrugs it off, which makes me cry harder. "Shhh, it's okay."

"I fucked everything, Mother."

"You know, when Teddy and I spoke earlier, he told me *you* were the greatest adventure he ever had," she says.

He was mine.

Until I destroyed it.

Nine
The Versatility of Men

Teddy Hughes

Nothing is better than sinking my fingers into fresh soil.

The perfect way to recharge, remind myself what's important. A palate cleanser.

I don't have much left, but I have exactly what I need to get lost in caring for my plant babies. Even if only for a short while.

It's a hell of a lot better than sitting cross-legged and stoned in my half-empty apartment, surrounded by a mountain of packed boxes. The last seven years of my life in neatly labeled cardboard, most of which say "DONATE" in big thick Sharpied letters. That's what my thirties have amounted to: boxes and empty spaces, a mass of collected junk I'll never use again, a city full of cemented regret.

New York City is many things to many people. But for me,

it's been the place that has broken my heart over and over again. It's an island of concrete and steel and glass and man-made parks with suffocated trees that gasp for oxygen. Kit asks me if I'll miss the city, and I say I will because she's here, but Cole taught me you can only pretend for so long. Nothing good grows here organically; weeds sprout through cracked cement and twist, mutate, until they become something else entirely.

I think about him and how he became something I never expected, but Kit is right. I have a tendency to lose myself—my livelihood, in Murray's case—in these rich men and their glitzy, glittery worlds.

All I'm taking with me is one suitcase of clothes, a box of mementos I should burn ceremoniously—including the water-logged pic of Murray and me, and the rose quartz Cole gave me, a backpack with my laptop and whatever books I'm not donating, including a couple remaining first editions of the *Plant Daddy* books, and my favorite succulent terrarium. The jungle of other plants I've collected I'm forcing Kit to take with her when she officially moves in with Naomi and Tara at the end of next month. They'll give my babies a good home in their Brooklyn loft with the natural sunlight. It would be impractical to rent a moving truck for plants, and Tara has good plant-lesbian vibes, so it's a win.

Brigitte was right. It's not easy to make love work, and it has never looked the way I thought it would when I was a child hoping for the sweeping romance I saw in heterolove movies. Falling in love isn't a grand romantic gesture that can be fortified with a boom box over your shoulder; it's a means of cracking open your chest in an act of ultimate vulnerability that sometimes opens old wounds that never quite healed.

The risks I've taken have never been worth the inevitable heartbreak, the excruciating, chest-thumping anxiety that accompanies the pain of losing love. In the end, I always end up here, on the floor of Kit's apartment, trying to pick up the pieces of my broken heart and put them back together.

So I cry.

Remembering what I had once upon a time with Murray.

Missing the life I lost.

Mourning for Plant Daddy.

Realizing the protective shell I never quite had before is finally starting to harden.

Hating that it is.

And my tears have nothing and everything to do with Cole Fucking Vivien.

Cole Vivien

"I'm lost," I tell Mother as she strokes my hair like she did when I was young, *shhhing* me to sleep on her shoulder.

"Everything lost can be found again, if we know where to look."

When I wake up alone in Château Deplantier with a cashmere blanket draped over and tucked in around me, a fluffy pillow where Mother once was, I wander toward the room that was once my childhood bedroom. I haven't been here in years, so it startles me when I realize how much of me existed in this space from a young age: exquisitely framed authentic design sketches from Givenchy, Valentino, Versace, and Galliano, all bought at an auction when I was in high school. Everything is black-and-white. Sleek, hard lines, traces of the man I would become. I remember feeling like I kept so much of myself tucked away in closets and drawers, in sketchbooks and journals where I planned my great escapes. I would become a fashion designer, travel the world on my terms.

Outwardly, I played the game.

Pretended the family business was my goal to keep Father happy.

Pretended not to hear my parents argue.

Pretended not to love people because I thought it would protect me.

Pretended I didn't need anyone, when all I've ever needed are people to love, and love me back.

I thought I was guarding myself, but all that pretending did was lead to me not trusting anyone, except the wrong person, and hurting the right ones.

It's time to come home.

Being a Deplantier has its perks.

With Father's name carrying the weight it does around here, I immediately gain access to new and exclusive real estate, houses not yet on the market.

The second the Realtor steps out of the room, Mallory gushes. "I love this place!" She's been house shopping with me the past few days while Mikey finishes his final class before their honeymoon. "It's perfect! I can totally see you here."

"You've said that about the last three houses," I say. "None of which were perfect."

But every house I've seen is not a home. They've all been new constructions, cookie-cutter mini McMansions with the same stark white kitchens and wood floors and cold steel appliances. I have that already in LA. I want something that allows me to dream again, to make me feel like I did for a few brief moments at the Airbnb with Teddy.

That's this house.

Mallory is right, it is perfect.

It's in the middle of a mountain on five acres, with plenty of space for a large multilevel garden. There's a stream running through the property, and the nearest neighbor is far down the road. It's not a large house by any stretch of the imagination, but it has an open floor plan, and *character*. The first—and top—floor is the living space with a Craftsman kitchen with butcher block counters and mismatched hardware on distressed teal cabinets with a farmhouse sink and a state-of-the-art gas oven with copper hood and matching pot rack hanging from the ceiling. The far wall in the living room is one giant window overlooking an endless, untouched forest and the stream. The layout is wonky and niche and unique, a labyrinth of rooms with a master bathroom designed to look like a spa on Italy's Amalfi coast. The Realtor tells us it was owned by a custom jewelry maker, and she embedded precious gemstones all around the property, which I saw immediately when we walked out the French doors in the master bedroom and into a private sitting area. In the pathway, cemented into the foundation, were small gems. The more I look around at the copper detailing in some of the rooms, the display cases built into some of the walls, the more I see her hard at work, creating pieces of art, and the more I see myself doing the same.

Creating a fashion line in this small artist's retreat in the mountains.

Maybe I'll even take up gardening.

"I know that look," Mallory says, her body trembling with kinetic energy. "You love it, don't you?"

"You don't know me," I say defiantly.

"I'm rubber and you're glue, and please say you're buying this place and moving back home because your older sister would love to have her brother back. I haven't allowed myself to believe you're serious because you hate every single house, except—"

"For this one."

I walk to the center of the empty living room, close my eyes, and try to visualize myself here:

Warm winter nights by the fireplace watching the snow fall over the mountain. With Teddy.

A work room where I could design clothes. I remember telling Mallory about Alessandro Arcobaleno, that we're collaborating on a line together, and how she squealed with unbridled joy. "*C'est incroyable, petit frère!* How did that happen?" *Teddy.*

A man smiling at me from behind the island in the kitchen as he pours us wine to take outside to a bonfire where we'll snuggle up in hoodies and warm wool blankets on cool spring nights. Teddy.

My own garden where I can learn how to plant.

Teddy, Teddy, Teddy.

I do what I can to push him out of my mind, shove him into a box and tape the lid shut. Toss it into the stream behind the house and watch it float away.

The Realtor walks back in. "What do we think? It's a

buyer's market, and this place won't last long once it's on the market—"

I cut her off. "I'll take it."

That stuns her into silence.

Mallory sucks in a breath.

"Full ask, all cash, quick close, no bullshit," I say. "I'm ready to start a new chapter. I leave for LA on Saturday, but I can fly back to close." I'll keep my apartment in LA, since VERSTL is based there, but I can run the company from any-where, and it'll be nice to be within driving distance to New York City as I branch out into fashion apparel.

"Excellent!" The Realtor has her phone out. "I'll get the offer to the seller's agent and we'll draw up the paperwork and go from there. Standard contingencies, based upon suc-cessful inspection—" she continues on with the terms of the offer, but it's all I can do not to think about Teddy.

Teddy in this house with me.

Teddy in the garden.

Teddy's laugh waking me up from a nap.

Teddy's face at Mallory's wedding, the horrible, disgusting things I said to him.

I've suppressed it for the last few days, but it's bubbling to the surface.

"How does that sound, Mr. Vivien?" the Realtor asks.

"Perfect. Mind if I step outside?" But I'm already out the door.

I dart for the railing of the wraparound porch. It's humid, which makes it harder to breathe, and the sun beats down hard on my skin, which prickles with sweat.

I'm light-headed. My breathing is heavy and quick.

I'm unable to focus on anything—the wooded, hilly land-scape looks pixelated; the willow tree in the distance is fuzzy, unfocused.

A hand on my back feels like it weighs three thousand pounds, and I nearly fold.

"Talk to me." Mallory's voice feels far away, like she's talk-ing through a plexiglass wall. She takes my hand and slides a green amethyst into my palm, and it's all I can do not to think about Teddy's eyes. Staring into them, finding a home in his green and blue amethysts, and watching them go cold when I turned him away.

That sends me over the edge.

"Oh, god, that was supposed to bring you serenity!" Mal-lory stammers. "Don't cry, *petit frère*, shhhh…" She rubs my back methodically. When I start to mellow, my breathing returning to a state of normalcy, and my vision restores, she says, "Talk to me."

I shake my head.

"Call *him*?" *Teddy.*

"He won't talk to me. *I* wouldn't talk to me," I explain.

"You'll never know if you don't try," she says. "That's your problem. You give up. Instead of trying, you run away."

Wow. Gut punch registered.

"If you'd stayed and talked to Father all those years ago—"

"I didn't want his money."

"It's not about money!" Her nostrils flare. "It's about fam-ily. Fighting for people who matter." Her gaze is far away. I never really took the time to think about how our fractured family has affected her. How my distance impacted her. Us. I take her hand, and she squeezes it back. I want to apologize, but I'm not sure the words would matter. That's why I want to move back here, to show her that I'm here.

"Father hasn't spoken to me since the wedding." The *Times* article. He's seething. "I've soiled his good name." Palming the green amethyst, I wish for serenity and stability.

"You haven't even tried to talk to him yet. If you want to stop running, start with him," she says. "Be the type of bigger person he could never be."

I chuck the amethyst into the woods; it bounces off a boulder and disappears into the stream.

"Did that make you feel better?" she asks. "You need to open yourself up to real possibilities, Vivièn. Not the ones you manufacture for yourself."

Teddy Hughes

Everything is quiet as the city gives us a moment of silence. Until Kit kills the vibe.

"Dearly beloved," she starts. "We are gathered here today to pay our respects to Edward 'Teddy' Hughes and Kit Davis as roommates." Her words start to break, but she shakes off her emotions. Our once-shared space is empty. "It's the end of an era."

"Is that a bad thing?"

"I guess for you, it isn't," she says. "But I'm going to miss the fuck out of you." She squeezes my arm tight. "And what about me? I'm moving in with my girlfriends. I'm going to be, like, a kept woman or something? I'm not a house cat!"

"You're going to thrive," I say.

"As are you," she assures. "How was the consult call, by the way?"

After my breakdown post–Cole, I realized I never allowed myself to fully grieve and process Murray tossing me to the curb, especially since my focus was on (failing to save) Plant Daddy. The worst part is that I realized I love Cole more than I ever loved Murray. That fucking floored me. I'm talking bottle of wine blackout at Naomi and Tara's. After that display of utter weakness, they all sat me down and told me they would pay for me to see a therapist knowing that, without health insurance, I wouldn't be able to afford therapy on my own. I hugged them so tight I never wanted to let them go. Kit and I spent that day looking up therapists in and around New Orleans, and I've had a few consultation calls, but I was holding out for the one I had set up for this morning. They're a queer psychotherapist who specializes in LGBTQ+ clients, sex, non-traditional relationship models, and family trauma.

"The consult was a dream," I say. "It was like winning the lottery at a Charli XCX concert in the middle of Provincetown during Bear Week. I love them. We set up our first session for next Friday, once I'm home."

Home. The word burrows into my head.

"I'm proud of you," she says.

"I'll be thanking you and the girls until my dying breath," I say.

"Thank us by visiting."

I don't tell her I probably won't be back for a while. I'm going to miss Kit more than I care to think about. She's been my heart and soul and lifeline for as long as I can remember, and the thought of not seeing her every day slaughters me. Who will water me the way she does? Care for me? Shower me with the sunlight I need to feel nourished? She's so much stronger than I am—she'll continue to thrive, take on the art world and dominate in ways she can't even fathom. Her love with the girls will blossom because she doesn't do anything half-assed. I'm heartsick that I won't physically be here to witness it all. But maybe it's time I learn how to root myself without her. "Of course."

"I know you won't," she says, reading my thoughts. "But a girl can dream. So what is the game plan for your last night tomorrow? American Trash?"

"Oh god, no."

She laughs. "You don't want to see Sugar one last time?"

"What's he gonna do when you're in Brooklyn?"

"I'm sure he'll survive."

"Straight men always do," I say. "Like roaches."

She raises one hand in prayer like she's in church. "Did you write at all today?"

Once I started researching therapists, my mind started to wander. Maybe it was the act of moving toward dealing with my shit that jump-started my brain, but, "I couldn't stop thinking about a potential new book idea. It marinated in my mind for two days, and it was all I could do to focus on getting it out. It's speculative fiction, a dystopic take on 'Jack and the Beanstalk,' but gay. A bag of magic seeds he'll never be able to plant because there is no soil. Until he meets a man who can physically change the landscape for him."

Kit hums. "No allegories there."

"None at all."

Over the last couple days, instead of sleeping and eating (unless a jumbo-sized bag of Haribo gummy bears counts), I wrote a ten-thousand-word book proposal. I have no idea if it's any good, but right now, escaping into fiction sounds sublime.

"You'll be proud of me because guess who fired off an email to his literary agent?" I point to myself. "This bitch right here."

Kit squeals and tackles me, and I topple over. "You big, beautiful author!"

"Don't get too excited. She'll probably read my email thinking, 'I still represent this loser?' Or worse, that a genre switch from nonfiction to fiction is grounds for a dissolution of partnership!"

Eyes wide, she clacks her tongue. "Dramatic much? The negative self-talk is not working for me—focus on that in therapy. Besides, I'm sure she's reading it right now going, 'I'm going to offer him one million dollars!'"

"Okay, Dr. Evil." I turn out my palm and put my pinky to my lips and do my best Mike Meyers. "One million dollars for a book? How about one trillion billion dollars?!"

Kit's lips curl. "Groovy, baby."

"I wish that's how publishing worked," I say. "Agents don't pay for books. She'd have to sell it. But it's been literal *years* since I published anything. I'm basically starting fresh, in fiction, so it's not like we can just sell it on proposal. I need to write the whole thing first. It's like planting magical beans and hoping for a beanstalk."

Eyes rolling, she says, "Has anybody ever told you that your stark realism is a total buzzkill? What happened to my favorite gaydreamer?"

"He can't come to the phone right now." I make the sign for phone with my pinky and thumb and motion to hang it up.

"Maybe this will help. Give you a cushion so you can write

once you get back to Nawlins." She plops a wad of cash, the seven thousand dollars from Cole, into my lap.

"Why do you have this? I told you to leave it at the Airbnb when we went back for my shit!"

"It's seven fucking grand!" Kit shouts. "You need it more than he does!"

"I don't want his blood money."

"Blood money? Jesus, Teddy. Take it," she commands. "You fucking earned it."

It makes me feel queasy. "When're you leaving?" I half joke.

"Hey," she says. "I'm proud of you. You're stronger now than you were with Murray, and even though you were with that dickwad for a third of your life, I know you love Cole more."

I'm not sure my strength is the badge of honor she thinks it is.

"You sure you want to spend tonight alone? I really don't want to leave you. Naomi and Tara will have all of me soon enough."

"I need time to meditate," I assure her. "I was surrounded by people the last week, and I haven't had any time to reflect. I'm going to transplant the plants I'm leaving with you, in-spect the roots and give them new soil. Make sure they have the best shot once I'm gone." I don't want to cry. I need her to get used to being without me. Or maybe I need to get used to being without her.

"I'll be back tomorrow for our last night." She kisses my forehead, slings her bag over her shoulder, and heads toward the door. "It'll be perfect. A fairy-tale end!"

If there's one thing I've learned from all the shit I've been through in my life, it's that fairy tales aren't real.

Cole Vivien

Waiting outside Father's office at Château Deplantier, I feel once again like the insolent child who had to have punishment "hearings" penciled into his calendar. Buried memories are interrupted by the double doors to Father's office opening, a whoosh of air rushing past.

"Vivièn," Father says. "Come in."

I follow him inside, and I expect him to go right for his desk chair, his throne, and to fold his fingers together in expectation, the way he would when I would come home from school with a C on a math test. Except he swerves and leads me to the stiff white couch on the far end of the room next to his bar cart. Wordlessly, he eyes the crystal decanter with auburn liquor and I nod, triggering his swift, effortless pours.

Handing it to me, he says, "*Santé*," and I echo his cheers.

He looks me directly in the eye. As a child, he taught me to stare everyone in their eyes, to never look away. It's a tactic of both respect and intimidation.

"I know why you're here," he says in French. "What I can't understand is why it took you so long to come to me about the *Times* article."

Wasting no time, I see.

My fight-or-flight instinct kicks in, and I reflexively start to defend VERSTL. But he puts his hand up and I immediately clam up. He still has that power over me.

"I can't pretend I'm happy with your choice of vocation," he says. "But knowledge is power, son. And from what I read, a good deal of your company is devoted to safety and protections, both health—physical and mental—and financial.

Good business sense, that is. Beyond that, I did some digging. What you've built, this company and application, is impressive. Your profits are staggering." He sits back in his chair and tips his glass. "*Santé*."

It's the closest I've come to him saying he's proud of me. Though I still desperately long to hear the actual words. So I push him. "Does that mean you approve?"

He swirls the liquid around his glass. "Would I have preferred *you* sitting in that chair one day?" He points to his throne. "Yes, of course. But I believe Mallory will make a better successor." Reaching forward, he grabs hold of my kneecap and squeezes, saying he's proud of us without uttering the actual words.

That's all I need.

"Mallory informed me that she tried to kill the mention of your name in the article. Of all the things I could possibly be mad about, you giving up my name, that hurts the most. Though I understand the reasons."

I don't dare look away, maintaining eye contact.

But he does.

And I'm floored.

It's only for a second, but my resolve crumbles.

"I didn't know any other way," I offer.

"I didn't give you much of a choice, did I?" He leans back, allows his posture to relax, if only a bit.

"Can I ask you something?"

He hums and a familiar feeling of anxiety bubbles in my chest.

"Mother always used to tell us she loved us. She believed

so fiercely in love, and I didn't. Not that I didn't feel it, but it felt impermanent. I think it's because I never heard *you* say it."

"Is that another damnation?" His voice is thinner.

"No, sir," I stammer, sitting against the hard back of the couch.

"I've been in love three times. You, your sister, and Brigitte."

My heart swells. "Why don't you ever say it?"

"Because!" He scoffs, taking a swig. "The feelings I have for you and your sister, I don't know if there are words to express. *Love* is not enough. I've done my best to provide and protect, but even then, I understand now that when I lost my son all those years ago through inaction and words that *love*, as I knew it, was not enough. So, until words come to me…" He goes silent.

I get it.

Maybe I don't need him to say the words. Because they're merely words. I see it in his face. He's proud of me. He loves me, but can't express it in the way I always imagined was "normal." In his own ways, he always loved me.

I've had it wrong this whole time.

Love is more than a declaration.

It's action.

Commitment to not giving up, to fighting for what seems impossible to sustain because eventually, everything ends, hearts break.

But is that any reason not to love?

My mind drifts to the man I never expected to meet but have been waiting for my entire adult life.

And I know exactly what I need to do, but it'll require Mallory *and* Kit's help.

Ten
Rooted

Teddy Hughes

While taping my last box, a key clicks in the lock, the heavy metal door creaks open.

Kit's bag drops on the floor with a thud. "Honey, I'm home!"

"Time for our two-person goodbye shindig!" I jump up. "Dicks and tequila."

She hugs me from behind, resting her chin on my shoulder.

"Brave faces and all," I confess. "So! American Trash? The Eagle? Get plastered and watch rom-coms all night while crying into cartons of Chunky Monkey?"

"Not the Kit and Teddy post-breakup special!"

"You're right," I concede. "We need to go balls to the walls, I was thinking—"

She reaches for her bag and hands me an envelope. "I wasn't sure if I should give you this or not."

"Oooo! A present? I didn't get you anything." I snatch it from her. "Looks like your standard-issue greeting card. A gift card? Money holder? One of those Adopt-a-Sloth certificates from Costa Rica?"

Teetering on her heels, she confesses, "It's not from me."

On the back is a red wax seal with the Deplantier name stamped into it.

My heart stops.

"I do love a wax seal." My voice shakes. "How did you get this?"

"Hand delivered." She giggles nervously as she tells me she's been texting with Mallory since the wedding, and that Mal reached out on Cole's behalf. "He's in the city. One night only."

"You saw him?"

"Briefly."

"How'd he look?"

"Honestly?" she asks. "Delicious. Sorry, but he's a snack."

"Not helpful." I wave it around in the air. "Do I open this?" I want to. So badly.

"That's not my decision!"

"I want your input. No, need. Desperately."

"Fine. Yes. You love him," she says for me. "And you owe it to yourself to have that. Real love. Even if it's just the potential for it."

"Last week, you hated him."

"I was being protective of you. But I saw you two together. I've been talking with Mal and I think I understand Cole better."

"Help me do that," I beg. "Can I turn off those feelings?"

"Nope." She makes a ticktock, ticktock sound with her tongue. "Whatever you decide, I'm here as your dedicated hypelesbian."

"What if I get hurt again?"

"You *will* get hurt again," she says. "You think my triad is free from pain? You don't think I stay up some nights riddled with insecurity because Naomi and Tara are legally married and they're sleeping together in the same bed in Brooklyn while I'm here in plant purgatory? We all fight, but the worst part is when they go home together, and I come back here. Part of me wonders if I'll ever feel like I have a place in their relationship."

"I never knew any of that," I say.

"Why would you?" Kit looks at the floor. "It's so fucking hard being part of a throuple, knowing people don't even know what that word means. And if they do, they always wonder, 'Who is the original couple,' and it feels like I'm always excluded. Even though they don't make me feel that way, I carry that around. And when I fight with one of them, I question whether or not we're solid enough to last."

"Kit—"

"The point is," she cuts me off, "love is not solid. It's a concept. A work in progress. Something you fight for every day. And something you get wrong sometimes. All you need to answer is, do you love him?"

Can it be that simple?

A letter, an apology, a proverbial boom box declaration? Love?

Once a seed sprouts, it can never go back inside its shell.

I slide my finger through the back of the envelope and pull out the card.

Teddy,

There is so much I wish I could say, but words don't matter. Only actions. I could spend the rest of my life showing you how sorry I am for what I said to you, and how I pulled you into my life only to let you walk away when things got a little bit tough.

I don't deserve you or your time. You may be far away from New York by the time you read this so if this is my last chance before I fly to LA, I have to say it: I love you.

I love you I love you I love you, Teddy Hughes.

-Cole

If on the off chance you love me too, come to the place you took me the night we met XOXO

Teardrops drip onto the card, blurring Cole's pen streaks. I furiously try to dry it, to preserve his words, but that makes it worse, smudging his declarations like bruises on skin—

I love you, I love you, I love you.

Letting him go feels so permanent. And it can't be over.

I'm afraid of losing myself to him, but I'm afraid to lose him more.

I look up and meet Kit's nail-biting gaze. "Are you going?"

Cole Vivien

This was a colossally asinine idea.

I never should have let Mallory talk me into a whole Grand Romantic Gesture. I'm not a Prince Charming, and Teddy is not a damsel in distress. Her first idea was to show up to his apartment hanging out of a stretch limousine with roses and chocolates blasting a love ballad like we're in some cheesy '80s rom-com.

Teddy needs to decide if he wants to see me at all. I remembered how he told me about the photoSYNTHESIS exhibit at The Metropolitan Museum of Art. *Nature as living art*, he said. As Mal reminded me, the Deplantier name gives me the ability to bribe a museum to stay open for a private tour after hours.

The idea was simple: Mallory arranged with Kit for me to drop off the letter with her when I came into the city for my flight back to LA. The letter, a small gesture to test the waters, would prompt him to come to The Met, where a ticket awaits him, allowing after-hours entry into the museum.

I've been here all day now and the museum's been closed for a good hour. I'm not sure how much longer I can wait on the off chance that Teddy will show.

So far, I've seen hundreds of people, none of which are Teddy Hughes.

It's a breathtaking exhibit, and I can see why Teddy would clamor to see this. The walls of the space are covered in living plants—vines and flowers—from all over the world. There's an app that pairs with the plant species, and if you scan something, it'll tell you what region it comes from, and how it thrives in its ecosystem. The floor is raised twelve inches under a plexiglass platform, and beneath it, the ground is covered in rich soil, and the area between soil and plexiglass is technologically outfitted to mirror a greenhouse, so tiny seeds were spread from wall to wall, and if you come back multiple times, you can watch the seeds sprout and grow. There's a Venus fly trap, and more exotic plants carefully attended to by the exhibit's creators, and a treehouse built around an artificial, but biodegradable, tree to climb up into and survey the jungle of the exhibit from a bird's-eye view. Then there is the sustainability exhibit, where guests can pay to plant seeds of local plants and flowers, and at the end of every day, the horticulturists will take the beds and bring them to plant-starved areas in need of natural vegetation. I could spend all day studying here and still find something beautiful and breathtaking with every new second. That's how I feel about Teddy.

Checking the time, I'm now certain he's not coming.

My flight back to LA boards soon.

Time to declare it a loss, and call a car to the airport.

Teddy Hughes

Lacing up my Converse, I'm primed to speed walk to The Met. I have no idea what I'll say to him, but I figure it'll come to me when I get there and see him. Brigitte DuBois's voice rings in my head: *The greatest gift you can offer someone, if you love them, is grace.*

Kit yells after me as I race down the apartment staircase.

"I admire you, Teddy! You always leap headfirst. You love with your whole heart!"

"Look where that's gotten me!" I shout back, nearly tripping over the last few stairs. Someone in a nearby apartment shouts for us to "shut the fuck up."

"Love, Teddy!" she shouts as I fling open the heavy door to the street; it's all the adrenaline-fueled encouragement I need.

Sprinting through busy streets.

I dodge cars and rogue taxis and Ubers, irritable men in suits with briefcases, annoying small dogs leashed to oblivious owners who won't get the fuck out of my way!

Don't they know this is life and death!

Okay, maybe not. But they don't know what I'm up against.

Time slows as I run, fire burning in my lungs. All my morning jogs prepared me for this very propulsion forward.

By the time I reach The Met, my chest is heaving, my thighs and calves wailing, throbbing in pain.

Frank, the intimidating, Italian mobster of a doorman from The Mark Hotel is waiting at the exact spot Cole and I sat, standing at attention. "Mr. Hughes."

The fuck is he doing here?

I don't remember giving him my last name, but maybe that means Cole is still here and expecting me.

"Frank—" I'm panting. "Cole. Vivien. Is he. Here?" I hold up a finger for him to give me a second, and I nearly keel over.

He doesn't move. Stoic as ever.

With my hands on my hips, I bend over to see if that'll help the sharp pangs in my stomach. I look up at him. "I'm fine, by the way. Don't worry. I'm only dying." Sweat drips from my cut-off thrifted *Beverly Hills, 90210* tee. I shake out my legs; my thighs chafed from my skintight four-inch jean shorts.

He looks me up and down, unamused.

"Mr. Vivien left this for you." He pulls a slender white envelope out of his breast pocket and tips his head in acknowledgement of my receipt. Cole's handwriting is on the front: Teddy.

"You would've been a great mob boss, you know that?"

Frank doesn't blink. "Who says I'm not?" He reveals the tiniest smile, and winks. "Go get him, stud."

Floored by his sudden gayness—but not surprised, the vibes were always strong—I salute him. "Thanks, Frankie."

Inside the envelope is a single bright red ticket to photo-SYNTHESIS, the interactive gardening experience here I told him about the night we met.

The entrance time: Whenever You Get Here.

Cole Vivien

Estimated time of arrival of the car to the airport: five minutes.

A single tear trickles down my face as I look around, knowing that this is as close to Teddy as I'll ever be again.

Rubber soles squeak against the floors echoing through the halls of the empty museum. I look up, toward the entrance of the exhibit, and there he is. Quiet strength in his cut-off white tee showcasing his thick arms, ripped jean shorts accentuating his juicy thighs and delicious calves, and Converse.

A tangled mess of curly coppery hair. All big, beautiful blue and green amethyst eyes, and tentative smiles.

Neither of us moves.

We stand at opposite ends of the space, which, when crowded with onlookers seems so small, but now feels like an Olympic stadium.

"You came," I say.

He crosses his arms, and I can tell it's taking all his strength not to look around.

"Do you want to walk around with me?" I ask as my phone alerts me to the arrival of the car I called, which I ignore. Nothing matters but Teddy. I'll book a new flight later.

He still doesn't say anything as I start toward him, slowly, so as to not spook him.

We take our time. Teddy studies each plant, naming every single one without looking at the app, until it turns into a quiz, where he waits for me to check the app for confirmation. Then I start testing him, asking him to name them while I have the answers on my screen. Little by little, his shoulders relax until he's dashing between flora, spouting out genus and species like a kid on Christmas morning tearing through presents and tossing wrapping paper into the air, unable to focus on one present for long because there's a newer, shinier gift to open.

I soak up everything, every part of him, like it's the last chance I'll have. Observing him in this environment, even though it's artificial, it's as close to the real Teddy I've gotten. I'm ready to relinquish control and let him dictate what happens next.

This is his part of the story to write.

At the treehouse exhibit, he grabs hold of the ladder, and looks at me.

"After you," I say.

Carefully, he makes his way up each rung, reaching out to different vines that hang from nearby branches to hold them delicately in his hands.

At the top, he sits wide-eyed and looks out over the exhibit, feet dangling joyfully.

"What do you think?" he asks, and it's the first time he's talking directly to me in a way that requires me to answer. "Of all this, I mean."

"I've been here most of the day, and this sounds weird, but I feel lighter. I can breathe easier. They must be pumping drugs in here because as sad as I've been, being in here has made me feel happy."

He rolls his eyes. "Such a cynic." He licks his lips and applies some ChapStick. "As someone who loves crystals so much, I would think this would be obvious."

"What do you mean?"

"Plants are healing, Cole. Flowers increase positivity. Plants not only produce a calming effect on people, but they generate oxygen. *Photosynthesis*." He gestures around at the space. "Get it?"

"I didn't pay much attention in chemistry."

He smacks his forehead in frustration. "Clearly."

I grimace.

"You're lucky you're pretty." He knocks into my shoulder, and electricity runs through us. Despite everything we've done together, it feels like we're two teens in the quad at recess accidentally touching for the first time.

"I accept that as a compliment."

He laughs. It's small, so small, but I'll take it.

With a held breath, I say, "Thanks for coming."

"I wasn't sure if I mentally could," he says. "At first."

"And now?"

He gnaws his upper lip, and I notice that he's still wearing the twisted chain I gave him before the dinner with Alessandro. The bracelet is around his wrist, too.

"What is it that you want, Cole?" he asks.

"What do *you* want?"

"I *know* what I want, but I need you to be honest with me about what you *really* want, so I can make an informed decision."

That's actually rather…pragmatic. I appreciate that.

His hands tremble. "I let you dictate the terms of our 'agreement.' You said it was a business proposition. We fucked. I met your family. And then *you* kiss *me* for the first time and Jesus, Cole, it was the most intense, incredible kiss of my entire life, and you tell me you love me but five minutes later you're tossing me out of your life like a cheap whore. Whalton showing up sent you into a tailspin, thinking I was conning you, especially after Jason—"

"I know you," I say. "I know your heart."

He sighs. "Thank you. But I don't want an agreement. I want an equal partner, someone who isn't afraid to love me. I can't keep losing myself to men who throw me away like I'm expendable."

"You're not expendable. Not to me. You're everything. A beautiful work of art. Teddy, honestly, you took my breath away that night we met, and I've been trying my best to get air back into my lungs ever since. I wasn't expecting you. I don't do this—" I gesture around us. "This is all new." I grab hold of his hand. "I'm so sorry I wasn't there for you. I didn't listen, or wait for you. Or give you a chance. I don't really know what I'm doing. I've never done relationships, but I'm not afraid to love you anymore."

He pulls my hand to his lips, pressing it there, but not kissing it.

"It took meeting you to make me realize I've been running from myself." I swivel toward him, and our knees touch, sparking. "You rescued me. I'm done running. No more propositions or rules. I'm fucking terrified because I don't know how to do this next part, but—" I want to ask him *how*, in order to think through it logically, but maybe this isn't something that can be methodically thought through. This is something I'm going to have to stay rooted for, right here, with him, and experience in the moment. Change the coding in my system, reroute my output.

"Promise," he requests.

"That's the easiest agreement I can subscribe to. I love *you*." His eyes well.

"I'll do whatever it takes. I'll quit sex work, I'll—"

He places his free hand on my leg, and my body shudders. "What you do is important. I hope you know this was never about you being a sex worker. I admire what you do and what you've built. No, it was about how *I* was treated. I'm not someone you need to run from, who will judge you or pretend they love you when they don't. And I expect the same from you. Because I want you to continue doing what *you* want to do. Not that you need my support, but you one thousand percent have it."

"Thank you," I say. "And I *will* earn your love, too."

"You have my love, Vivièn DuBois-Deplantier. It's what you do with it next." He holds my face in his hand, so gingerly.

My arms wrap around his waist and pull him closer until our noses graze and our foreheads touch.

"I love you," he says. "I love you so fucking much."

And we kiss.

Kiss and kiss and kiss and it's the best kiss of my entire life.

It's soft at first, hesitant, gentle, like nothing else in the world matters. Everything around us has disappeared—The Met, the city, North America, the entire earth is gone and all that remains is Teddy and me at the center of the universe, floating weightlessly and silently among infinite galaxies.

Then the heat between us rises and he grabs at me harder, pawing at me like a ravenous bear, and our tongues wrestle with each other until we're breathing so heavy we have to take a break.

Panting, I wipe his saliva from the corners of my mouth. His cheeks are all red, nearly hiding his freckles, and he gives me a boyish grin. I reach forward and stroke his soft copper beard. "I missed you."

"Me too," he says. "Thank you for not giving up on me."

"I should be thanking you," I say. "Speaking of which, there is something I wanted to do with you here."

"We can't do *that*!" Teddy gasps. "I'm a lady! Plus, running a billion miles made me all sweaty."

"That's fucking hot." I bite my tongue.

"We have the rest of our lives for that." He catches himself, clamming up like he let a secret out. He scratches his head and laughs. Then looks at the time on my watch. "What time is your flight?"

"Flights come and go. This is what matters right now." I fight the urge to ask him what happens after today, for us, but maybe that's the Deplantier in me wanting control.

He follows me back down the ladder and toward the sustainability exhibit until we're standing in front of a large plot of untouched soil, waist-high. There are seven bags of labeled seeds, and behind them are nursery labels with the corresponding plant type.

Together, we sink our hands into the soil. It's warm and cold at once, mushy and gritty and full of life. It releases a pungent, earthy musk.

"Show me what to do," I ask.

He rakes the plot with his fingers until it looks like a small crop field. "It loosens the soil, so the roots have more access to nutrients and water."

I follow suit, roughly digging in, and though the dirt makes my muscles clench and my anxiety fire on all cylinders, I grin and bear it.

"Not too rough. Don't overdo it. Find your rhythm. Feel the soil, and what it needs. Read its energy." He places his hand over mine and guides me, gently. "You don't have to go down too far. Only deep enough for the seeds to catch once they sprout."

One by one, we plant the seeds, burying them, and when we're done, we use the provided sprinkling can to water them.

"I wish we would be able to see them grow," I say, meticulously wiping my hands, though the dirt under my nails is wedged in too deep.

"Give it time." He turns into me, leans in close, and stops my nervous hands.

Our noses graze, and he trembles. His breath makes my body ache. My lips tease his until gravity pulls us together, and we're a tangle of arms and lips and soil.

Finally rooted.

★ ★ ★ ★ ★

Acknowledgements

Chris, you rooted me. I love you, Bubs. You're my favorite, and my biggest supporter. I'm beyond lucky to grow, bloom, and blossom with you every day. We did it!!

This book wouldn't exist without my incredible superstar agent and personal cheerleader, Jess Regel. Jess, your support is invaluable and always exactly what I need, especially when I'm spiraling or uncertain. Your love and enthusiasm of Cole and Teddy's story fueled me to write this modern gay retelling of *Pretty Woman* with an empowering financial flip, a story I've always wanted to tell. Thank you for believing in me and for steering my ship.

The biggest, most enthusiastic round of applause and endless thank you's go to my brilliant, wonderful, and insightful editor John Jacobson! Your love of Cole and Teddy, and vision for this book have pushed me to make this into the book

I'm most proud of. My writing has never been tighter and stronger, and I'm forever grateful to you for championing this story. You—and the team at Harlequin—are the best!! I'm so honored to be part of Afterglow Books! Additionally, to everyone at Harlequin who had a hand in bringing this book to life: The beautiful cover art by Michelle Kwon that brought my guys to life with help from Amy Wetton and Tara Scarcello! To the editorial team, including copyeditors, proofreaders, sales and marketing and everyone in between, thank you from the bottom of my heart! Special thanks to Katherine Rushby, Stacy Boyd, Errin Toma, Bonnie Lo, Stephanie Van de Vooren, Amanda Roberts, Monica Czerepak, Shana Mongroo, Sara Marinac, and Stephanie Tzogas.

To my family and friends who nourish me: I love you all so much. Nicolas DiDomizio, my ride-or-die critique partner and one of my best friends. I would not be here without you. I truly love you, and I have such a deep admiration for your friendship *and* your talent. For Sam, my romcom queen bestie, the Kit Davis to my Teddy Hughes, for introducing me to *Pretty Woman* in high school: If I could have a second dedication, it would be to you—love you to the moon! For all my friends, especially Steve, Marissa, Nikki, Liz, and the rest of my beautiful family who have never stopped believing in me and pushing me to keep telling my stories.

I can't *not* acknowledge THE legend Julia Roberts, who doesn't know I exist (yet!), but whose strength and iconic characters have informed so much of my formative years! Thank you! I hope Cole Vivien does Vivian Ward proud!

Finally, to all the queer folks both cis and trans and everyone in between pushing sex work forward and working tirelessly to destigmatize it and change the narratives and what it means to love and own your body and personhood: I admire you all so, so much. This book was written for gay readers, and I hope you can find pieces of yourself in Cole and Teddy and Kit and her triad, and if not, I hope you enjoy the ride *and* the love.

Never forget the love. It exists everywhere. It's what roots us.